J.R.R. TOLKIEN

THE LORD OF THE RINGS
comprising:

BOOK ONE
THE RING SETS OUT

BOOK TWO
THE RING GOES SOUTH

BOOK THREE
THE TREASON OF ISENGARD

BOOK FOUR
THE RING GOES EAST

BOOK FIVE
THE WAR OF THE RING

BOOK SIX
THE END OF THE THIRD AGE

and

APPENDICES

THE WAR
OF THE RING

BEING THE FIFTH BOOK OF
THE LORD OF THE RINGS

BY

J.R.R. TOLKIEN

HarperCollins*Publishers*

HarperCollins*Publishers*
77–85 Fulham Palace Road,
Hammersmith, London W6 8JB
www.**fire**and**water**.com

Seven-volume edition 1999
1 3 5 7 9 8 6 4 2

First published in Great Britain by
George Allen & Unwin 1955
Second edition 1966
This new reset edition published
by HarperCollins*Publishers* 1994

 ® is a registered trademark of
The J.R.R. Tolkien Estate Limited

ISBN 0 261 10397 0

Set in Postscript Monotype Plantin Light by
Rowland Phototypesetting Ltd,
Bury St Edmunds, Suffolk

Printed and bound in Great Britain by
Clays Ltd, St Ives plc

CONTENTS

Three Rings for the Elven-kings under the sky,
  Seven for the Dwarf-lords in their halls of stone,
Nine for Mortal Men doomed to die,
  One for the Dark Lord on his dark throne
In the Land of Mordor where the Shadows lie.
  One Ring to rule them all, One Ring to find them,
  One Ring to bring them all and in the darkness bind them
In the Land of Mordor where the Shadows lie.

CHAPTER I

MINAS TIRITH

Pippin looked out from the shelter of Gandalf's cloak. He wondered if he was awake or still sleeping, still in the swift-moving dream in which he had been wrapped so long since the great ride began. The dark world was rushing by and the wind sang loudly in his ears. He could see nothing but the wheeling stars, and away to his right vast shadows against the sky where the mountains of the South marched past. Sleepily he tried to reckon the times and stages of their journey, but his memory was drowsy and uncertain.

There had been the first ride at terrible speed without a halt, and then in the dawn he had seen a pale gleam of gold, and they had come to the silent town and the great empty house on the hill. And hardly had they reached its shelter when the winged shadow had passed over once again, and men wilted with fear. But Gandalf had spoken soft words to him, and he had slept in a corner, tired but uneasy, dimly aware of comings and goings and of men talking and Gandalf giving orders. And then again riding, riding in the night. This was the second, no, the third night since he had looked in the Stone. And with that hideous memory he woke fully, and shivered, and the noise of the wind became filled with menacing voices.

A light kindled in the sky, a blaze of yellow fire behind dark barriers. Pippin cowered back, afraid for a moment, wondering into what dreadful country Gandalf was bearing him. He rubbed his eyes, and then he saw that it was the moon rising above the eastern shadows, now almost at the full. So the night was not yet old and for hours the dark journey would go on. He stirred and spoke.

'Where are we, Gandalf?' he asked.

'In the realm of Gondor,' the wizard answered. 'The land of Anórien is still passing by.'

There was a silence again for a while. Then, 'What is that?' cried Pippin suddenly, clutching at Gandalf's cloak. 'Look! Fire, red fire! Are there dragons in this land? Look, there is another!'

For answer Gandalf cried aloud to his horse. 'On, Shadowfax! We must hasten. Time is short. See! The beacons of Gondor are alight, calling for aid. War is kindled. See, there is the fire on Amon Dîn, and flame on Eilenach; and there they go speeding west: Nardol, Erelas, Min-Rimmon, Calenhad, and the Halifirien on the borders of Rohan.'

But Shadowfax paused in his stride, slowing to a walk, and then he lifted up his head and neighed. And out of the darkness the answering neigh of other horses came; and presently the thudding of hoofs was heard, and three riders swept up and passed like flying ghosts in the moon and vanished into the West. Then Shadowfax gathered himself together and sprang away, and the night flowed over him like a roaring wind.

Pippin became drowsy again and paid little attention to Gandalf telling him of the customs of Gondor, and how the Lord of the City had beacons built on the tops of outlying hills along both borders of the great range, and maintained posts at these points where fresh horses were always in readiness to bear his errand-riders to Rohan in the North, or to Belfalas in the South. 'It is long since the beacons of the North were lit,' he said; 'and in the ancient days of Gondor they were not needed, for they had the Seven Stones.' Pippin stirred uneasily.

'Sleep again, and do not be afraid!' said Gandalf. 'For you are not going like Frodo to Mordor, but to Minas Tirith, and there you will be as safe as you can be anywhere in these days. If Gondor falls, or the Ring is taken, then the Shire will be no refuge.'

'You do not comfort me,' said Pippin, but nonetheless

sleep crept over him. The last thing that he remembered before he fell into deep dream was a glimpse of high white peaks, glimmering like floating isles above the clouds as they caught the light of the westering moon. He wondered where Frodo was, and if he was already in Mordor, or if he was dead; and he did not know that Frodo from far away looked on that same moon as it set beyond Gondor ere the coming of the day.

Pippin woke to the sound of voices. Another day of hiding and a night of journey had fleeted by. It was twilight: the cold dawn was at hand again, and chill grey mists were about them. Shadowfax stood steaming with sweat, but he held his neck proudly and showed no sign of weariness. Many tall men heavily cloaked stood beside him, and behind them in the mist loomed a wall of stone. Partly ruinous it seemed, but already before the night was passed the sound of hurried labour could be heard: beat of hammers, clink of trowels, and the creak of wheels. Torches and flares glowed dully here and there in the fog. Gandalf was speaking to the men that barred his way, and as he listened Pippin became aware that he himself was being discussed.

'Yea truly, we know you, Mithrandir,' said the leader of the men, 'and you know the pass-words of the Seven Gates and are free to go forward. But we do not know your companion. What is he? A dwarf out of the mountains in the North? We wish for no strangers in the land at this time, unless they be mighty men of arms in whose faith and help we can trust.'

'I will vouch for him before the seat of Denethor,' said Gandalf. 'And as for valour, that cannot be computed by stature. He has passed through more battles and perils than you have, Ingold, though you be twice his height; and he comes now from the storming of Isengard, of which we bear tidings, and great weariness is on him, or I would wake him. His name is Peregrin, a very valiant man.'

'Man?' said Ingold dubiously, and the others laughed.

'Man!' cried Pippin, now thoroughly roused. 'Man! Indeed not! I am a hobbit and no more valiant than I am a man, save perhaps now and again by necessity. Do not let Gandalf deceive you!'

'Many a doer of great deeds might say no more,' said Ingold. 'But what is a hobbit?'

'A Halfling,' answered Gandalf. 'Nay, not the one that was spoken of,' he added seeing the wonder in the men's faces. 'Not he, yet one of his kindred.'

'Yes, and one who journeyed with him,' said Pippin. 'And Boromir of your City was with us, and he saved me in the snows of the North, and at the last he was slain defending me from many foes.'

'Peace!' said Gandalf. 'The news of that grief should have been told first to the father.'

'It has been guessed already,' said Ingold; 'for there have been strange portents here of late. But pass on now quickly! For the Lord of Minas Tirith will be eager to see any that bear the latest tidings of his son, be he man or———'

'Hobbit,' said Pippin. 'Little service can I offer to your lord, but what I can do, I would do, remembering Boromir the brave.'

'Fare you well!' said Ingold; and the men made way for Shadowfax, and he passed through a narrow gate in the wall. 'May you bring good counsel to Denethor in his need, and to us all, Mithrandir!' Ingold cried. 'But you come with tidings of grief and danger, as is your wont, they say.'

'Because I come seldom but when my help is needed,' answered Gandalf. 'And as for counsel, to you I would say that you are over-late in repairing the wall of the Pelennor. Courage will now be your best defence against the storm that is at hand – that and such hope as I bring. For not all the tidings that I bring are evil. But leave your trowels and sharpen your swords!'

'The work will be finished ere evening,' said Ingold. 'This is the last portion of the wall to be put in defence: the least open to attack, for it looks towards our friends of Rohan. Do you know aught of them? Will they answer the summons, think you?'

'Yes, they will come. But they have fought many battles at your back. This road and no road looks towards safety any longer. Be vigilant! But for Gandalf Stormcrow you would have seen a host of foes coming out of Anórien and no Riders of Rohan. And you may yet. Fare you well, and sleep not!'

Gandalf passed now into the wide land beyond the Rammas Echor. So the men of Gondor called the out-wall that they had built with great labour, after Ithilien fell under the shadow of their Enemy. For ten leagues or more it ran from the mountains' feet and so back again, enclosing in its fence the fields of the Pelennor: fair and fertile townlands on the long slopes and terraces falling to the deep levels of the Anduin. At its furthest point from the Great Gate of the City, north-eastward, the wall was four leagues distant, and there from a frowning bank it overlooked the long flats beside the river, and men had made it high and strong; for at that point, upon a walled causeway, the road came in from the fords and bridges of Osgiliath and passed through a guarded gate between embattled towers. At its nearest point the wall was little more than one league from the City, and that was south-eastward. There Anduin, going in a wide knee about the hills of Emyn Arnen in South Ithilien, bent sharply west, and the out-wall rose upon its very brink; and beneath it lay the quays and landings of the Harlond for craft that came upstream from the southern fiefs.

The townlands were rich, with wide tilth and many orchards, and homesteads there were with oast and garner, fold and byre, and many rills rippling through the green from the highlands down to Anduin. Yet the herdsmen and husbandmen that dwelt there were not many, and the most part of the people of Gondor lived in the seven circles of the City, or in the high vales of the mountain-borders, in

Lossarnach, or further south in fair Lebennin with its five swift streams. There dwelt a hardy folk between the mountains and the sea. They were reckoned men of Gondor, yet their blood was mingled, and there were short and swarthy folk among them whose sires came more from the forgotten men who housed in the shadow of the hills in the Dark Years ere the coming of the kings. But beyond, in the great fief of Belfalas, dwelt Prince Imrahil in his castle of Dol Amroth by the sea, and he was of high blood, and his folk also, tall men and proud with sea-grey eyes.

Now after Gandalf had ridden for some time the light of day grew in the sky, and Pippin roused himself and looked up. To his left lay a sea of mist, rising to a bleak shadow in the East; but to his right great mountains reared their heads, ranging from the West to a steep and sudden end, as if in the making of the land the River had burst through a great barrier, carving out a mighty valley to be a land of battle and debate in times to come. And there where the White Mountains of Ered Nimrais came to their end he saw, as Gandalf had promised, the dark mass of Mount Mindolluin, the deep purple shadows of its high glens, and its tall face whitening in the rising day. And upon its out-thrust knee was the Guarded City, with its seven walls of stone so strong and old that it seemed to have been not builded but carven by giants out of the bones of the earth.

Even as Pippin gazed in wonder the walls passed from looming grey to white, blushing faintly in the dawn; and suddenly the sun climbed over the eastern shadow and sent forth a shaft that smote the face of the City. Then Pippin cried aloud, for the Tower of Ecthelion, standing high within the topmost wall, shone out against the sky, glimmering like a spike of pearl and silver, tall and fair and shapely, and its pinnacle glittered as if it were wrought of crystals; and white banners broke and fluttered from the battlements in the morning breeze, and high and far he heard a clear ringing as of silver trumpets.

*   *   *

So Gandalf and Peregrin rode to the Great Gate of the Men of Gondor at the rising of the sun, and its iron doors rolled back before them.

'Mithrandir! Mithrandir!' men cried. 'Now we know that the storm is indeed nigh!'

'It is upon you,' said Gandalf. 'I have ridden on its wings. Let me pass! I must come to your Lord Denethor, while his stewardship lasts. Whatever betide, you have come to the end of the Gondor that you have known. Let me pass!'

Then men fell back before the command of his voice and questioned him no further, though they gazed in wonder at the hobbit that sat before him and at the horse that bore him. For the people of the City used horses very little and they were seldom seen in their streets, save only those ridden by the errand-riders of their lord. And they said: 'Surely that is one of the great steeds of the King of Rohan? Maybe the Rohirrim will come soon to strengthen us.' But Shadowfax walked proudly up the long winding road.

For the fashion of Minas Tirith was such that it was built on seven levels, each delved into the hill, and about each was set a wall, and in each wall was a gate. But the gates were not set in a line: the Great Gate in the City Wall was at the east point of the circuit, but the next faced half south, and the third half north, and so to and fro upwards; so that the paved way that climbed towards the Citadel turned first this way and then that across the face of the hill. And each time that it passed the line of the Great Gate it went through an arched tunnel, piercing a vast pier of rock whose huge out-thrust bulk divided in two all the circles of the City save the first. For partly in the primeval shaping of the hill, partly by the mighty craft and labour of old, there stood up from the rear of the wide court behind the Gate a towering bastion of stone, its edge sharp as a ship-keel facing east. Up it rose, even to the level of the topmost circle, and there was crowned by a battlement; so that those in the Citadel might, like mariners in a mountainous ship, look from its peak sheer down upon the Gate seven hundred feet below. The entrance to the Citadel also looked eastward, but was delved in the heart of the rock; thence a long lamp-lit slope ran up to the seventh gate. Thus men reached at last the High Court, and the Place of the Fountain before the feet of the White Tower: tall and shapely, fifty fathoms from its base to the pinnacle, where the banner of the Stewards floated a thousand feet above the plain.

A strong citadel it was indeed, and not to be taken by a host of enemies, if there were any within that could hold weapons; unless some foe could come behind and scale the lower skirts of Mindolluin, and so come upon the narrow shoulder that joined the Hill of Guard to the mountain mass. But that shoulder, which rose to the height of the fifth wall, was hedged with great ramparts right up to the precipice that overhung its western end; and in that space stood the houses and domed tombs of bygone kings and lords, for ever silent between the mountain and the tower.

Pippin gazed in growing wonder at the great stone city, vaster and more splendid than anything that he had dreamed of; greater and stronger than Isengard, and far more beautiful. Yet it was in truth falling year by year into decay; and already it lacked half the men that could have dwelt at ease there. In every street they passed some great house or court over whose doors and arched gates were carved many fair letters of strange and ancient shapes: names Pippin guessed of great men and kindreds that had once dwelt there; and yet now they were silent, and no footsteps rang on their wide pavements, nor voice was heard in their halls, nor any face looked out from door or empty window.

At last they came out of shadow to the seventh gate, and the warm sun that shone down beyond the river, as Frodo walked in the glades of Ithilien, glowed here on the smooth walls and rooted pillars, and the great arch with keystone carven in the likeness of a crowned and kingly head. Gandalf dismounted, for no horse was allowed in the Citadel, and

Shadowfax suffered himself to be led away at the soft word of his master.

The Guards of the gate were robed in black, and their helms were of strange shape, high-crowned, with long cheek-guards close-fitting to the face, and above the cheek-guards were set the white wings of sea-birds; but the helms gleamed with a flame of silver, for they were indeed wrought of *mithril*, heirlooms from the glory of old days. Upon the black surcoats were embroidered in white a tree blossoming like snow beneath a silver crown and many-pointed stars. This was the livery of the heirs of Elendil, and none wore it now in all Gondor, save the Guards of the Citadel before the Court of the Fountain where the White Tree once had grown.

Already it seemed that word of their coming had gone before them; and at once they were admitted, silently, and without question. Quickly Gandalf strode across the white-paved court. A sweet fountain played there in the morning sun, and a sward of bright green lay about it; but in the midst, drooping over the pool, stood a dead tree, and the falling drops dripped sadly from its barren and broken branches back into the clear water.

Pippin glanced at it as he hurried after Gandalf. It looked mournful, he thought, and he wondered why the dead tree was left in this place where everything else was well tended.

Seven stars and seven stones and one white tree.

The words that Gandalf had murmured came back into his mind. And then he found himself at the doors of the great hall beneath the gleaming tower; and behind the wizard he passed the tall silent door-wardens and entered the cool echoing shadows of the house of stone.

They walked down a paved passage, long and empty, and as they went Gandalf spoke softly to Pippin. 'Be careful of your words, Master Peregrin! This is no time for hobbit pertness. Théoden is a kindly old man. Denethor is of another sort, proud and subtle, a man of far greater lineage and power, though he is not called a king. But he will speak most to you, and question you much, since you can tell him of his son Boromir. He loved him greatly: too much perhaps; and the more so because they were unlike. But under cover of this love he will think it easier to learn what he wishes from you rather than from me. Do not tell him more than you need, and leave quiet the matter of Frodo's errand. I will deal with that in due time. And say nothing about Aragorn either, unless you must.'

'Why not? What is wrong with Strider?' Pippin whispered. 'He meant to come here, didn't he? And he'll be arriving soon himself, anyway.'

'Maybe, maybe,' said Gandalf. 'Though if he comes, it is likely to be in some way that no one expects, not even Denethor. It will be better so. At least he should come unheralded by us.'

Gandalf halted before a tall door of polished metal. 'See, Master Pippin, there is no time to instruct you now in the history of Gondor; though it might have been better, if you had learned something of it, when you were still birds-nesting and playing truant in the woods of the Shire. Do as I bid! It is scarcely wise when bringing the news of the death of his heir to a mighty lord to speak over much of the coming of one who will, if he comes, claim the kingship. Is that enough?'

'Kingship?' said Pippin amazed.

'Yes,' said Gandalf. 'If you have walked all these days with closed ears and mind asleep, wake up now!' He knocked on the door.

The door opened, but no one could be seen to open it. Pippin looked into a great hall. It was lit by deep windows in the wide aisles at either side, beyond the rows of tall pillars that upheld the roof. Monoliths of black marble, they rose to great capitals carved in many strange figures of beasts and leaves; and far above in shadow the wide vaulting gleamed with dull gold, inset with flowing traceries of many colours. No hangings nor storied webs, nor any things of woven stuff or of wood, were to be seen in that long solemn hall; but

between the pillars there stood a silent company of tall images
graven in cold stone.

Suddenly Pippin was reminded of the hewn rocks of
Argonath, and awe fell on him, as he looked down that avenue
of kings long dead. At the far end upon a dais of many steps
was set a high throne under a canopy of marble shaped like
a crowned helm; behind it was carved upon the wall and set
with gems an image of a tree in flower. But the throne was
empty. At the foot of the dais, upon the lowest step which
was broad and deep, there was a stone chair, black and
unadorned, and on it sat an old man gazing at his lap. In his
hand was a white rod with a golden knob. He did not look
up. Solemnly they paced the long floor towards him, until
they stood three paces from his footstool. Then Gandalf
spoke.

'Hail, Lord and Steward of Minas Tirith, Denethor son
of Ecthelion! I am come with counsel and tidings in this dark
hour.'

Then the old man looked up. Pippin saw his carven face
with its proud bones and skin like ivory, and the long curved
nose between the dark deep eyes; and he was reminded not
so much of Boromir as of Aragorn. 'Dark indeed is the hour,'
said the old man, 'and at such times you are wont to come,
Mithrandir. But though all the signs forebode that the doom
of Gondor is drawing nigh, less now to me is that darkness
than my own darkness. It has been told to me that you bring
with you one who saw my son die. Is this he?'

'It is,' said Gandalf. 'One of the twain. The other is with
Théoden of Rohan and may come hereafter. Halflings they
are, as you see, yet this is not he of whom the omens spoke.'

'Yet a Halfling still,' said Denethor grimly, 'and little love
do I bear the name, since those accursed words came to
trouble our counsels and drew away my son on the wild
errand to his death. My Boromir! Now we have need of you.
Faramir should have gone in his stead.'

'He would have gone,' said Gandalf. 'Be not unjust in your
grief! Boromir claimed the errand and would not suffer any

other to have it. He was a masterful man, and one to take what he desired. I journeyed far with him and learned much of his mood. But you speak of his death. You have had news of that ere we came?'

'I have received this,' said Denethor, and laying down his rod he lifted from his lap the thing that he had been gazing at. In each hand he held up one half of a great horn cloven through the middle: a wild-ox horn bound with silver.

'That is the horn that Boromir always wore!' cried Pippin.

'Verily,' said Denethor. 'And in my turn I bore it, and so did each eldest son of our house, far back into the vanished years before the failing of the kings, since Vorondil father of Mardil hunted the wild kine of Araw in the far fields of Rhûn. I heard it blowing dim upon the northern marches thirteen days ago, and the River brought it to me, broken: it will wind no more.' He paused and there was a heavy silence. Suddenly he turned his black glance upon Pippin. 'What say you to that, Halfling?'

'Thirteen, thirteen days,' faltered Pippin. 'Yes, I think that would be so. Yes, I stood beside him, as he blew the horn. But no help came. Only more orcs.'

'So,' said Denethor, looking keenly at Pippin's face. 'You were there? Tell me more! Why did no help come? And how did you escape, and yet he did not, so mighty a man as he was, and only orcs to withstand him?'

Pippin flushed and forgot his fear. 'The mightiest man may be slain by one arrow,' he said; 'and Boromir was pierced by many. When last I saw him he sank beside a tree and plucked a black-feathered shaft from his side. Then I swooned and was made captive. I saw him no more, and know no more. But I honour his memory, for he was very valiant. He died to save us, my kinsman Meriadoc and myself, waylaid in the woods by the soldiery of the Dark Lord; and though he fell and failed, my gratitude is none the less.'

Then Pippin looked the old man in the eye, for pride stirred strangely within him, still stung by the scorn and suspicion in that cold voice. 'Little service, no doubt, will so great a lord of Men think to find in a hobbit, a halfling from the northern Shire; yet such as it is, I will offer it, in payment of my debt.' Twitching aside his grey cloak, Pippin drew forth his small sword and laid it at Denethor's feet.

A pale smile, like a gleam of cold sun on a winter's evening, passed over the old man's face; but he bent his head and held out his hand, laying the shards of the horn aside. 'Give me the weapon!' he said.

Pippin lifted it and presented the hilt to him. 'Whence came this?' said Denethor. 'Many, many years lie on it. Surely this is a blade wrought by our own kindred in the North in the deep past?'

'It came out of the mounds that lie on the borders of my country,' said Pippin. 'But only evil wights dwell there now, and I will not willingly tell more of them.'

'I see that strange tales are woven about you,' said Denethor, 'and once again it is shown that looks may belie the man – or the halfling. I accept your service. For you are not daunted by words; and you have courteous speech, strange though the sound of it may be to us in the South. And we shall have need of all folk of courtesy, be they great or small, in the days to come. Swear to me now!'

'Take the hilt,' said Gandalf, 'and speak after the Lord, if you are resolved on this.'

'I am,' said Pippin.

The old man laid the sword along his lap, and Pippin put his hand to the hilt, and said slowly after Denethor:

'Here do I swear fealty and service to Gondor, and to the Lord and Steward of the realm, to speak and to be silent, to do and to let be, to come and to go, in need or plenty, in peace or war, in living or dying, from this hour henceforth, until my lord release me, or death take me, or the world end. So say I, Peregrin son of Paladin of the Shire of the Halflings.'

'And this do I hear, Denethor son of Ecthelion, Lord of Gondor, Steward of the High King, and I will not forget it, nor fail to reward that which is given: fealty with love, valour with honour, oath-breaking with vengeance.' Then Pippin received back his sword and put it in its sheath.

'And now,' said Denethor, 'my first command to you: speak and be not silent! Tell me your full tale, and see that you recall all that you can of Boromir, my son. Sit now and begin!' As he spoke he struck a small silver gong that stood near his footstool, and at once servants came forward. Pippin saw then that they had been standing in alcoves on either side of the door, unseen as he and Gandalf entered.

'Bring wine and food and seats for the guests,' said Denethor, 'and see that none trouble us for one hour.'

'It is all that I have to spare, for there is much else to heed,' he said to Gandalf. 'Much of more import, it may seem, and yet to me less pressing. But maybe we can speak again at the end of the day.'

'And earlier, it is to be hoped,' said Gandalf. 'For I have not ridden hither from Isengard, one hundred and fifty leagues, with the speed of wind, only to bring you one small warrior, however courteous. Is it naught to you that Théoden has fought a great battle, and that Isengard is overthrown, and that I have broken the staff of Saruman?'

'It is much to me. But I know already sufficient of these deeds for my own counsel against the menace of the East.' He turned his dark eyes on Gandalf, and now Pippin saw a likeness between the two, and he felt the strain between them, almost as if he saw a line of smouldering fire, drawn from eye to eye, that might suddenly burst into flame.

Denethor looked indeed much more like a great wizard than Gandalf did, more kingly, beautiful, and powerful; and older. Yet by a sense other than sight Pippin perceived that Gandalf had the greater power and the deeper wisdom, and a majesty that was veiled. And he was older, far older. 'How much older?' he wondered, and then he thought how odd it was that he had never thought about it before. Treebeard had said something about wizards, but even then he had not thought of Gandalf as one of them. What was Gandalf? In what far time and place did he come into the world, and when would he leave it? And then his musings broke off, and he saw that Denethor and Gandalf still looked each other in the eye, as if reading the other's mind. But it was Denethor who first withdrew his gaze.

'Yea,' he said; 'for though the Stones be lost, they say, still the lords of Gondor have keener sight than lesser men, and many messages come to them. But sit now!'

Then men came bearing a chair and a low stool, and one brought a salver with a silver flagon and cups, and white cakes. Pippin sat down, but he could not take his eyes from the old lord. Was it so, or had he only imagined it, that as he spoke of the Stones a sudden gleam of his eye had glanced upon Pippin's face?

'Now tell me your tale, my liege,' said Denethor, half kindly, half mockingly. 'For the words of one whom my son so befriended will be welcome indeed.'

Pippin never forgot that hour in the great hall under the piercing eye of the Lord of Gondor, stabbed ever and anon by his shrewd questions, and all the while conscious of Gandalf at his side, watching and listening, and (so Pippin felt) holding in check a rising wrath and impatience. When the hour was over and Denethor again rang the gong, Pippin felt worn out. 'It cannot be more than nine o'clock,' he thought. 'I could now eat three breakfasts on end.'

'Lead the Lord Mithrandir to the housing prepared for him,' said Denethor, 'and his companion may lodge with him for the present, if he will. But be it known that I have now sworn him to my service, and he shall be known as Peregrin son of Paladin and taught the lesser pass-words. Send word to the Captains that they shall wait on me here, as soon as may be after the third hour has rung.

'And you, my Lord Mithrandir, shall come too, as and when you will. None shall hinder your coming to me at any time, save only in my brief hours of sleep. Let your wrath at an old man's folly run off, and then return to my comfort!'

'Folly?' said Gandalf. 'Nay, my lord, when you are a dotard

you will die. You can use even your grief as a cloak. Do you think that I do not understand your purpose in questioning for an hour one who knows the least, while I sit by?'

'If you understand it, then be content,' returned Denethor. 'Pride would be folly that disdained help and counsel at need; but you deal out such gifts according to your own designs. Yet the Lord of Gondor is not to be made the tool of other men's purposes, however worthy. And to him there is no purpose higher in the world as it now stands than the good of Gondor; and the rule of Gondor, my lord, is mine and no other man's, unless the king should come again.'

'Unless the king should come again?' said Gandalf. 'Well, my lord Steward, it is your task to keep some kingdom still against that event, which few now look to see. In that task you shall have all the aid that you are pleased to ask for. But I will say this: the rule of no realm is mine, neither of Gondor nor any other, great or small. But all worthy things that are in peril as the world now stands, those are my care. And for my part, I shall not wholly fail of my task, though Gondor should perish, if anything passes through this night that can still grow fair or bear fruit and flower again in days to come. For I also am a steward. Did you not know?' And with that he turned and strode from the hall with Pippin running at his side.

Gandalf did not look at Pippin or speak a word to him as they went. Their guide brought them from the doors of the hall, and then led them across the Court of the Fountain into a lane between tall buildings of stone. After several turns they came to a house close to the wall of the citadel upon the north side, not far from the shoulder that linked the hill with the mountain. Within, upon the first floor above the street, up a wide carven stair, he showed them to a fair room, light and airy, with goodly hangings of dull gold sheen unfigured. It was sparely furnished, having but a small table, two chairs and a bench; but at either side there were curtained alcoves and well-clad beds within with vessels and basins for washing. There were three high narrow windows that looked northward over the great curve of Anduin, still shrouded in mists, towards the Emyn Muil and Rauros far away. Pippin had to climb on the bench to look out over the deep stone sill.

'Are you angry with me, Gandalf?' he said, as their guide went out and closed the door. 'I did the best I could.'

'You did indeed!' said Gandalf, laughing suddenly; and he came and stood beside Pippin, putting his arm about the hobbit's shoulders, and gazing out of the window. Pippin glanced in some wonder at the face now close beside his own, for the sound of that laugh had been gay and merry. Yet in the wizard's face he saw at first only lines of care and sorrow; though as he looked more intently he perceived that under all there was a great joy: a fountain of mirth enough to set a kingdom laughing, were it to gush forth.

'Indeed you did your best,' said the wizard; 'and I hope that it may be long before you find yourself in such a tight corner again between two such terrible old men. Still the Lord of Gondor learned more from you than you may have guessed, Pippin. You could not hide the fact that Boromir did not lead the Company from Moria, and that there was one among you of high honour who was coming to Minas Tirith; and that he had a famous sword. Men think much about the stories of old days in Gondor; and Denethor has given long thought to the rhyme and to the words *Isildur's Bane*, since Boromir went away.

'He is not as other men of this time, Pippin, and whatever be his descent from father to son, by some chance the blood of Westernesse runs nearly true in him; as it does in his other son, Faramir, and yet did not in Boromir whom he loved best. He has long sight. He can perceive, if he bends his will thither, much of what is passing in the minds of men, even of those that dwell far off. It is difficult to deceive him, and dangerous to try.

'Remember that! For you are now sworn to his service. I do not know what put it into your head, or your heart, to do that. But it was well done. I did not hinder it, for generous deed should not be checked by cold counsel. It touched his heart, as well (may I say it) as pleasing his humour. And at least you are free now to move about as you will in Minas Tirith – when you are not on duty. For there is another side to it. You are at his command; and he will not forget. Be wary still!'

He fell silent and sighed. 'Well, no need to brood on what tomorrow may bring. For one thing, tomorrow will be certain to bring worse than today, for many days to come. And there is nothing more that I can do to help it. The board is set, and the pieces are moving. One piece that I greatly desire to find is Faramir, now the heir of Denethor. I do not think that he is in the City; but I have had no time to gather news. I must go, Pippin. I must go to this lords' council and learn what I can. But the Enemy has the move, and he is about to open his full game. And pawns are likely to see as much of it as any, Peregrin son of Paladin, soldier of Gondor. Sharpen your blade!'

Gandalf went to the door, and there he turned. 'I am in haste, Pippin,' he said. 'Do me a favour when you go out. Even before you rest, if you are not too weary. Go and find Shadowfax and see how he is housed. These people are kindly to beasts, for they are a good and wise folk, but they have less skill with horses than some.'

With that Gandalf went out; and as he did so, there came the note of a clear sweet bell ringing in a tower of the citadel. Three strokes it rang, like silver in the air, and ceased: the third hour from the rising of the sun.

After a minute Pippin went to the door and down the stair and looked about the street. The sun was now shining warm and bright, and the towers and tall houses cast long clear-cut shadows westward. High in the blue air Mount Mindolluin lifted its white helm and snowy cloak. Armed men went to and fro in the ways of the City, as if going at the striking of the hour to changes of post and duty.

'Nine o'clock we'd call it in the Shire,' said Pippin aloud to himself. 'Just the time for a nice breakfast by the open window in spring sunshine. And how I should like breakfast! Do these people ever have it, or is it over? And when do they have dinner, and where?'

Presently he noticed a man, clad in black and white, coming along the narrow street from the centre of the citadel towards him. Pippin felt lonely and made up his mind to speak as the man passed; but he had no need. The man came straight up to him.

'You are Peregrin the Halfling?' he said. 'I am told that you have been sworn to the service of the Lord and of the City. Welcome!' He held out his hand and Pippin took it.

'I am named Beregond son of Baranor. I have no duty this morning, and I have been sent to you to teach you the pass-words, and to tell you some of the many things that no doubt you will wish to know. And for my part, I would learn of you also. For never before have we seen a halfling in this land and though we have heard rumour of them, little is said of them in any tale that we know. Moreover you are a friend of Mithrandir. Do you know him well?'

'Well,' said Pippin. 'I have known *of* him all my short life, as you might say; and lately I have travelled far with him. But there is much to read in that book, and I cannot claim to have seen more than a page or two. Yet perhaps I know him as well as any but a few. Aragorn was the only one of our Company, I think, who really knew him.'

'Aragorn?' said Beregond. 'Who is he?'

'Oh,' stammered Pippin, 'he was a man who went about with us. I think he is in Rohan now.'

'You have been in Rohan, I hear. There is much that I would ask you of that land also; for we put much of what little hope we have in its people. But I am forgetting my errand, which was first to answer what you would ask. What would you know, Master Peregrin?'

'Er well,' said Pippin, 'if I may venture to say so, rather a burning question in my mind at present is, well, what about breakfast and all that? I mean, what are the meal-times, if you understand me, and where is the dining-room, if there

is one? And the inns? I looked, but never a one could I see
as we rode up, though I had been borne up by the hope of
a draught of ale as soon as we came to the homes of wise
and courtly men.'

Beregond looked at him gravely. 'An old campaigner, I
see,' he said. 'They say that men who go warring afield look
ever to the next hope of food and of drink; though I am not
a travelled man myself. Then you have not yet eaten today?'

'Well, yes, to speak in courtesy, yes,' said Pippin. 'But no
more than a cup of wine and a white cake or two by the
kindness of your lord; but he racked me for it with an hour
of questions, and that is hungry work.'

Beregond laughed. 'At the table small men may do the
greater deeds, we say. But you have broken your fast as well
as any man in the Citadel, and with greater honour. This is
a fortress and a tower of guard and is now in posture of war.
We rise ere the Sun, and take a morsel in the grey light, and
go to our duties at the opening hour. But do not despair!'
He laughed again, seeing the dismay in Pippin's face. 'Those
who have had *heavy* duty take somewhat to refresh their
strength in the mid-morning. Then there is the nuncheon,
at noon or after as duties allow; and men gather for the
daymeal, and such mirth as there still may be, about the hour
of sunset.

'Come! We will walk a little and then go find us some
refreshment, and eat and drink on the battlement, and survey
the fair morning.'

'One moment!' said Pippin blushing. 'Greed, or hunger
by your courtesy, put it out of my mind. But Gandalf,
Mithrandir as you call him, asked me to see to his horse –
Shadowfax, a great steed of Rohan, and the apple of the
king's eye, I am told, though he has given him to Mithrandir
for his services. I think his new master loves the beast better
than he loves many men, and if his good will is of any value
to this city, you will treat Shadowfax with all honour: with
greater kindness than you have treated this hobbit, if it is
possible.'

'Hobbit?' said Beregond.

'That is what we call ourselves,' said Pippin.

'I am glad to learn it,' said Beregond, 'for now I may say that strange accents do not mar fair speech, and hobbits are a fair-spoken folk. But come! You shall make me acquainted with this good horse. I love beasts, and we see them seldom in this stony city; for my people came from the mountain-vales, and before that from Ithilien. But fear not! The visit shall be short, a mere call of courtesy, and we will go thence to the butteries.'

Pippin found that Shadowfax had been well housed and tended. For in the sixth circle, outside the walls of the citadel, there were some fair stables where a few swift horses were kept, hard by the lodgings of the errand-riders of the Lord: messengers always ready to go at the urgent command of Denethor or his chief captains. But now all the horses and the riders were out and away.

Shadowfax whinnied as Pippin entered the stable and turned his head. 'Good morning!' said Pippin. 'Gandalf will come as soon as he may. He is busy, but he sends greetings, and I am to see that all is well with you; and you resting, I hope, after your long labours.'

Shadowfax tossed his head and stamped. But he allowed Beregond to handle his head gently and stroke his great flanks.

'He looks as if he were spoiling for a race, and not newly come from a great journey,' said Beregond. 'How strong and proud he is! Where is his harness? It should be rich and fair.'

'None is rich and fair enough for him,' said Pippin. 'He will have none. If he will consent to bear you, bear you he does; and if not, well, no bit, bridle, whip, or thong will tame him. Farewell, Shadowfax! Have patience. Battle is coming.'

Shadowfax lifted up his head and neighed, so that the stable shook, and they covered their ears. Then they took their leave, seeing that the manger was well filled.

'And now for our manger,' said Beregond, and he led

Pippin back to the citadel, and so to a door in the north side of the great tower. There they went down a long cool stair into a wide alley lit with lamps. There were hatches in the walls at the side, and one of these was open.

'This is the storehouse and buttery of my company of the Guard,' said Beregond. 'Greetings, Targon!' he called through the hatch. 'It is early yet, but here is a newcomer that the Lord has taken into his service. He has ridden long and far with a tight belt, and has had sore labour this morning, and he is hungry. Give us what you have!'

They got there bread, and butter, and cheese and apples: the last of the winter store, wrinkled but sound and sweet; and a leather flagon of new-drawn ale, and wooden platters and cups. They put all into a wicker basket and climbed back into the sun; and Beregond brought Pippin to a place at the east end of the great out-thrust battlement where there was an embrasure in the walls with a stone seat beneath the sill. From there they could look out on the morning over the world.

They ate and drank; and they talked now of Gondor and its ways and customs, now of the Shire and the strange countries that Pippin had seen. And ever as they talked Beregond was more amazed, and looked with greater wonder at the hobbit, swinging his short legs as he sat on the seat, or standing tiptoe upon it to peer over the sill at the lands below.

'I will not hide from you, Master Peregrin,' said Beregond, 'that to us you look almost as one of our children, a lad of nine summers or so; and yet you have endured perils and seen marvels that few of our greybeards could boast of. I thought it was the whim of our Lord to take him a noble page, after the manner of the kings of old, they say. But I see that it is not so, and you must pardon my foolishness.'

'I do,' said Pippin. 'Though you are not far wrong. I am still little more than a boy in the reckoning of my own people, and it will be four years yet before I "come of age", as we say in the Shire. But do not bother about me. Come and look and tell me what I can see.'

*   *   *

The sun was now climbing, and the mists in the vale below had been drawn up. The last of them were floating away, just overhead, as wisps of white cloud borne on the stiffening breeze from the East, that was now flapping and tugging the flags and white standards of the citadel. Away down in the valley-bottom, five leagues or so as the eye leaps, the Great River could now be seen grey and glittering, coming out of the north-west, and bending in a mighty sweep south and west again, till it was lost to view in a haze and shimmer, far beyond which lay the Sea fifty leagues away.

Pippin could see all the Pelennor laid out before him, dotted into the distance with farmsteads and little walls, barns and byres, but nowhere could he see any kine or other beasts. Many roads and tracks crossed the green fields, and there was much coming and going: wains moving in lines towards the Great Gate, and others passing out. Now and again a horseman would ride up, and leap from the saddle and hasten into the City. But most of the traffic went out along the chief highway, and that turned south, and then bending swifter than the River skirted the hills and passed soon from sight. It was wide and well-paved, and along its eastern edge ran a broad green riding-track, and beyond that a wall. On the ride horsemen galloped to and fro, but all the street seemed to be choked with great covered wains going south. But soon Pippin saw that all was in fact well-ordered: the wains were moving in three lines, one swifter drawn by horses; another slower, great waggons with fair housings of many colours, drawn by oxen; and along the west rim of the road many smaller carts hauled by trudging men.

'That is the road to the vales of Tumladen and Lossarnach, and the mountain-villages, and then on to Lebennin,' said Beregond. 'There go the last of the wains that bear away to refuge the aged, the children, and the women that must go with them. They must all be gone from the Gate and the road clear for a league before noon: that was the order. It is a sad necessity.' He sighed. 'Few, maybe, of those now sundered will meet again. And there were always too few children in this city; but now there are none – save some young lads that will not depart, and may find some task to do: my own son is one of them.'

They fell silent for a while. Pippin gazed anxiously eastward, as if at any moment he might see thousands of orcs pouring over the fields. 'What can I see there?' he asked, pointing down to the middle of the great curve of the Anduin. 'Is that another city, or what is it?'

'It was a city,' said Beregond, 'the chief city of Gondor, of which this was only a fortress. For that is the ruin of Osgiliath on either side of Anduin, which our enemies took and burned long ago. Yet we won it back in the days of the youth of Denethor: not to dwell in, but to hold as an outpost, and to rebuild the bridge for the passage of our arms. And then came the Fell Riders out of Minas Morgul.'

'The Black Riders?' said Pippin, opening his eyes, and they were wide and dark with an old fear re-awakened.

'Yes, they were black,' said Beregond, 'and I see that you know something of them, though you have not spoken of them in any of your tales.'

'I know of them,' said Pippin softly, 'but I will not speak of them now, so near, so near.' He broke off and lifted his eyes above the River, and it seemed to him that all he could see was a vast and threatening shadow. Perhaps it was mountains looming on the verge of sight, their jagged edges softened by wellnigh twenty leagues of misty air; perhaps it was but a cloud-wall, and beyond that again a yet deeper gloom. But even as he looked it seemed to his eyes that the gloom was growing and gathering, very slowly, slowly rising to smother the regions of the sun.

'So near to Mordor?' said Beregond quietly. 'Yes, there it lies. We seldom name it; but we have dwelt ever in sight of that shadow: sometimes it seems fainter and more distant; sometimes nearer and darker. It is growing and darkening now; and therefore our fear and disquiet grow too. And the Fell Riders, less than a year ago they won back the crossings, and many of our best men were slain. Boromir it was that

drove the enemy at last back from this western shore, and
we hold still the near half of Osgiliath. For a little while.
But we await now a new onslaught there. Maybe the chief
onslaught of the war that comes.'

'When?' said Pippin. 'Have you a guess? For I saw the
beacons last night and the errand-riders; and Gandalf said
that it was a sign that war had begun. He seemed in a desperate hurry. But now everything seems to have slowed up
again.'

'Only because everything is now ready,' said Beregond. 'It
is but the deep breath before the plunge.'

'But why were the beacons lit last night?'

'It is over-late to send for aid when you are already
besieged,' answered Beregond. 'But I do not know the counsel of the Lord and his captains. They have many ways of
gathering news. And the Lord Denethor is unlike other men:
he sees far. Some say that as he sits alone in his high chamber
in the Tower at night, and bends his thought this way and
that, he can read somewhat of the future; and that he will at
times search even the mind of the Enemy, wrestling with
him. And so it is that he is old, worn before his time. But
however that may be, my lord Faramir is abroad, beyond the
River on some perilous errand, and he may have sent tidings.

'But if you would know what I think set the beacons ablaze,
it was the news that came yestereve out of Lebennin. There
is a great fleet drawing near to the mouths of Anduin, manned
by the corsairs of Umbar in the South. They have long ceased
to fear the might of Gondor, and they have allied them with
the Enemy, and now make a heavy stroke in his cause. For
this attack will draw off much of the help that we looked to
have from Lebennin and Belfalas, where folk are hardy and
numerous. All the more do our thoughts go north to Rohan;
and the more glad are we for these tidings of victory that
you bring.

'And yet' – he paused and stood up, and looked round,
north, east, and south – 'the doings at Isengard should warn
us that we are caught now in a great net and strategy. This

is no longer a bickering at the fords, raiding from Ithilien and from Anórien, ambushing and pillaging. This is a great war long-planned, and we are but one piece in it, whatever pride may say. Things move in the far East beyond the Inland Sea, it is reported; and north in Mirkwood and beyond; and south in Harad. And now all realms shall be put to the test, to stand, or fall – under the Shadow.

'Yet, Master Peregrin, we have this honour: ever we bear the brunt of the chief hatred of the Dark Lord, for that hatred comes down out of the depths of time and over the deeps of the Sea. Here will the hammer-stroke fall hardest. And for that reason Mithrandir came hither in such haste. For if we fall, who shall stand? And, Master Peregrin, do you see any hope that we shall stand?'

Pippin did not answer. He looked at the great walls, and the towers and brave banners, and the sun in the high sky, and then at the gathering gloom in the East; and he thought of the long fingers of that Shadow: of the orcs in the woods and the mountains, the treason of Isengard, the birds of evil eye, and the Black Riders even in the lanes of the Shire – and of the winged terror, the Nazgûl. He shuddered, and hope seemed to wither. And even at that moment the sun for a second faltered and was obscured, as though a dark wing had passed across it. Almost beyond hearing he thought he caught, high and far up in the heavens, a cry: faint, but heart-quelling, cruel and cold. He blanched and cowered against the wall.

'What was that?' asked Beregond. 'You also felt something?'

'Yes,' muttered Pippin. 'It is the sign of our fall, and the shadow of doom, a Fell Rider of the air.'

'Yes, the shadow of doom,' said Beregond. 'I fear that Minas Tirith shall fall. Night comes. The very warmth of my blood seems stolen away.'

For a time they sat together with bowed heads and did not speak. Then suddenly Pippin looked up and saw that the sun was still shining and the banners still streaming in the breeze. He shook himself. 'It is passed,' he said. 'No, my heart will not yet despair. Gandalf fell and has returned and is with us. We may stand, if only on one leg, or at least be left still upon our knees.'

'Rightly said!' cried Beregond, rising and striding to and fro. 'Nay, though all things must come utterly to an end in time, Gondor shall not perish yet. Not though the walls be taken by a reckless foe that will build a hill of carrion before them. There are still other fastnesses, and secret ways of escape into the mountains. Hope and memory shall live still in some hidden valley where the grass is green.'

'All the same, I wish it was over for good or ill,' said Pippin. 'I am no warrior at all and dislike any thought of battle; but waiting on the edge of one that I can't escape is worst of all. What a long day it seems already! I should be happier, if we were not obliged to stand and watch, making no move, striking nowhere first. No stroke would have been struck in Rohan, I think, but for Gandalf.'

'Ah, there you lay your finger on the sore that many feel!' said Beregond. 'But things may change when Faramir returns. He is bold, more bold than many deem; for in these days men are slow to believe that a captain can be wise and learned in the scrolls of lore and song, as he is, and yet a man of hardihood and swift judgement in the field. But such is Faramir. Less reckless and eager than Boromir, but not less resolute. Yet what indeed can he do? We cannot assault the mountains of – of yonder realm. Our reach is shortened, and we cannot strike till some foe comes within it. Then our hand must be heavy!' He smote the hilt of his sword.

Pippin looked at him: tall and proud and noble, as all the men that he had yet seen in that land; and with a glitter in his eye as he thought of the battle. 'Alas! my own hand feels as light as a feather,' he thought, but he said nothing. 'A pawn did Gandalf say? Perhaps; but on the wrong chessboard.'

So they talked until the sun reached its height, and suddenly the noon-bells were rung, and there was a stir in the citadel; for all save the watchmen were going to their meal.

'Will you come with me?' said Beregond. 'You may join my mess for this day. I do not know to what company you will be assigned; or the Lord may hold you at his own command. But you will be welcome. And it will be well to meet as many men as you may, while there is yet time.'

'I shall be glad to come,' said Pippin. 'I am lonely, to tell you the truth. I left my best friend behind in Rohan, and I have had no one to talk to or jest with. Perhaps I could really join your company? Are you the captain? If so, you could take me on, or speak for me?'

'Nay, nay,' Beregond laughed, 'I am no captain. Neither office nor rank nor lordship have I, being but a plain man of arms of the Third Company of the Citadel. Yet, Master Peregrin, to be only a man of arms of the Guard of the Tower of Gondor is held worthy in the City, and such men have honour in the land.'

'Then it is far beyond me,' said Pippin. 'Take me back to our room, and if Gandalf is not there, I will go where you like – as your guest.'

Gandalf was not in the lodging and had sent no message; so Pippin went with Beregond and was made known to the men of the Third Company. And it seemed that Beregond got as much honour from it as his guest, for Pippin was very welcome. There had already been much talk in the citadel about Mithrandir's companion and his long closeting with the Lord; and rumour declared that a Prince of the Halflings had come out of the North to offer allegiance to Gondor and five thousand swords. And some said that when the Riders came from Rohan each would bring behind him a halfling warrior, small maybe, but doughty.

Though Pippin had regretfully to destroy this hopeful tale, he could not be rid of his new rank, only fitting, men thought, to one befriended by Boromir and honoured by the Lord

Denethor; and they thanked him for coming among them, and hung on his words and stories of the outlands, and gave him as much food and ale as he could wish. Indeed his only trouble was to be 'wary' according to the counsel of Gandalf, and not to let his tongue wag freely after the manner of a hobbit among friends.

At length Beregond rose. 'Farewell for this time!' he said. 'I have duty now till sundown, as have all the others here, I think. But if you are lonely, as you say, maybe you would like a merry guide about the City. My son would go with you gladly. A good lad, I may say. If that pleases you, go down to the lowest circle and ask for the Old Guesthouse in the Rath Celerdain, the Lampwrights' Street. You will find him there with other lads that are remaining in the City. There may be things worth seeing down at the Great Gate ere the closing.'

He went out, and soon after all the others followed. The day was still fine, though it was growing hazy, and it was hot for March, even so far southwards. Pippin felt sleepy, but the lodging seemed cheerless, and he decided to go down and explore the City. He took a few morsels that he had saved to Shadowfax, and they were graciously accepted, though the horse seemed to have no lack. Then he walked on down many winding ways.

People stared much as he passed. To his face men were gravely courteous, saluting him after the manner of Gondor with bowed head and hands upon the breast; but behind him he heard many calls, as those out of doors cried to others within to come and see the Prince of the Halflings, the companion of Mithrandir. Many used some other tongue than the Common Speech, but it was not long before he learned at least what was meant by *Ernil i Pheriannath* and knew that his title had gone down before him into the City.

He came at last by arched streets and many fair alleys and pavements to the lowest and widest circle, and there he was directed to the Lampwrights' Street, a broad way running towards the Great Gate. In it he found the Old Guesthouse, a large building of grey weathered stone with two wings running back from the street, and between them a narrow greensward, behind which was the many-windowed house, fronted along its whole width by a pillared porch and a flight of steps down on to the grass. Boys were playing among the pillars, the only children that Pippin had seen in Minas Tirith, and he stopped to look at them. Presently one of them caught sight of him, and with a shout he sprang across the grass and came into the street, followed by several others. There he stood in front of Pippin, looking him up and down.

'Greetings!' said the lad. 'Where do you come from? You are a stranger in the City.'

'I was,' said Pippin; 'but they say I have become a man of Gondor.'

'Oh come!' said the lad. 'Then we are all men here. But how old are you, and what is your name? I am ten years already, and shall soon be five feet. I am taller than you. But then my father is a Guard, one of the tallest. What is your father?'

'Which question shall I answer first?' said Pippin. 'My father farms the lands round Whitwell near Tuckborough in the Shire. I am nearly twenty-nine, so I pass you there; though I am but four feet, and not likely to grow any more, save sideways.'

'Twenty-nine!' said the lad and whistled. 'Why, you are quite old! As old as my uncle Iorlas. Still,' he added hopefully, 'I wager I could stand you on your head or lay you on your back.'

'Maybe you could, if I let you,' said Pippin with a laugh. 'And maybe I could do the same to you: we know some wrestling tricks in my little country. Where, let me tell you, I am considered uncommonly large and strong; and I have never allowed anyone to stand me on my head. So if it came to a trial and nothing else would serve, I might have to kill you. For when you are older, you will learn that folk are not always what they seem; and though you may have taken me for a soft stranger-lad and easy prey, let me warn you: I am not, I am a halfling, hard, bold, and wicked!' Pippin pulled such a grim face that the boy stepped back a pace, but at once he returned with clenched fists and the light of battle in his eye.

'No!' Pippin laughed. 'Don't believe what strangers say of themselves either! I am not a fighter. But it would be politer in any case for the challenger to say who he is.'

The boy drew himself up proudly. 'I am Bergil son of Beregond of the Guards,' he said.

'So I thought,' said Pippin, 'for you look like your father. I know him and he sent me to find you.'

'Then why did you not say so at once?' said Bergil, and suddenly a look of dismay came over his face. 'Do not tell me that he has changed his mind, and will send me away with the maidens! But no, the last wains have gone.'

'His message is less bad than that, if not good,' said Pippin. 'He says that if you would prefer it to standing me on my head, you might show me round the City for a while and cheer my loneliness. I can tell you some tales of far countries in return.'

Bergil clapped his hands, and laughed with relief. 'All is well,' he cried. 'Come then! We were soon going to the Gate to look on. We will go now.'

'What is happening there?'

'The Captains of the Outlands are expected up the South Road ere sundown. Come with us and you will see.'

Bergil proved a good comrade, the best company Pippin had had since he parted from Merry, and soon they were laughing and talking gaily as they went about the streets, heedless of the many glances that men gave them. Before long they found themselves in a throng going towards the Great Gate. There Pippin went up much in the esteem of Bergil, for when he spoke his name and the pass-word the guard saluted him and let him pass through; and what was more, he allowed him to take his companion with him.

'That is good!' said Bergil. 'We boys are no longer allowed to pass the Gate without an elder. Now we shall see better.'

Beyond the Gate there was a crowd of men along the verge of the road and of the great paved space into which all the ways to Minas Tirith ran. All eyes were turned southwards, and soon a murmur rose: 'There is dust away there! They are coming!'

Pippin and Bergil edged their way forward to the front of the crowd, and waited. Horns sounded at some distance, and the noise of cheering rolled towards them like a gathering wind. Then there was a loud trumpet-blast, and all about them people were shouting.

'Forlong! Forlong!' Pippin heard men calling. 'What do they say?' he asked.

'Forlong has come,' Bergil answered; 'old Forlong the Fat, the Lord of Lossarnach. That is where my grandsire lives. Hurrah! Here he is. Good old Forlong!'

Leading the line there came walking a big thick-limbed horse, and on it sat a man of wide shoulders and huge girth, but old and grey-bearded, yet mail-clad and black-helmed and bearing a long heavy spear. Behind him marched proudly a dusty line of men, well-armed and bearing great battle-axes; grim-faced they were, and shorter and somewhat swarthier than any men that Pippin had yet seen in Gondor.

'Forlong!' men shouted. 'True heart, true friend! Forlong!' But when the men of Lossarnach had passed they muttered: 'So few! Two hundreds, what are they? We hoped for ten times the number. That will be the new tidings of the black fleet. They are sparing only a tithe of their strength. Still every little is a gain.'

And so the companies came and were hailed and cheered and passed through the Gate, men of the Outlands marching to defend the City of Gondor in a dark hour; but always too few, always less than hope looked for or need asked. The men of Ringló Vale behind the son of their lord, Dervorin

striding on foot: three hundreds. From the uplands of Morthond, the great Blackroot Vale, tall Duinhir with his sons,
Duilin and Derufin, and five hundred bowmen. From the
Anfalas, the Langstrand far away, a long line of men of many
sorts, hunters and herdsmen and men of little villages, scantily
equipped save for the household of Golasgil their lord. From
Lamedon, a few grim hillmen without a captain. Fisher-folk
of the Ethir, some hundred or more spared from the ships.
Hirluin the Fair of the Green Hills from Pinnath Gelin with
three hundreds of gallant green-clad men. And last and
proudest, Imrahil, Prince of Dol Amroth, kinsman of the
Lord, with gilded banners bearing his token of the Ship and
the Silver Swan, and a company of knights in full harness
riding grey horses; and behind them seven hundreds of men
at arms, tall as lords, grey-eyed, dark-haired, singing as they
came.

And that was all, less than three thousands full told. No
more would come. Their cries and the tramp of their feet
passed into the City and died away. The onlookers stood
silent for a while. Dust hung in the air, for the wind had died
and the evening was heavy. Already the closing hour was
drawing nigh, and the red sun had gone behind Mindolluin.
Shadow came down on the City.

Pippin looked up, and it seemed to him that the sky had
grown ashen-grey, as if a vast dust and smoke hung above
them, and light came dully through it. But in the West the
dying sun had set all the fume on fire, and now Mindolluin
stood black against a burning smoulder flecked with embers.
'So ends a fair day in wrath!' he said, forgetful of the lad at
his side.

'So it will, if I have not returned before the sundown-bells,'
said Bergil. 'Come! There goes the trumpet for the closing
of the Gate.'

Hand in hand they went back into the City, the last to
pass the Gate before it was shut; and as they reached the
Lampwrights' Street all the bells in the towers tolled solemnly.

Lights sprang in many windows, and from the houses and
wards of the men at arms along the walls there came the
sound of song.

'Farewell for this time,' said Bergil. 'Take my greetings to
my father, and thank him for the company that he sent.
Come again soon, I beg. Almost I wish now that there was
no war, for we might have had some merry times. We might
have journeyed to Lossarnach, to my grandsire's house; it is
good to be there in Spring, the woods and fields are full of
flowers. But maybe we will go thither together yet. They will
never overcome our Lord, and my father is very valiant.
Farewell and return!'

They parted and Pippin hurried back towards the citadel.
It seemed a long way, and he grew hot and very hungry; and
night closed down swift and dark. Not a star pricked the sky.
He was late for the daymeal in the mess, and Beregond
greeted him gladly, and sat him at his side to hear news of
his son. After the meal Pippin stayed a while, and then took
his leave, for a strange gloom was on him, and now he desired
very much to see Gandalf again.

'Can you find your way?' said Beregond at the door of the
small hall, on the north side of the citadel, where they had
sat. 'It is a black night, and all the blacker since orders came
that lights are to be dimmed within the City, and none are
to shine out from the walls. And I can give you news of
another order: you will be summoned to the Lord Denethor
early tomorrow. I fear you will not be for the Third Company.
Still we may hope to meet again. Farewell and sleep in peace!'

The lodging was dark, save for a little lantern set on the
table. Gandalf was not there. Gloom settled still more heavily
on Pippin. He climbed on the bench and tried to peer out
of a window, but it was like looking into a pool of ink. He
got down and closed the shutter and went to bed. For a while
he lay and listened for sounds of Gandalf's return, and then
he fell into an uneasy sleep.

In the night he was wakened by a light, and he saw that
Gandalf had come and was pacing to and fro in the room

beyond the curtain of the alcove. There were candles on the table and rolls of parchment. He heard the wizard sigh, and mutter: 'When will Faramir return?'

'Hullo!' said Pippin, poking his head round the curtain. 'I thought you had forgotten all about me. I am glad to see you back. It has been a long day.'

'But the night will be too short,' said Gandalf. 'I have come back here, for I must have a little peace, alone. You should sleep, in a bed while you still may. At the sunrise I shall take you to the Lord Denethor again. No, when the summons comes, not at sunrise. The Darkness has begun. There will be no dawn.'

CHAPTER II

THE PASSING OF THE GREY COMPANY

Gandalf was gone, and the thudding hoofs of Shadowfax were lost in the night, when Merry came back to Aragorn. He had only a light bundle, for he had lost his pack at Parth Galen, and all he had was a few useful things he had picked up among the wreckage of Isengard. Hasufel was already saddled. Legolas and Gimli with their horse stood close by.

'So four of the Company still remain,' said Aragorn. 'We will ride on together. But we shall not go alone, as I thought. The king is now determined to set out at once. Since the coming of the winged shadow, he desires to return to the hills under cover of night.'

'And then whither?' said Legolas.

'I cannot say yet,' Aragorn answered. 'As for the king, he will go to the muster that he commanded at Edoras, four nights from now. And there, I think, he will hear tidings of war, and the Riders of Rohan will go down to Minas Tirith. But for myself, and any that will go with me . . .'

'I for one!' cried Legolas. 'And Gimli with him!' said the Dwarf.

'Well, for myself,' said Aragorn, 'it is dark before me. I must go down also to Minas Tirith, but I do not yet see the road. An hour long prepared approaches.'

'Don't leave me behind!' said Merry. 'I have not been of much use yet; but I don't want to be laid aside, like baggage to be called for when all is over. I don't think the Riders will want to be bothered with me now. Though, of course, the king did say that I was to sit by him when he came to his house and tell him all about the Shire.'

'Yes,' said Aragorn, 'and your road lies with him, I think, Merry. But do not look for mirth at the ending. It will be long, I fear, ere Théoden sits at ease again in Meduseld. Many hopes will wither in this bitter Spring.'

Soon all were ready to depart: twenty-four horses, with Gimli behind Legolas, and Merry in front of Aragorn. Presently they were riding swiftly through the night. They had not long passed the mounds at the Fords of Isen, when a Rider galloped up from the rear of their line.

'My lord,' he said to the king, 'there are horsemen behind us. As we crossed the fords I thought that I heard them. Now we are sure. They are overtaking us, riding hard.'

Théoden at once called a halt. The Riders turned about and seized their spears. Aragorn dismounted and set Merry on the ground, and drawing his sword he stood by the king's stirrup. Éomer and his esquire rode back to the rear. Merry felt more like unneeded baggage than ever, and he wondered, if there was a fight, what he should do. Supposing the king's small escort was trapped and overcome, but he escaped into the darkness – alone in the wild fields of Rohan with no idea of where he was in all the endless miles? 'No good!' he thought. He drew his sword and tightened his belt.

The sinking moon was obscured by a great sailing cloud, but suddenly it rode out clear again. Then they all heard the sound of hoofs, and at the same moment they saw dark shapes coming swiftly on the path from the fords. The moonlight glinted here and there on the points of spears. The number of the pursuers could not be told, but they seemed no fewer than the king's escort, at the least.

When they were some fifty paces off, Éomer cried in a loud voice: 'Halt! Halt! Who rides in Rohan?'

The pursuers brought their steeds to a sudden stand. A silence followed; and then in the moonlight, a horseman could be seen dismounting and walking slowly forward. His hand showed white as he held it up, palm outward, in token of peace; but the king's men gripped their weapons. At ten paces the man stopped. He was tall, a dark standing shadow. Then his clear voice rang out.

'Rohan? Rohan did you say? That is a glad word. We seek that land in haste from long afar.'

'You have found it,' said Éomer. 'When you crossed the fords yonder you entered it. But it is the realm of Théoden the King. None ride here save by his leave. Who are you? And what is your haste?'

'Halbarad Dúnadan, Ranger of the North I am,' cried the man. 'We seek one Aragorn son of Arathorn, and we heard that he was in Rohan.'

'And you have found him also!' cried Aragorn. Giving his reins to Merry, he ran forward and embraced the newcomer. 'Halbarad!' he said. 'Of all joys this is the least expected!'

Merry breathed a sigh of relief. He had thought that this was some last trick of Saruman's, to waylay the king while he had only a few men about him; but it seemed that there would be no need to die in Théoden's defence, not yet at any rate. He sheathed his sword.

'All is well,' said Aragorn, turning back. 'Here are some of my own kin from the far land where I dwelt. But why they come, and how many they be, Halbarad shall tell us.'

'I have thirty with me,' said Halbarad. 'That is all of our kindred that could be gathered in haste; but the brethren Elladan and Elrohir have ridden with us, desiring to go to the war. We rode as swiftly as we might when your summons came.'

'But I did not summon you,' said Aragorn, 'save only in wish. My thoughts have often turned to you, and seldom more than tonight; yet I have sent no word. But come! All such matters must wait. You find us riding in haste and danger. Ride with us now, if the king will give his leave.'

Théoden was indeed glad of the news. 'It is well!' he said. 'If these kinsmen be in any way like to yourself, my lord Aragorn, thirty such knights will be a strength that cannot be counted by heads.'

Then the Riders set out again, and Aragorn for a while rode with the Dúnedain; and when they had spoken of tidings in the North and in the South, Elrohir said to him:

'I bring word to you from my father: *The days are short. If thou art in haste, remember the Paths of the Dead.*'

'Always my days have seemed to me too short to achieve my desire,' answered Aragorn. 'But great indeed will be my haste ere I take that road.'

'That will soon be seen,' said Elrohir. 'But let us speak no more of these things upon the open road!'

And Aragorn said to Halbarad: 'What is that that you bear, kinsman?' For he saw that instead of a spear he bore a tall staff, as it were a standard, but it was close-furled in a black cloth bound about with many thongs.

'It is a gift that I bring you from the Lady of Rivendell,' answered Halbarad. 'She wrought it in secret, and long was the making. But she also sends word to you: *The days now are short. Either our hope cometh, or all hopes end. Therefore I send thee what I have made for thee. Fare well, Elfstone!*'

And Aragorn said: 'Now I know what you bear. Bear it still for me a while!' And he turned and looked away to the North under the great stars, and then he fell silent and spoke no more while the night's journey lasted.

The night was old and the East grey when they rode up at last from Deeping-coomb and came back to the Hornburg. There they were to lie and rest for a brief while and take counsel.

Merry slept until he was roused by Legolas and Gimli. 'The Sun is high,' said Legolas. 'All others are up and doing. Come, Master Sluggard, and look at this place while you may!'

'There was a battle here three nights ago,' said Gimli, 'and here Legolas and I played a game that I won only by a single orc. Come and see how it was! And there are caves, Merry, caves of wonder! Shall we visit them, Legolas, do you think?'

'Nay! There is no time,' said the Elf. 'Do not spoil the wonder with haste! I have given you my word to return hither with you, if a day of peace and freedom comes again. But it is now near to noon, and at that hour we eat, and then set out again, I hear.'

Merry got up and yawned. His few hours' sleep had not been nearly enough; he was tired and rather dismal. He missed Pippin, and felt that he was only a burden, while everybody was making plans for speed in a business that he did not fully understand. 'Where is Aragorn?' he asked.

'In a high chamber of the Burg,' said Legolas. 'He has neither rested nor slept, I think. He went thither some hours ago, saying that he must take thought, and only his kinsman, Halbarad, went with him; but some dark doubt or care sits on him.'

'They are a strange company, these newcomers,' said Gimli. 'Stout men and lordly they are, and the Riders of Rohan look almost as boys beside them; for they are grim men of face, worn like weathered rocks for the most part, even as Aragorn himself; and they are silent.'

'But even as Aragorn they are courteous, if they break their silence,' said Legolas. 'And have you marked the brethren Elladan and Elrohir? Less sombre is their gear than the others', and they are fair and gallant as Elven-lords; and that is not to be wondered at in the sons of Elrond of Rivendell.'

'Why have they come? Have you heard?' asked Merry. He had now dressed, and he flung his grey cloak about his shoulders; and the three passed out together towards the ruined gate of the Burg.

'They answered a summons, as you heard,' said Gimli. 'Word came to Rivendell, they say: *Aragorn has need of his kindred. Let the Dúnedain ride to him in Rohan!* But whence this message came they are now in doubt. Gandalf sent it, I would guess.'

'Nay, Galadriel,' said Legolas. 'Did she not speak through Gandalf of the ride of the Grey Company from the North?'

'Yes, you have it,' said Gimli. 'The Lady of the Wood! She read many hearts and desires. Now why did not we wish for some of our own kinsfolk, Legolas?'

Legolas stood before the gate and turned his bright eyes away north and east, and his fair face was troubled. 'I do not think that any would come,' he answered. 'They have no need to ride to war; war already marches on their own lands.'

For a while the three companions walked together, speaking of this and that turn of the battle, and they went down from the broken gate, and passed the mounds of the fallen on the greensward beside the road, until they stood on Helm's Dike and looked into the Coomb. The Death Down already stood there, black and tall and stony, and the great trampling and scoring of the grass by the Huorns could be plainly seen. The Dunlendings and many men of the garrison of the Burg were at work on the Dike or in the fields and about the battered walls behind; yet all seemed strangely quiet: a weary valley resting after a great storm. Soon they turned back and went to the midday meal in the hall of the Burg.

The king was already there, and as soon as they entered he called for Merry and had a seat set for him at his side. 'It is not as I would have it,' said Théoden; 'for this is little like my fair house in Edoras. And your friend is gone, who should also be here. But it may be long ere we sit, you and I, at the high table in Meduseld; there will be no time for feasting when I return thither. But come now! Eat and drink, and let us speak together while we may. And then you shall ride with me.'

'May I?' said Merry, surprised and delighted. 'That would be splendid!' He had never felt more grateful for any kindness in words. 'I am afraid I am only in everybody's way,' he stammered; 'but I should like to do anything I could, you know.'

'I doubt it not,' said the king. 'I have had a good hill-pony made ready for you. He will bear you as swift as any horse by the roads that we shall take. For I will ride from the Burg by mountain paths, not by the plain, and so come to Edoras by way of Dunharrow where the Lady Éowyn awaits me.

You shall be my esquire, if you will. Is there gear of war in this place, Éomer, that my sword-thain could use?'

'There are no great weapon-hoards here, lord,' answered Éomer. 'Maybe a light helm might be found to fit him; but we have no mail or sword for one of his stature.'

'I have a sword,' said Merry, climbing from his seat, and drawing from its black sheath his small bright blade. Filled suddenly with love for this old man, he knelt on one knee, and took his hand and kissed it. 'May I lay the sword of Meriadoc of the Shire on your lap, Théoden King?' he cried. 'Receive my service, if you will!'

'Gladly will I take it,' said the king; and laying his long old hands upon the brown hair of the hobbit, he blessed him. 'Rise now, Meriadoc, esquire of Rohan of the household of Meduseld!' he said. 'Take your sword and bear it unto good fortune!'

'As a father you shall be to me,' said Merry.

'For a little while,' said Théoden.

They talked then together as they ate, until presently Éomer spoke. 'It is near the hour that we set for our going, lord,' he said. 'Shall I bid men sound the horns? But where is Aragorn? His place is empty and he has not eaten.'

'We will make ready to ride,' said Théoden; 'but let word be sent to the Lord Aragorn that the hour is nigh.'

The king with his guard and Merry at his side passed down from the gate of the Burg to where the Riders were assembling on the green. Many were already mounted. It would be a great company; for the king was leaving only a small garrison in the Burg, and all who could be spared were riding to the weapontake at Edoras. A thousand spears had indeed already ridden away at night; but still there would be some five hundred more to go with the king, for the most part men from the fields and dales of Westfold.

A little apart the Rangers sat, silent, in an ordered company, armed with spear and bow and sword. They were clad in cloaks of dark grey, and their hoods were cast now over helm and head. Their horses were strong and of proud bearing, but rough-haired; and one stood there without a rider, Aragorn's own horse that they had brought from the North; Roheryn was his name. There was no gleam of stone or gold, nor any fair thing in all their gear and harness; nor did their riders bear any badge or token, save only that each cloak was pinned upon the left shoulder by a brooch of silver shaped like a rayed star.

The king mounted his horse, Snowmane, and Merry sat beside him on his pony: Stybba was his name. Presently Éomer came out from the gate, and with him was Aragorn, and Halbarad bearing the great staff close-furled in black, and two tall men, neither young nor old. So much alike were they, the sons of Elrond, that few could tell them apart: dark-haired, grey-eyed, and their faces elven-fair, clad alike in bright mail beneath cloaks of silver-grey. Behind them walked Legolas and Gimli. But Merry had eyes only for Aragorn, so startling was the change that he saw in him, as if in one night many years had fallen on his head. Grim was his face, grey-hued and weary.

'I am troubled in mind, lord,' he said, standing by the king's horse. 'I have heard strange words, and I see new perils far off. I have laboured long in thought, and now I fear that I must change my purpose. Tell me, Théoden, you ride now to Dunharrow, how long will it be ere you come there?'

'It is now a full hour past noon,' said Éomer. 'Before the night of the third day from now we should come to the Hold. The Moon will then be one night past his full, and the muster that the king commanded will be held the day after. More speed we cannot make, if the strength of Rohan is to be gathered.'

Aragorn was silent for a moment. 'Three days,' he murmured, 'and the muster of Rohan will only be begun. But I see that it cannot now be hastened.' He looked up, and it seemed that he had made some decision; his face was less troubled. 'Then, by your leave, lord, I must take new counsel for myself and my kindred. We must ride our own road, and no longer in secret. For me the time of stealth has passed. I will ride east by the swiftest way, and I will take the Paths of the Dead.'

'The Paths of the Dead!' said Théoden, and trembled. 'Why do you speak of them?' Éomer turned and gazed at Aragorn, and it seemed to Merry that the faces of the Riders that sat within hearing turned pale at the words. 'If there be in truth such paths,' said Théoden, 'their gate is in Dunharrow; but no living man may pass it.'

'Alas! Aragorn my friend!' said Éomer. 'I had hoped that we should ride to war together; but if you seek the Paths of the Dead, then our parting is come, and it is little likely that we shall ever meet again under the Sun.'

'That road I will take, nonetheless,' said Aragorn. 'But I say to you, Éomer, that in battle we may yet meet again, though all the hosts of Mordor should stand between.'

'You will do as you will, my lord Aragorn,' said Théoden. 'It is your doom, maybe, to tread strange paths that others dare not. This parting grieves me, and my strength is lessened by it; but now I must take the mountain-roads and delay no longer. Farewell!'

'Farewell, lord!' said Aragorn. 'Ride unto great renown! Farewell, Merry! I leave you in good hands, better than we hoped when we hunted the orcs to Fangorn. Legolas and Gimli will still hunt with me, I hope; but we shall not forget you.'

'Good-bye!' said Merry. He could find no more to say. He felt very small, and he was puzzled and depressed by all these gloomy words. More than ever he missed the unquenchable cheerfulness of Pippin. The Riders were ready, and their horses were fidgeting; he wished they would start and get it over.

Now Théoden spoke to Éomer, and he lifted up his hand and cried aloud, and with that word the Riders set forth. They rode over the Dike and down the Coomb, and then, turning swiftly eastwards, they took a path that skirted the foothills for a mile or so, until bending south it passed back among the hills and disappeared from view. Aragorn rode to the Dike and watched till the king's men were far down the Coomb. Then he turned to Halbarad.

'There go three that I love, and the smallest not the least,' he said. 'He knows not to what end he rides; yet if he knew, he still would go on.'

'A little people, but of great worth are the Shire-folk,' said Halbarad. 'Little do they know of our long labour for the safekeeping of their borders, and yet I grudge it not.'

'And now our fates are woven together,' said Aragorn. 'And yet, alas! here we must part. Well, I must eat a little, and then we also must hasten away. Come, Legolas and Gimli! I must speak with you as I eat.'

Together they went back into the Burg; yet for some time Aragorn sat silent at the table in the hall, and the others waited for him to speak. 'Come!' said Legolas at last. 'Speak and be comforted, and shake off the shadow! What has happened since we came back to this grim place in the grey morning?'

'A struggle somewhat grimmer for my part than the battle of the Hornburg,' answered Aragorn. 'I have looked in the Stone of Orthanc, my friends.'

'You have looked in that accursed stone of wizardry!' exclaimed Gimli with fear and astonishment in his face. 'Did you say aught to – him? Even Gandalf feared that encounter.'

'You forget to whom you speak,' said Aragorn sternly, and his eyes glinted. 'What do you fear that I should say to him? Did I not openly proclaim my title before the doors of Edoras? Nay, Gimli,' he said in a softer voice, and the grimness left his face, and he looked like one who has laboured in sleepless pain for many nights. 'Nay, my friends, I am the lawful master of the Stone, and I had both the right and the strength to use it, or so I judged. The right cannot be doubted. The strength was enough – barely.'

He drew a deep breath. 'It was a bitter struggle, and the weariness is slow to pass. I spoke no word to him, and in the end I wrenched the Stone to my own will. That alone he will find hard to endure. And he beheld me. Yes, Master Gimli, he saw me, but in other guise than you see me here. If that will aid him, then I have done ill. But I do not think so. To know that I lived and walked the earth was a blow to his heart, I deem; for he knew it not till now. The eyes in Orthanc did not see through the armour of Théoden; but Sauron has not forgotten Isildur and the sword of Elendil. Now in the very hour of his great designs the heir of Isildur and the Sword are revealed; for I showed the blade re-forged to him. He is not so mighty yet that he is above fear; nay, doubt ever gnaws him.'

'But he wields great dominion, nonetheless,' said Gimli; 'and now he will strike more swiftly.'

'The hasty stroke goes oft astray,' said Aragorn. 'We must press our Enemy, and no longer wait upon him for the move. See my friends, when I had mastered the Stone, I learned many things. A grave peril I saw coming unlooked-for upon Gondor from the South that will draw off great strength from the defence of Minas Tirith. If it is not countered swiftly, I deem that the City will be lost ere ten days be gone.'

'Then lost it must be,' said Gimli. 'For what help is there to send thither, and how could it come there in time?'

'I have no help to send, therefore I must go myself,' said Aragorn. 'But there is only one way through the mountains that will bring me to the coastlands before all is lost. That is the Paths of the Dead.'

'The Paths of the Dead!' said Gimli. 'It is a fell name; and little to the liking to the Men of Rohan, as I saw. Can the living use such a road and not perish? And even if you pass that way, what will so few avail to counter the strokes of Mordor?'

'The living have never used that road since the coming of the Rohirrim,' said Aragorn, 'for it is closed to them. But in this dark hour the heir of Isildur may use it, if he dare. Listen! This is the word that the sons of Elrond bring to me from their father in Rivendell, wisest in lore: *Bid Aragorn remember the words of the seer, and the Paths of the Dead.*'

'And what may be the words of the seer?' said Legolas.

'Thus spoke Malbeth the Seer, in the days of Arvedui, last king at Fornost,' said Aragorn:

> *Over the land there lies a long shadow,*
> *westward reaching wings of darkness.*
> *The Tower trembles; to the tombs of kings*
> *doom approaches. The Dead awaken;*
> *for the hour is come for the oathbreakers:*
> *at the Stone of Erech they shall stand again*
> *and hear there a horn in the hills ringing.*
> *Whose shall the horn be? Who shall call them*
> *from the grey twilight, the forgotten people?*
> *The heir of him to whom the oath they swore.*
> *From the North shall he come, need shall drive him:*
> *he shall pass the Door to the Paths of the Dead.*

'Dark ways, doubtless,' said Gimli, 'but no darker than these staves are to me.'

'If you would understand them better, then I bid you come with me,' said Aragorn; 'for that way I now shall take. But I do not go gladly; only need drives me. Therefore, only of your free will would I have you come, for you will find both toil and great fear, and maybe worse.'

'I will go with you even on the Paths of the Dead, and to whatever end they may lead,' said Gimli.

'I also will come,' said Legolas, 'for I do not fear the Dead.'

'I hope that the forgotten people will not have forgotten how to fight,' said Gimli; 'for otherwise I see not why we should trouble them.'

'That we shall know if ever we come to Erech,' said Aragorn. 'But the oath that they broke was to fight against Sauron, and they must fight therefore, if they are to fulfil it. For at Erech there stands yet a black stone that was brought, it was said, from Númenor by Isildur; and it was set upon a hill, and upon it the King of the Mountains swore allegiance to him in the beginning of the realm of Gondor. But when

Sauron returned and grew in might again, Isildur summoned the Men of the Mountains to fulfil their oath, and they would not: for they had worshipped Sauron in the Dark Years.

'Then Isildur said to their king: "Thou shalt be the last king. And if the West prove mightier than thy Black Master, this curse I lay upon thee and thy folk: to rest never until your oath is fulfilled. For this war will last through years uncounted, and you shall be summoned once again ere the end." And they fled before the wrath of Isildur, and did not dare to go forth to war on Sauron's part; and they hid themselves in secret places in the mountains and had no dealings with other men, but slowly dwindled in the barren hills. And the terror of the Sleepless Dead lies about the Hill of Erech and all places where that people lingered. But that way I must go, since there are none living to help me.'

He stood up. 'Come!' he cried, and drew his sword, and it flashed in the twilit hall of the Burg. 'To the Stone of Erech! I seek the Paths of the Dead. Come with me who will!'

Legolas and Gimli made no answer, but they rose and followed Aragorn from the hall. On the green there waited, still and silent, the hooded Rangers. Legolas and Gimli mounted. Aragorn sprang upon Roheryn. Then Halbarad lifted a great horn, and the blast of it echoed in Helm's Deep: and with that they leapt away, riding down the Coomb like thunder, while all the men that were left on Dike or Burg stared in amaze.

And while Théoden went by slow paths in the hills, the Grey Company passed swiftly over the plain, and on the next day in the afternoon they came to Edoras; and there they halted only briefly, ere they passed up the valley, and so came to Dunharrow as darkness fell.

The Lady Éowyn greeted them and was glad of their coming; for no mightier men had she seen than the Dúnedain and the fair sons of Elrond; but on Aragorn most of all her eyes rested. And when they sat at supper with her, they talked together, and she heard of all that had passed since Théoden rode away, concerning which only hasty tidings had yet reached her; and when she heard of the battle in Helm's Deep and the great slaughter of their foes, and of the charge of Théoden and his knights, then her eyes shone.

But at last she said: 'Lords, you are weary and shall now go to your beds with such ease as can be contrived in haste. But tomorrow fairer housing shall be found for you.'

But Aragorn said: 'Nay, lady, be not troubled for us! If we may lie here tonight and break our fast tomorrow, it will be enough. For I ride on an errand most urgent, and with the first light of morning we must go.'

She smiled on him and said: 'Then it was kindly done, lord, to ride so many miles out of your way to bring tidings to Éowyn, and to speak with her in her exile.'

'Indeed no man would count such a journey wasted,' said Aragorn; 'and yet, lady, I could not have come hither, if it were not that the road which I must take leads me to Dunharrow.'

And she answered as one that likes not what is said: 'Then, lord, you are astray; for out of Harrowdale no road runs east or south; and you had best return as you came.'

'Nay, lady,' said he, 'I am not astray; for I walked in this land ere you were born to grace it. There is a road out of this valley, and that road I shall take. Tomorrow I shall ride by the Paths of the Dead.'

Then she stared at him as one that is stricken, and her face blanched, and for long she spoke no more, while all sat silent. 'But, Aragorn,' she said at last, 'is it then your errand to seek death? For that is all that you will find on that road. They do not suffer the living to pass.'

'They may suffer me to pass,' said Aragorn; 'but at the least I will adventure it. No other road will serve.'

'But this is madness,' she said. 'For here are men of renown and prowess, whom you should not take into the shadows, but should lead to war, where men are needed. I beg you to

remain and ride with my brother; for then all our hearts will
be gladdened, and our hope be the brighter.'

'It is not madness, lady,' he answered; 'for I go on a path
appointed. But those who follow me do so of their free will;
and if they wish now to remain and ride with the Rohirrim,
they may do so. But I shall take the Paths of the Dead, alone,
if needs be.'

Then they said no more, and they ate in silence; but her
eyes were ever upon Aragorn, and the others saw that she
was in great torment of mind. At length they arose, and took
their leave of the Lady, and thanked her for her care, and
went to their rest.

But as Aragorn came to the booth where he was to lodge
with Legolas and Gimli, and his companions had gone in,
there came the Lady Éowyn after him and called to him. He
turned and saw her as a glimmer in the night, for she was
clad in white; but her eyes were on fire.

'Aragorn,' she said, 'why will you go on this deadly road?'

'Because I must,' he said. 'Only so can I see any hope of
doing my part in the war against Sauron. I do not choose
paths of peril, Éowyn. Were I to go where my heart dwells,
far in the North I would now be wandering in the fair valley
of Rivendell.'

For a while she was silent, as if pondering what this might
mean. Then suddenly she laid her hand on his arm. 'You
are a stern lord and resolute,' she said; 'and thus do men win
renown.' She paused. 'Lord,' she said, 'if you must go, then
let me ride in your following. For I am weary of skulking in
the hills, and wish to face peril and battle.'

'Your duty is with your people,' he answered.

'Too often have I heard of duty,' she cried. 'But am I not
of the House of Eorl, a shieldmaiden and not a dry-nurse? I
have waited on faltering feet long enough. Since they falter
no longer, it seems, may I not now spend my life as I will?'

'Few may do that with honour,' he answered. 'But as for
you, lady: did you not accept the charge to govern the people
until their lord's return? If you had not been chosen, then

some marshal or captain would have been set in the same place, and he could not ride away from his charge, were he weary of it or no.'

'Shall I always be chosen?' she said bitterly. 'Shall I always be left behind when the Riders depart, to mind the house while they win renown, and find food and beds when they return?'

'A time may come soon,' said he, 'when none will return. Then there will be need of valour without renown, for none shall remember the deeds that are done in the last defence of your homes. Yet the deeds will not be less valiant because they are unpraised.'

And she answered: 'All your words are but to say: you are a woman, and your part is in the house. But when the men have died in battle and honour, you have leave to be burned in the house, for the men will need it no more. But I am of the House of Eorl and not a serving-woman. I can ride and wield blade, and I do not fear either pain or death.'

'What do you fear, lady?' he asked.

'A cage,' she said. 'To stay behind bars, until use and old age accept them, and all chance of doing great deeds is gone beyond recall or desire.'

'And yet you counselled me not to adventure on the road that I had chosen, because it is perilous?'

'So may one counsel another,' she said. 'Yet I do not bid you flee from peril, but to ride to battle where your sword may win renown and victory. I would not see a thing that is high and excellent cast away needlessly.'

'Nor would I,' he said. 'Therefore I say to you, lady: Stay! For you have no errand to the South.'

'Neither have those others who go with thee. They go only because they would not be parted from thee – because they love thee.' Then she turned and vanished into the night.

When the light of day was come into the sky but the sun was not yet risen above the high ridges in the East, Aragorn made ready to depart. His company was all mounted, and he was about to leap into the saddle, when the Lady Éowyn came to bid them farewell. She was clad as a Rider and girt with a sword. In her hand she bore a cup, and she set it to her lips and drank a little, wishing them good speed; and then she gave the cup to Aragorn, and he drank, and he said: 'Farewell, Lady of Rohan! I drink to the fortunes of your House, and of you, and of all your people. Say to your brother: beyond the shadows we may meet again!'

Then it seemed to Gimli and Legolas who were nearby that she wept, and in one so stern and proud that seemed the more grievous. But she said: 'Aragorn, wilt thou go?'

'I will,' he said.

'Then wilt thou not let me ride with this company, as I have asked?'

'I will not, lady,' he said. 'For that I could not grant without leave of the king and of your brother; and they will not return until tomorrow. But I count now every hour, indeed every minute. Farewell!'

Then she fell on her knees, saying: 'I beg thee!'

'Nay, lady,' he said, and taking her by the hand he raised her. Then he kissed her hand, and sprang into the saddle, and rode away, and did not look back; and only those who knew him well and were near to him saw the pain that he bore.

But Éowyn stood still as a figure carven in stone, her hands clenched at her sides, and she watched them until they passed into the shadows under the black Dwimorberg, the Haunted Mountain, in which was the Door of the Dead. When they were lost to view, she turned, stumbling as one that is blind, and went back to her lodging. But none of her folk saw this parting, for they hid themselves in fear and would not come forth until the day was up, and the reckless strangers were gone.

And some said: 'They are Elvish wights. Let them go where they belong, into the dark places, and never return. The times are evil enough.'

*   *   *

The light was still grey as they rode, for the sun had not yet climbed over the black ridges of the Haunted Mountain before them. A dread fell on them, even as they passed between the lines of ancient stones and so came to the Dimholt. There under the gloom of black trees that not even Legolas could long endure they found a hollow place opening at the mountain's root, and right in their path stood a single mighty stone like a finger of doom.

'My blood runs chill,' said Gimli, but the others were silent, and his voice fell dead on the dank fir-needles at his feet. The horses would not pass the threatening stone, until the riders dismounted and led them about. And so they came at last deep into the glen; and there stood a sheer wall of rock, and in the wall the Dark Door gaped before them like the mouth of night. Signs and figures were carved above its wide arch too dim to read, and fear flowed from it like a grey vapour.

The company halted, and there was not a heart among them that did not quail, unless it were the heart of Legolas of the Elves, for whom the ghosts of Men have no terror.

'This is an evil door,' said Halbarad, 'and my death lies beyond it. I will dare to pass it nonetheless; but no horse will enter.'

'But we must go in, and therefore the horses must go too,' said Aragorn. 'For if ever we come through this darkness, many leagues lie beyond, and every hour that is lost there will bring the triumph of Sauron nearer. Follow me!'

Then Aragorn led the way, and such was the strength of his will in that hour that all the Dúnedain and their horses followed him. And indeed the love that the horses of the Rangers bore for their riders was so great that they were willing to face even the terror of the Door, if their masters' hearts were steady as they walked beside them. But Arod, the horse of Rohan, refused the way, and he stood sweating and trembling in a fear that was grievous to see. Then Legolas laid his hands on his eyes and sang some words that went soft in the gloom, until he suffered himself to be led, and

Legolas passed in. And there stood Gimli the Dwarf left all alone.

His knees shook, and he was wroth with himself. 'Here is a thing unheard of!' he said. 'An Elf will go underground and a Dwarf dare not!' With that he plunged in. But it seemed to him that he dragged his feet like lead over the threshold; and at once a blindness came upon him, even upon Gimli Glóin's son who had walked unafraid in many deep places of the world.

Aragorn had brought torches from Dunharrow, and now he went ahead bearing one aloft; and Elladan with another went at the rear, and Gimli, stumbling behind, strove to overtake him. He could see nothing but the dim flame of the torches; but if the company halted, there seemed an endless whisper of voices all about him, a murmur of words in no tongue that he had ever heard before.

Nothing assailed the company nor withstood their passage, and yet steadily fear grew on the Dwarf as he went on: most of all because he knew now that there could be no turning back; all the paths behind were thronged by an unseen host that followed in the dark.

So time unreckoned passed, until Gimli saw a sight that he was ever afterwards loth to recall. The road was wide, as far as he could judge, but now the company came suddenly into a great empty space, and there were no longer any walls upon either side. The dread was so heavy on him that he could hardly walk. Away to the left something glittered in the gloom as Aragorn's torch drew near. Then Aragorn halted and went to look what it might be.

'Does he feel no fear?' muttered the Dwarf. 'In any other cave Gimli Glóin's son would have been the first to run to the gleam of gold. But not here! Let it lie!'

Nonetheless he drew near, and saw Aragorn kneeling, while Elladan held aloft both torches. Before him were the bones of a mighty man. He had been clad in mail, and still his harness lay there whole; for the cavern's air was as dry as dust, and his hauberk was gilded. His belt was of gold and garnets, and rich with gold was the helm upon his bony head face downward on the floor. He had fallen near the far wall of the cave, as now could be seen, and before him stood a stony door closed fast: his finger-bones were still clawing at the cracks. A notched and broken sword lay by him, as if he had hewn at the rock in his last despair.

Aragorn did not touch him, but after gazing silently for a while he rose and sighed. 'Hither shall the flowers of *simbelmynë* come never unto world's end,' he murmured. 'Nine mounds and seven there are now green with grass, and through all the long years he has lain at the door that he could not unlock. Whither does it lead? Why would he pass? None shall ever know!

'For that is not my errand!' he cried, turning back and speaking to the whispering darkness behind. 'Keep your hoards and your secrets hidden in the Accursed Years! Speed only we ask. Let us pass, and then come! I summon you to the Stone of Erech!'

There was no answer, unless it were an utter silence more dreadful than the whispers before; and then a chill blast came in which the torches flickered and went out, and could not be rekindled. Of the time that followed, one hour or many, Gimli remembered little. The others pressed on, but he was ever hindmost, pursued by a groping horror that seemed always just about to seize him; and a rumour came after him like the shadow-sound of many feet. He stumbled on until he was crawling like a beast on the ground and felt that he could endure no more: he must either find an ending and escape or run back in madness to meet the following fear.

Suddenly he heard the tinkle of water, a sound hard and clear as a stone falling into a dream of dark shadow. Light grew, and lo! the company passed through another gateway, high-arched and broad, and a rill ran out beside them; and beyond, going steeply down, was a road between sheer cliffs, knife-edged against the sky far above. So deep and narrow was that chasm that the sky was dark, and in it small stars glinted. Yet as Gimli after learned it was still two hours ere sunset of the day on which they had set out from Dunharrow; though for all that he could then tell it might have been twilight in some later year, or in some other world.

The Company now mounted again, and Gimli returned to Legolas. They rode in file, and evening came on and a deep blue dusk; and still fear pursued them. Legolas turning to speak to Gimli looked back and the Dwarf saw before his face the glitter in the Elf's bright eyes. Behind them rode Elladan, last of the Company, but not the last of those that took the downward road.

'The Dead are following,' said Legolas. 'I see shapes of Men and of horses, and pale banners like shreds of cloud, and spears like winter-thickets on a misty night. The Dead are following.'

'Yes, the Dead ride behind. They have been summoned,' said Elladan.

The Company came at last out of the ravine, as suddenly as if they had issued from a crack in a wall; and there lay the uplands of a great vale before them, and the stream beside them went down with a cold voice over many falls.

'Where in Middle-earth are we?' said Gimli; and Elladan answered: 'We have descended from the uprising of the Morthond, the long chill river that flows at last to the sea that washes the walls of Dol Amroth. You will not need to ask hereafter how comes its name: Blackroot men call it.'

The Morthond Vale made a great bay that beat up against the sheer southern faces of the mountains. Its steep slopes were grass-grown; but all was grey in that hour, for the sun had gone, and far below lights twinkled in the homes of Men. The vale was rich and many folk dwelt there.

Then without turning Aragorn cried aloud so that all could hear: 'Friends, forget your weariness! Ride now, ride! We must come to the Stone of Erech ere this day passes, and long still is the way.' So without looking back they rode the mountain-fields, until they came to a bridge over the growing torrent and found a road that went down into the land.

Lights went out in house and hamlet as they came, and doors were shut, and folk that were afield cried in terror and ran wild like hunted deer. Ever there rose the same cry in the gathering night: 'The King of the Dead ! The King of the Dead is come upon us!'

Bells were ringing far below, and all men fled before the face of Aragorn; but the Grey Company in their haste rode like hunters, until their horses were stumbling with weariness. And thus, just ere midnight, and in a darkness as black as the caverns in the mountains, they came at last to the Hill of Erech.

Long had the terror of the Dead lain upon that hill and upon the empty fields about it. For upon the top stood a black stone, round as a great globe, the height of a man, though its half was buried in the ground. Unearthly it looked, as though it had fallen from the sky, as some believed; but those who remembered still the lore of Westernesse told that it had been brought out of the ruin of Númenor and there set by Isildur at his landing. None of the people of the valley dared to approach it, nor would they dwell near; for they said that it was a trysting-place of the Shadow-men and there they would gather in times of fear, thronging round the Stone and whispering.

To that Stone the Company came and halted in the dead of night. Then Elrohir gave to Aragorn a silver horn, and he blew upon it; and it seemed to those that stood near that they heard a sound of answering horns, as if it was an echo in deep caves far away. No other sound they heard, and yet they were aware of a great host gathered all about the hill on which they stood; and a chill wind like the breath of ghosts came down from the mountains. But Aragorn dismounted, and standing by the Stone he cried in a great voice:

'Oathbreakers, why have ye come?'

And a voice was heard out of the night that answered him, as if from far away:

'To fulfil our oath and have peace.'

Then Aragorn said: 'The hour is come at last. Now I go to Pelargir upon Anduin, and ye shall come after me. And when all this land is clean of the servants of Sauron, I will hold the oath fulfilled, and ye shall have peace and depart for ever. For I am Elessar, Isildur's heir of Gondor.'

And with that he bade Halbarad unfurl the great standard which he had brought; and behold! it was black, and if there was any device upon it, it was hidden in the darkness. Then there was silence, and not a whisper nor a sigh was heard again all the long night. The Company camped beside the Stone, but they slept little, because of the dread of the Shadows that hedged them round.

But when the dawn came, cold and pale, Aragorn rose at once, and he led the Company forth upon the journey of greatest haste and weariness that any among them had known, save he alone, and only his will held them to go on. No other mortal Men could have endured it, none but the Dúnedain of the North, and with them Gimli the Dwarf and Legolas of the Elves.

They passed Tarlang's Neck and came into Lamedon; and the Shadow Host pressed behind and fear went on before them, until they came to Calembel upon Ciril, and the sun went down like blood behind Pinnath Gelin away in the West behind them. The township and the fords of Ciril they found deserted, for many men had gone away to war, and all that were left fled to the hills at the rumour of the coming of the King of the Dead. But the next day there came no dawn, and the Grey Company passed on into the darkness of the Storm of Mordor and were lost to mortal sight; but the Dead followed them.

CHAPTER III

THE MUSTER OF ROHAN

Now all roads were running together to the East to meet the coming of war and the onset of the Shadow. And even as Pippin stood at the Great Gate of the City and saw the Prince of Dol Amroth ride in with his banners, the King of Rohan came down out of the hills.

Day was waning. In the last rays of the sun the Riders cast long pointed shadows that went on before them. Darkness had already crept beneath the murmuring fir-woods that clothed the steep mountain-sides. The king rode now slowly at the end of the day. Presently the path turned round a huge bare shoulder of rock and plunged into the gloom of soft-sighing trees. Down, down they went in a long winding file. When at last they came to the bottom of the gorge they found that evening had fallen in the deep places. The sun was gone. Twilight lay upon the waterfalls.

All day far below them a leaping stream had run down from the high pass behind, cleaving its narrow way between pine-clad walls; and now through a stony gate it flowed out and passed into a wider vale. The Riders followed it, and suddenly Harrowdale lay before them, loud with the noise of waters in the evening. There the white Snowbourn, joined by the lesser stream, went rushing, fuming on the stones, down to Edoras and the green hills and the plains. Away to the right at the head of the great dale the mighty Starkhorn loomed up above its vast buttresses swathed in cloud; but its jagged peak, clothed in everlasting snow, gleamed far above the world, blue-shadowed upon the East, red-stained by the sunset in the West.

Merry looked out in wonder upon this strange country, of which he had heard many tales upon their long road. It was a skyless world, in which his eye, through dim gulfs of shad-owy air, saw only ever-mounting slopes, great walls of stone behind great walls, and frowning precipices wreathed with mist. He sat for a moment half dreaming, listening to the noise of water, the whisper of dark trees, the crack of stone, and the vast waiting silence that brooded behind all sound. He loved mountains, or he had loved the thought of them marching on the edge of stories brought from far away; but now he was borne down by the insupportable weight of Middle-earth. He longed to shut out the immensity in a quiet room by a fire.

He was very tired, for though they had ridden slowly, they had ridden with very little rest. Hour after hour for nearly three weary days he had jogged up and down, over passes, and through long dales, and across many streams. Sometimes where the way was broader he had ridden at the king's side, not noticing that many of the Riders smiled to see the two together: the hobbit on his little shaggy grey pony, and the Lord of Rohan on his great white horse. Then he had talked to Théoden, telling him about his home and the doings of the Shire-folk, or listening in turn to tales of the Mark and its mighty men of old. But most of the time, especially on this last day, Merry had ridden by himself just behind the king, saying nothing, and trying to understand the slow son-orous speech of Rohan that he heard the men behind him using. It was a language in which there seemed to be many words that he knew, though spoken more richly and strongly than in the Shire, yet he could not piece the words together. At times some Rider would lift up his clear voice in stirring song, and Merry felt his heart leap, though he did not know what it was about.

All the same he had been lonely, and never more so than now at the day's end. He wondered where in all this strange world Pippin had got to; and what would become of Aragorn and Legolas and Gimli. Then suddenly like a cold touch on his heart he thought of Frodo and Sam. 'I am forgetting them!' he said to himself reproachfully. 'And yet they are more important than all the rest of us. And I came to help them; but now they must be hundreds of miles away, if they are still alive.' He shivered.

'Harrowdale at last!' said Éomer. 'Our journey is almost at an end.' They halted. The paths out of the narrow gorge fell steeply. Only a glimpse, as through a tall window, could be seen of the great valley in the gloaming below. A single small light could be seen twinkling by the river.

'This journey is over, maybe,' said Théoden, 'but I have far yet to go. Last night the moon was full, and in the morning I shall ride to Edoras to the gathering of the Mark.'

'But if you would take my counsel,' said Éomer in a low voice, 'you would then return hither, until the war is over, lost or won.'

Théoden smiled. 'Nay, my son, for so I will call you, speak not the soft words of Wormtongue in my old ears!' He drew himself up and looked back at the long line of his men fading into the dusk behind. 'Long years in the space of days it seems since I rode west; but never will I lean on a staff again. If the war is lost, what good will be my hiding in the hills? And if it is won, what grief will it be, even if I fall, spending my last strength? But we will leave this now. Tonight I will lie in the Hold of Dunharrow. One evening of peace at least is left us. Let us ride on!'

In the deepening dusk they came down into the valley. Here the Snowbourn flowed near to the western walls of the dale, and soon the path led them to a ford where the shallow waters murmured loudly on the stones. The ford was guarded. As the king approached many men sprang up out of the shadow of the rocks; and when they saw the king they cried with glad voices: 'Théoden King! Théoden King! The King of the Mark returns!'

Then one blew a long call on a horn. It echoed in the valley. Other horns answered it, and lights shone out across the river.

And suddenly there rose a great chorus of trumpets from high above, sounding from some hollow place, as it seemed, that gathered their notes into one voice and sent it rolling and beating on the walls of stone.

So the King of the Mark came back victorious out of the West to Dunharrow beneath the feet of the White Mountains. There he found the remaining strength of his people already assembled; for as soon as his coming was known captains rode to meet him at the ford, bearing messages from Gandalf. Dúnhere, chieftain of the folk of Harrowdale, was at their head.

'At dawn three days ago, lord,' he said, 'Shadowfax came like a wind out of the West to Edoras, and Gandalf brought tidings of your victory to gladden our hearts. But he brought also word from you to hasten the gathering of the Riders. And then came the winged Shadow.'

'The winged Shadow?' said Théoden. 'We saw it also, but that was in the dead of night before Gandalf left us.'

'Maybe, lord,' said Dúnhere. 'Yet the same, or another like to it, a flying darkness in the shape of a monstrous bird, passed over Edoras that morning, and all men were shaken with fear. For it stooped upon Meduseld, and as it came low, almost to the gable, there came a cry that stopped our hearts. Then it was that Gandalf counselled us not to assemble in the fields, but to meet you here in the valley under the mountains. And he bade us to kindle no more lights or fires than barest need asked. So it has been done. Gandalf spoke with great authority. We trust that it is as you would wish. Naught has been seen in Harrowdale of these evil things.'

'It is well,' said Théoden. 'I will ride now to the Hold, and there before I go to rest I will meet the marshals and captains. Let them come to me as soon as may be!'

The road now led eastward straight across the valley, which was at that point little more than half a mile in width. Flats and meads of rough grass, grey now in the falling night, lay all about, but in front on the far side of the dale Merry saw a

frowning wall, a last outlier of the great roots of the Starkhorn,
cloven by the river in ages past.

On all the level spaces there was great concourse of men.
Some thronged to the roadside, hailing the king and the riders
from the West with glad cries; but stretching away into the
distance behind there were ordered rows of tents and booths,
and lines of picketed horses, and great store of arms, and
piled spears bristling like thickets of new-planted trees. Now
all the great assembly was falling into shadow, and yet, though
the night-chill blew cold from the heights, no lanterns glowed,
no fires were lit. Watchmen heavily cloaked paced to and
fro.

Merry wondered how many Riders there were. He could
not guess their number in the gathering gloom, but it looked
to him like a great army, many thousands strong. While he
was peering from side to side the king's party came up under
the looming cliff on the eastern side of the valley; and there
suddenly the path began to climb, and Merry looked up in
amazement. He was on a road the like of which he had never
seen before, a great work of men's hands in years beyond
the reach of song. Upwards it wound, coiling like a snake,
boring its way across the sheer slope of rock. Steep as a stair,
it looped backwards and forwards as it climbed. Up it horses
could walk, and wains could be slowly hauled; but no enemy
could come that way, except out of the air, if it was defended
from above. At each turn of the road there were great standing stones that had been carved in the likeness of men, huge
and clumsy-limbed, squatting cross-legged with their stumpy
arms folded on fat bellies. Some in the wearing of the years
had lost all features save the dark holes of their eyes that still
stared sadly at the passers-by. The Riders hardly glanced at
them. The Púkel-men they called them, and heeded them
little: no power or terror was left in them; but Merry gazed
at them with wonder and a feeling almost of pity, as they
loomed up mournfully in the dusk.

After a while he looked back and found that he had already
climbed some hundreds of feet above the valley, but still far

below he could dimly see a winding line of Riders crossing the ford and filing along the road towards the camp prepared for them. Only the king and his guard were going up into the Hold.

At last the king's company came to a sharp brink, and the climbing road passed into a cutting between walls of rock, and so went up a short slope and out on to a wide upland. The Firienfeld men called it, a green mountain-field of grass and heath, high above the deep-delved courses of the Snowbourn, laid upon the lap of the great mountains behind: the Starkhorn southwards, and northwards the saw-toothed mass of Írensaga, between which there faced the riders, the grim black wall of the Dwimorberg, the Haunted Mountain rising out of steep slopes of sombre pines. Dividing the upland into two there marched a double line of unshaped standing stones that dwindled into the dusk and vanished in the trees. Those who dared to follow that road came soon to the black Dimholt under Dwimorberg, and the menace of the pillar of stone, and the yawning shadow of the forbidden door.

Such was the dark Dunharrow, the work of long-forgotten men. Their name was lost and no song or legend remembered it. For what purpose they had made this place, as a town or secret temple or a tomb of kings, none in Rohan could say. Here they laboured in the Dark Years, before ever a ship came to the western shores, or Gondor of the Dúnedain was built; and now they had vanished, and only the old Púkel-men were left, still sitting at the turnings of the road.

Merry stared at the lines of marching stones: they were worn and black; some were leaning, some were fallen, some cracked or broken; they looked like rows of old and hungry teeth. He wondered what they could be, and he hoped that the king was not going to follow them into the darkness beyond. Then he saw that there were clusters of tents and booths on either side of the stony way; but these were not set near the trees, and seemed rather to huddle away from them towards the brink of the cliff. The greater number were on the right, where the Firienfeld was wider; and on the left there was a smaller camp, in the midst of which stood a tall pavilion. From this side a rider now came out to meet them, and they turned from the road.

As they drew near Merry saw that the rider was a woman with long braided hair gleaming in the twilight, yet she wore a helm and was clad to the waist like a warrior and girded with a sword.

'Hail, Lord of the Mark!' she cried. 'My heart is glad at your returning.'

'And you, Éowyn,' said Théoden, 'is all well with you?'

'All is well,' she answered; yet it seemed to Merry that her voice belied her, and he would have thought that she had been weeping, if that could be believed of one so stern of face. 'All is well. It was a weary road for the people to take, torn suddenly from their homes. There were hard words, for it is long since war has driven us from the green fields; but there have been no evil deeds. All is now ordered, as you see. And your lodging is prepared for you; for I have had full tidings of you and knew the hour of your coming.'

'So Aragorn has come then,' said Éomer. 'Is he still here?'

'No, he is gone,' said Éowyn turning away and looking at the mountains dark against the East and South.

'Whither did he go?' asked Éomer.

'I do not know,' she answered. 'He came at night, and rode away yestermorn, ere the Sun had climbed over the mountain-tops. He is gone.'

'You are grieved, daughter,' said Théoden. 'What has happened? Tell me, did he speak of that road?' He pointed away along the darkening lines of stones towards the Dwimorberg. 'Of the Paths of the Dead?'

'Yes, lord,' said Éowyn. 'And he has passed into the shadow from which none have returned. I could not dissuade him. He is gone.'

'Then our paths are sundered,' said Éomer. 'He is lost. We must ride without him, and our hope dwindles.'

*   *   *

Slowly they passed through the short heath and upland grass, speaking no more, until they came to the king's pavilion. There Merry found that everything was made ready, and that he himself was not forgotten. A little tent had been pitched for him beside the king's lodging; and there he sat alone, while men passed to and fro, going in to the king and taking counsel with him. Night came on and the half-seen heads of the mountains westward were crowned with stars, but the East was dark and blank. The marching stones faded slowly from sight, but still beyond them, blacker than the gloom, brooded the vast crouching shadow of the Dwimorberg.

'The Paths of the Dead,' he muttered to himself. 'The Paths of the Dead? What does all this mean? They have all left me now. They have all gone to some doom: Gandalf and Pippin to war in the East; and Sam and Frodo to Mordor; and Strider and Legolas and Gimli to the Paths of the Dead. But my turn will come soon enough, I suppose. I wonder what they are all talking about, and what the king means to do. For I must go where he goes now.'

In the midst of these gloomy thoughts he suddenly remembered that he was very hungry, and he got up to go and see if anyone else in this strange camp felt the same. But at that very moment a trumpet sounded, and a man came summoning him, the king's esquire, to wait at the king's board.

In the inner part of the pavilion was a small space, curtained off with broidered hangings, and strewn with skins; and there at a small table sat Théoden with Éomer and Éowyn, and Dúnhere, lord of Harrowdale. Merry stood beside the king's stool and waited on him, till presently the old man, coming out of deep thought, turned to him and smiled.

'Come, Master Meriadoc!' he said. 'You shall not stand. You shall sit beside me, as long as I remain in my own lands, and lighten my heart with tales.'

Room was made for the hobbit at the king's left hand, but no one called for any tale. There was indeed little speech, and they ate and drank for the most part in silence, until at last, plucking up courage, Merry asked the question that was tormenting him.

'Twice now, lord, I have heard of the Paths of the Dead,' he said. 'What are they? And where has Strider, I mean the Lord Aragorn, where has he gone?'

The king sighed, but no one answered, until at last Éomer spoke. 'We do not know, and our hearts are heavy,' he said. 'But as for the Paths of the Dead, you have yourself walked on their first steps. Nay, I speak no words of ill omen! The road that we have climbed is the approach to the Door, yonder in the Dimholt. But what lies beyond no man knows.'

'No man knows,' said Théoden: 'yet ancient legend, now seldom spoken, has somewhat to report. If these old tales speak true that have come down from father to son in the House of Eorl, then the Door under Dwimorberg leads to a secret way that goes beneath the mountain to some forgotten end. But none have ever ventured in to search its secrets, since Baldor, son of Brego, passed the Door and was never seen among men again. A rash vow he spoke, as he drained the horn at that feast which Brego made to hallow new-built Meduseld, and he came never to the high seat of which he was the heir.

'Folk say that Dead Men out of the Dark Years guard the way and will suffer no living man to come to their hidden halls; but at whiles they may themselves be seen passing out of the door like shadows and down the stony road. Then the people of Harrowdale shut fast their doors and shroud their windows and are afraid. But the Dead come seldom forth and only at times of great unquiet and coming death.'

'Yet it is said in Harrowdale,' said Éowyn in a low voice, 'that in the moonless nights but little while ago a great host in strange array passed by. Whence they came none knew, but they went up the stony road and vanished into the hill, as if they went to keep a tryst.'

'Then why has Aragorn gone that way?' asked Merry. 'Don't you know anything that would explain it?'

'Unless he has spoken words to you as his friend that we have not heard,' said Éomer, 'none now in the land of the living can tell his purpose.'

'Greatly changed he seemed to me since I saw him first in the king's house,' said Éowyn: 'grimmer, older. Fey I thought him, and like one whom the Dead call.'

'Maybe he was called,' said Théoden; 'and my heart tells me that I shall not see him again. Yet he is a kingly man of high destiny. And take comfort in this, daughter, since comfort you seem to need in your grief for this guest. It is said that when the Eorlingas came out of the North and passed at length up the Snowbourn, seeking strong places of refuge in time of need, Brego and his son Baldor climbed the Stair of the Hold and so came before the Door. On the threshold sat an old man, aged beyond guess of years; tall and kingly he had been, but now he was withered as an old stone. Indeed for stone they took him, for he moved not, and he said no word, until they sought to pass him by and enter. And then a voice came out of him, as it were out of the ground, and to their amaze it spoke in the western tongue: *The way is shut.*

'Then they halted and looked at him and saw that he lived still; but he did not look at them. *The way is shut,* his voice said again. *It was made by those who are Dead, and the Dead keep it, until the time comes. The way is shut.*

'*And when will that time be?* said Baldor. But no answer did he ever get. For the old man died in that hour and fell upon his face; and no other tidings of the ancient dwellers in the mountains have our folk ever learned. Yet maybe at last the time foretold has come, and Aragorn may pass.'

'But how shall a man discover whether that time be come or no, save by daring the Door?' said Éomer. 'And that way I would not go though all the hosts of Mordor stood before me, and I were alone and had no other refuge. Alas that a fey mood should fall on a man so greathearted in this hour of need! Are there not evil things enough abroad without seeking them under the earth? War is at hand.'

He paused, for at that moment there was a noise outside, a man's voice crying the name of Théoden, and the challenge of the guard.

Presently the captain of the Guard thrust aside the curtain. 'A man is here, lord,' he said, 'an errand-rider of Gondor. He wishes to come before you at once.'

'Let him come!' said Théoden.

A tall man entered, and Merry choked back a cry; for a moment it seemed to him that Boromir was alive again and had returned. Then he saw that it was not so; the man was a stranger, though as like to Boromir as if he were one of his kin, tall and grey-eyed and proud. He was clad as a rider with a cloak of dark green over a coat of fine mail; on the front of his helm was wrought a small silver star. In his hand he bore a single arrow, black-feathered and barbed with steel, but the point was painted red.

He sank on one knee and presented the arrow to Théoden. 'Hail, Lord of the Rohirrim, friend of Gondor!' he said. 'Hirgon I am, errand-rider of Denethor, who bring you this token of war. Gondor is in great need. Often the Rohirrim have aided us, but now the Lord Denethor asks for all your strength and all your speed, lest Gondor fall at last.'

'The Red Arrow!' said Théoden, holding it, as one who receives a summons long expected and yet dreadful when it comes. His hand trembled. 'The Red Arrow has not been seen in the Mark in all my years! Has it indeed come to that? And what does the Lord Denethor reckon that all my strength and all my speed may be?'

'That is best known to yourself, lord,' said Hirgon. 'But ere long it may well come to pass that Minas Tirith is surrounded, and unless you have the strength to break a siege of many powers, the Lord Denethor bids me say that he judges that the strong arms of the Rohirrim would be better within his walls than without.'

'But he knows that we are a people who fight rather upon horseback and in the open, and that we are also a scattered people and time is needed for the gathering of our Riders. Is it not true, Hirgon, that the Lord of Minas Tirith knows more than he sets in his message? For we are already at war, as you may have seen, and you do not find us all unprepared. Gandalf the Grey has been among us, and even now we are mustering for battle in the East.'

'What the Lord Denethor may know or guess of all these things I cannot say,' answered Hirgon. 'But indeed our case is desperate. My lord does not issue any command to you, he begs you only to remember old friendship and oaths long spoken, and for your own good to do all that you may. It is reported to us that many kings have ridden in from the East to the service of Mordor. From the North to the field of Dagorlad there is skirmish and rumour of war. In the South the Haradrim are moving, and fear has fallen on all our coastlands, so that little help will come to us thence. Make haste! For it is before the walls of Minas Tirith that the doom of our time will be decided, and if the tide be not stemmed there, then it will flow over all the fair fields of Rohan, and even in this Hold among the hills there shall be no refuge.'

'Dark tidings,' said Théoden, 'yet not all unguessed. But say to Denethor that even if Rohan itself felt no peril, still we would come to his aid. But we have suffered much loss in our battles with Saruman the traitor, and we must still think of our frontier to the north and east, as his own tidings make clear. So great a power as the Dark Lord seems now to wield might well contain us in battle before the City and yet strike with great force across the River away beyond the Gate of Kings.

'But we will speak no longer counsels of prudence. We will come. The weapontake was set for the morrow. When all is ordered we will set out. Ten thousand spears I might have sent riding over the plain to the dismay of your foes. It will be less now, I fear; for I will not leave my strongholds all unguarded. Yet six thousands at the least shall ride behind me. For say to Denethor that in this hour the King of the Mark himself will come down to the land of Gondor, though maybe he will not ride back. But it is a long road, and man and beast must reach the end with strength to fight. A week it may be from tomorrow's morn ere you hear the cry of the Sons of Eorl coming from the North.'

'A week!' said Hirgon. 'If it must be so, it must. But you are like to find only ruined walls in seven days from now, unless other help unlooked-for comes. Still, you may at the least disturb the Orcs and Swarthy Men from their feasting in the White Tower.'

'At the least we will do that,' said Théoden. 'But I myself am new-come from battle and long journey, and I will now go to rest. Tarry here this night. Then you shall look on the muster of Rohan and ride away the gladder for the sight, and the swifter for the rest. In the morning counsels are best, and night changes many thoughts.'

With that the king stood up, and they all rose. 'Go now each to your rest,' he said, 'and sleep well. And you, Master Meriadoc, I need no more tonight. But be ready to my call as soon as the Sun is risen.'

'I will be ready,' said Merry, 'even if you bid me ride with you on the Paths of the Dead.'

'Speak not words of omen!' said the king. 'For there may be more roads than one that could bear that name. But I did not say that I would bid you ride with me on any road. Good night!'

'I won't be left behind, to be called for on return!' said Merry. 'I won't be left, I won't.' And repeating this over and over again to himself he fell asleep at last in his tent.

He was wakened by a man shaking him. 'Wake up, wake up, Master Holbytla!' he cried; and at length Merry came out of deep dreams and sat up with a start. It still seemed very dark, he thought.

'What is the matter?' he asked.

'The king calls for you.'

'But the Sun has not risen, yet,' said Merry.

'No, and will not rise today, Master Holbytla. Nor ever again, one would think under this cloud. But time does not stand still, though the Sun be lost. Make haste!'

Flinging on some clothes, Merry looked outside. The world was darkling. The very air seemed brown, and all things about were black and grey and shadowless; there was a great stillness. No shape of cloud could be seen, unless it were far away westward, where the furthest groping fingers of the great gloom still crawled onwards and a little light leaked through them. Overhead there hung a heavy roof, sombre and featureless, and light seemed rather to be failing than growing.

Merry saw many folk standing, looking up and muttering; all their faces were grey and sad, and some were afraid. With a sinking heart he made his way to the king. Hirgon the rider of Gondor was there before him, and beside him stood now another man, like him and dressed alike, but shorter and broader. As Merry entered he was speaking to the king.

'It comes from Mordor, lord,' he said. 'It began last night at sunset. From the hills in the Eastfold of your realm I saw it rise and creep across the sky, and all night as I rode it came behind eating up the stars. Now the great cloud hangs over all the land between here and the Mountains of Shadow; and it is deepening. War has already begun.'

For a while the king sat silent. At last he spoke. 'So we come to it in the end,' he said: 'the great battle of our time, in which many things shall pass away. But at least there is no longer need for hiding. We will ride the straight way and the open road and with all our speed. The muster shall begin at once, and wait for none that tarry. Have you good store in Minas Tirith? For if we must ride now in all haste, then we must ride light, with but meal and water enough to last us into battle.'

'We have very great store long prepared,' answered Hirgon. 'Ride now as light and as swift as you may!'

'Then call the heralds, Éomer,' said Théoden. 'Let the Riders be marshalled!'

Éomer went out, and presently the trumpets rang in the Hold and were answered by many others from below; but their voices no longer sounded clear and brave as they had seemed to Merry the night before. Dull they seemed and harsh in the heavy air, braying ominously.

The king turned to Merry. 'I am going to war, Master Meriadoc,' he said. 'In a little while I shall take the road. I release you from my service, but not from my friendship. You shall abide here, and if you will, you shall serve the Lady Éowyn, who will govern the folk in my stead.'

'But, but, lord,' Merry stammered, 'I offered you my sword. I do not want to be parted from you like this, Théoden King. And as all my friends have gone to the battle, I should be ashamed to stay behind.'

'But we ride on horses tall and swift,' said Théoden; 'and great though your heart be, you cannot ride on such beasts.'

'Then tie me on to the back of one, or let me hang on a stirrup, or something,' said Merry. 'It is a long way to run; but run I shall, if I cannot ride, even if I wear my feet off and arrive weeks too late.'

Théoden smiled. 'Rather than that I would bear you with me on Snowmane,' he said. 'But at the least you shall ride with me to Edoras and look on Meduseld; for that way I shall go. So far Stybba can bear you: the great race will not begin till we reach the plains.'

Then Éowyn rose up. 'Come now, Meriadoc!' she said. 'I will show you the gear that I have prepared for you.' They went out together. 'This request only did Aragorn make to me,' said Éowyn, as they passed among the tents, 'that you should be armed for battle. I have granted it, as I could. For my heart tells me that you will need such gear ere the end.'

Now she led Merry to a booth among the lodges of the

king's guard; and there an armourer brought out to her a
small helm, and a round shield, and other gear.

'No mail have we to fit you,' said Éowyn, 'nor any time
for the forging of such a hauberk; but here is also a stout
jerkin of leather, a belt, and a knife. A sword you have.'

Merry bowed, and the lady showed him the shield, which
was like the shield that had been given to Gimli, and it bore
on it the device of the white horse. 'Take all these things,'
she said, 'and bear them to good fortune! Farewell now,
Master Meriadoc! Yet maybe we shall meet again, you and
I.'

So it was that amid a gathering gloom the King of the
Mark made ready to lead all his Riders on the eastward road.
Hearts were heavy and many quailed in the shadow. But they
were a stern people, loyal to their lord, and little weeping or
murmuring was heard, even in the camp in the Hold where
the exiles from Edoras were housed, women and children and
old men. Doom hung over them, but they faced it silently.

Two swift hours passed, and now the king sat upon his
white horse, glimmering in the half-light. Proud and tall he
seemed, though the hair that flowed beneath his high helm
was like snow; and many marvelled at him and took heart to
see him unbent and unafraid.

There on the wide flats beside the noisy river were marshalled in many companies well nigh five and fifty hundreds
of Riders fully armed, and many hundreds of other men with
spare horses lightly burdened. A single trumpet sounded.
The king raised his hand, and then silently the host of the
Mark began to move. Foremost went twelve of the king's
household-men, Riders of renown. Then the king followed
with Éomer on his right. He had said farewell to Éowyn
above in the Hold, and the memory was grievous; but now
he turned his mind to the road that lay ahead. Behind him
Merry rode on Stybba with the errand riders of Gondor, and
behind them again twelve more of the king's household. They
passed down the long ranks of waiting men with stern and

unmoved faces. But when they had come almost to the end
of the line one looked up glancing keenly at the hobbit. A
young man, Merry thought as he returned the glance, less
in height and girth than most. He caught the glint of clear
grey eyes; and then he shivered, for it came suddenly to him
that it was the face of one without hope who goes in search
of death.

On down the grey road they went beside the Snowbourn
rushing on its stones; through the hamlets of Underharrow
and Upbourn, where many sad faces of women looked out
from dark doors; and so without horn or harp or music of
men's voices the great ride into the East began with which
the songs of Rohan were busy for many long lives of men
thereafter.

> *From dark Dunharrow in the dim morning*
> *with thane and captain rode Thengel's son:*
> *to Edoras he came, the ancient halls*
> *of the Mark-wardens mist-enshrouded;*
> *golden timbers were in gloom mantled.*
> *Farewell he bade to his free people,*
> *hearth and high-seat, and the hallowed places,*
> *where long he had feasted ere the light faded.*
> *Forth rode the king, fear behind him,*
> *fate before him. Fealty kept he;*
> *oaths he had taken, all fulfilled them.*
> *Forth rode Théoden. Five nights and days*
> *east and onward rode the Eorlingas*
> *through Folde and Fenmarch and the Firienwood,*
> *six thousand spears to Sunlending,*
> *Mundburg the mighty under Mindolluin,*
> *Sea-kings' city in the South-kingdom*
> *foe-beleaguered, fire-encircled.*
> *Doom drove them on. Darkness took them,*
> *horse and horseman; hoofbeats afar*
> *sank into silence: so the songs tell us.*

It was indeed in deepening gloom that the king came to Edoras, although it was then but noon by the hour. There he halted only a short while and strengthened his host by some three score of Riders that came late to the weapontake. Now having eaten he made ready to set out again, and he wished his esquire a kindly farewell. But Merry begged for the last time not to be parted from him.

'This is no journey for such steeds as Stybba, as I have told you,' said Théoden. 'And in such a battle as we think to make on the fields of Gondor what would you do, Master Meriadoc, swordthain though you be, and greater of heart than of stature?'

'As for that, who can tell?' answered Merry. 'But why, lord, did you receive me as swordthain, if not to stay by your side? And I would not have it said of me in song only that I was always left behind!'

'I received you for your safe-keeping,' answered Théoden; 'and also to do as I might bid. None of my Riders can bear you as burden. If the battle were before my gates, maybe your deeds would be remembered by the minstrels; but it is a hundred leagues and two to Mundburg where Denethor is lord. I will say no more.'

Merry bowed and went away unhappily, and stared at the lines of horsemen. Already the companies were preparing to start: men were tightening girths, looking to saddles, caressing their horses; some gazed uneasily at the lowering sky. Unnoticed a Rider came up and spoke softly in the hobbit's ear.

'*Where will wants not, a way opens*, so we say,' he whispered; 'and so I have found myself.' Merry looked up and saw that it was the young Rider whom he had noticed in the morning. 'You wish to go whither the Lord of the Mark goes: I see it in your face.'

'I do,' said Merry.

'Then you shall go with me,' said the Rider. 'I will bear you before me, under my cloak until we are far afield, and this darkness is yet darker. Such good will should not be denied. Say no more to any man, but come!'

'Thank you indeed!' said Merry. 'Thank you, sir, though I do not know your name.'

'Do you not?' said the Rider softly. 'Then call me Dernhelm.'

Thus it came to pass that when the king set out, before Dernhelm sat Meriadoc the hobbit, and the great grey steed Windfola made little of the burden; for Dernhelm was less in weight than many men, though lithe and well-knit in frame.

On into the shadow they rode. In the willow-thickets where Snowbourn flowed into Entwash, twelve leagues east of Edoras, they camped that night. And then on again through the Folde; and through the Fenmarch, where to their right great oakwoods climbed on the skirts of the hills under the shades of dark Halifirien by the borders of Gondor; but away to their left the mists lay on the marshes fed by the mouths of Entwash. And as they rode rumour came of war in the North. Lone men, riding wild, brought word of foes assailing their east-borders, of orc-hosts marching in the Wold of Rohan.

'Ride on! Ride on!' cried Éomer. 'Too late now to turn aside. The fens of Entwash must guard our flank. Haste now we need. Ride on!'

And so King Théoden departed from his own realm, and mile by mile the long road wound away, and the beacon hills marched past: Calenhad, Min-Rimmon, Erelas, Nardol. But their fires were quenched. All the lands were grey and still; and ever the shadow deepened before them, and hope waned in every heart.

CHAPTER IV

THE SIEGE OF GONDOR

Pippin was roused by Gandalf. Candles were lit in their chamber, for only a dim twilight came through the windows; the air was heavy as with approaching thunder.

'What is the time?' said Pippin yawning.

'Past the second hour,' said Gandalf. 'Time to get up and make yourself presentable. You are summoned to the Lord of the City to learn your new duties.'

'And will he provide breakfast?'

'No! I have provided it: all that you will get till noon. Food is now doled out by order.'

Pippin looked ruefully at the small loaf and (he thought) very inadequate pat of butter which was set out for him, beside a cup of thin milk. 'Why did you bring me here?' he said.

'You know quite well,' said Gandalf. 'To keep you out of mischief; and if you do not like being here, you can remember that you brought it on yourself.' Pippin said no more.

Before long he was walking with Gandalf once more down the cold corridor to the door of the Tower Hall. There Denethor sat in a grey gloom, like an old patient spider, Pippin thought; he did not seem to have moved since the day before. He beckoned Gandalf to a seat, but Pippin was left for a while standing unheeded. Presently the old man turned to him:

'Well, Master Peregrin, I hope that you used yesterday to your profit, and to your liking? Though I fear that the board is barer in this city than you could wish.'

Pippin had an uncomfortable feeling that most of what he had said or done was somehow known to the Lord of the

City, and much was guessed of what he thought as well. He did not answer.

'What would you do in my service?'

'I thought, sir, that you would tell me my duties.'

'I will, when I learn what you are fit for,' said Denethor. 'But that I shall learn soonest, maybe, if I keep you beside me. The esquire of my chamber has begged leave to go to the out-garrison, so you shall take his place for a while. You shall wait on me, bear errands, and talk to me, if war and council leave me any leisure. Can you sing?'

'Yes,' said Pippin. 'Well, yes, well enough for my own people. But we have no songs fit for great halls and evil times, lord. We seldom sing of anything more terrible than wind or rain. And most of my songs are about things that make us laugh; or about food and drink, of course.'

'And why should such songs be unfit for my halls, or for such hours as these? We who have lived long under the Shadow may surely listen to echoes from a land untroubled by it? Then we may feel that our vigil was not fruitless, though it may have been thankless.'

Pippin's heart sank. He did not relish the idea of singing any song of the Shire to the Lord of Minas Tirith, certainly not the comic ones that he knew best; they were too, well, rustic for such an occasion. He was however spared the ordeal for the present. He was not commanded to sing. Denethor turned to Gandalf, asking questions about the Rohirrim and their policies, and the position of Éomer, the king's nephew. Pippin marvelled at the amount that the Lord seemed to know about a people that lived far away, though it must, he thought, be many years since Denethor himself had ridden abroad.

Presently Denethor waved to Pippin and dismissed him again for a while. 'Go to the armouries of the Citadel,' he said, 'and get you there the livery and gear of the Tower. It will be ready. It was commanded yesterday. Return when you are clad!'

It was as he said; and Pippin soon found himself arrayed

in strange garments, all of black and silver. He had a small
hauberk, its rings forged of steel, maybe, yet black as jet; and
a high-crowned helm with small raven-wings on either side,
set with a silver star in the centre of the circlet. Above the
mail was a short surcoat of black, but broidered on the breast
in silver with the token of the Tree. His old clothes were
folded and put away, but he was permitted to keep the grey
cloak of Lórien, though not to wear it when on duty. He
looked now, had he known it, verily *Ernil i Pheriannath*, the
Prince of the Halflings, that folk had called him; but he felt
uncomfortable. And the gloom began to weigh on his spirits.

It was dark and dim all day. From the sunless dawn until
evening the heavy shadow had deepened, and all hearts in
the City were oppressed. Far above a great cloud streamed
slowly westward from the Black Land, devouring light, borne
upon a wind of war; but below the air was still and breathless,
as if all the Vale of Anduin waited for the onset of a ruinous
storm.

About the eleventh hour, released at last for a while from
service, Pippin came out and went in search of food and
drink to cheer his heavy heart and make his task of waiting
more supportable. In the messes he met Beregond again, who
had just come from an errand over the Pelennor out to the
Guard-towers upon the Causeway. Together they strolled
out to the walls; for Pippin felt imprisoned indoors, and stifled
even in the lofty citadel. Now they sat side by side again in
the embrasure looking eastward, where they had eaten and
talked the day before.

It was the sunset-hour, but the great pall had now stretched
far into the West, and only as it sank at last into the Sea did
the Sun escape to send out a brief farewell gleam before the
night, even as Frodo saw it at the Cross-roads touching the
head of the fallen king. But to the fields of the Pelennor,
under the shadow of Mindolluin, there came no gleam: they
were brown and drear.

Already it seemed years to Pippin since he had sat there

before, in some half-forgotten time when he had still been a hobbit, a light-hearted wanderer touched little by the perils he had passed through. Now he was one small soldier in a city preparing for a great assault, clad in the proud but sombre manner of the Tower of Guard.

In some other time and place Pippin might have been pleased with his new array, but he knew now that he was taking part in no play; he was in deadly earnest the servant of a grim master in the greatest peril. The hauberk was burdensome, and the helm weighed upon his head. His cloak he had cast aside upon the seat. He turned his tired gaze away from the darkling fields below and yawned, and then he sighed.

'You are weary of this day?' said Beregond.

'Yes,' said Pippin, 'very: tired out with idleness and waiting. I have kicked my heels at the door of my master's chamber for many slow hours, while he has debated with Gandalf and the Prince and other great persons. And I'm not used, Master Beregond, to waiting hungry on others while they eat. It is a sore trial for a hobbit, that. No doubt you will think I should feel the honour more deeply. But what is the good of such honour? Indeed what is the good even of food and drink under this creeping shadow? What does it mean? The very air seems thick and brown! Do you often have such glooms when the wind is in the East?'

'Nay,' said Beregond, 'this is no weather of the world. This is some device of his malice; some broil of fume from the Mountain of Fire that he sends to darken hearts and counsel. And so it doth indeed. I wish the Lord Faramir would return. He would not be dismayed. But now, who knows if he will ever come back across the River out of the Darkness?'

'Yes,' said Pippin, 'Gandalf, too, is anxious. He was disappointed, I think, not to find Faramir here. And where has he got to himself? He left the Lord's council before the noon-meal, and in no good mood either, I thought. Perhaps he has some foreboding of bad news.'

*   *   *

Suddenly as they talked they were stricken dumb, frozen as it were to listening stones. Pippin cowered down with his hands pressed to his ears; but Beregond, who had been looking out from the battlement as he spoke of Faramir, remained there, stiffened, staring out with starting eyes. Pippin knew the shuddering cry that he had heard: it was the same that he had heard long ago in the Marish of the Shire, but now it was grown in power and hatred, piercing the heart with a poisonous despair.

At last Beregond spoke with an effort. 'They have come!' he said. 'Take courage and look! There are fell things below.'

Reluctantly Pippin climbed on to the seat and looked out over the wall. The Pelennor lay dim beneath him, fading away to the scarce guessed line of the Great River. But now wheeling swiftly across it, like shadows of untimely night, he saw in the middle airs below him five birdlike forms, horrible as carrion-fowl yet greater than eagles, cruel as death. Now they swooped near, venturing almost within bowshot of the walls, now they circled away.

'Black Riders!' muttered Pippin. 'Black Riders of the air! But see, Beregond!' he cried. 'They are looking for something, surely? See how they wheel and swoop, always down to that point over there! And can you see something moving on the ground? Dark little things. Yes, men on horses: four or five. Ah! I cannot stand it! Gandalf! Gandalf save us!'

Another long screech rose and fell, and he threw himself back again from the wall, panting like a hunted animal. Faint and seemingly remote through that shuddering cry he heard winding up from below the sound of a trumpet ending on a long high note.

'Faramir! The Lord Faramir! It is his call!' cried Beregond. 'Brave heart! But how can he win to the Gate, if these foul hell-hawks have other weapons than fear? But look! They hold on. They will make the Gate. No! the horses are running mad. Look! the men are thrown; they are running on foot. No, one is still up, but he rides back to the others. That will be the Captain: he can master both beasts and men. Ah! there one of the foul things is stooping on him. Help! help! Will no one go out to him? Faramir!'

With that Beregond sprang away and ran off into the gloom. Ashamed of his terror, while Beregond of the Guard thought first of the captain whom he loved, Pippin got up and peered out. At that moment he caught a flash of white and silver coming from the North, like a small star down on the dusky fields. It moved with the speed of an arrow and grew as it came, converging swiftly with the flight of the four men towards the Gate. It seemed to Pippin that a pale light was spread about it and the heavy shadows gave way before it; and then as it drew near he thought that he heard, like an echo in the walls, a great voice calling.

'Gandalf!' he cried. 'Gandalf! He always turns up when things are darkest. Go on! Go on, White Rider! Gandalf, Gandalf!' he shouted wildly, like an onlooker at a great race urging on a runner who is far beyond encouragement.

But now the dark swooping shadows were aware of the newcomer. One wheeled towards him; but it seemed to Pippin that he raised his hand, and from it a shaft of white light stabbed upwards. The Nazgûl gave a long wailing cry and swerved away; and with that the four others wavered, and then rising in swift spirals they passed away eastward vanishing into the lowering cloud above; and down on the Pelennor it seemed for a while less dark.

Pippin watched, and he saw the horseman and the White Rider meet and halt, waiting for those on foot. Men now hurried out to them from the City; and soon they all passed from sight under the outer walls, and he knew that they were entering the Gate. Guessing that they would come at once to the Tower and the Steward, he hurried to the entrance of the citadel. There he was joined by many others who had watched the race and the rescue from the high walls.

It was not long before a clamour was heard in the streets leading up from the outer circles, and there was much cheering and crying of the names of Faramir and Mithrandir.

Presently Pippin saw torches, and followed by a press of people two horsemen riding slowly: one was in white but shining no longer, pale in the twilight as if his fire was spent or veiled; the other was dark and his head was bowed. They dismounted, and as grooms took Shadowfax and the other horse, they walked forward to the sentinel at the gate: Gandalf steadily, his grey cloak flung back, and a fire still smouldering in his eyes; the other, clad all in green, slowly, swaying a little as a weary or a wounded man.

Pippin pressed forward as they passed under the lamp beneath the gate-arch, and when he saw the pale face of Faramir he caught his breath. It was the face of one who has been assailed by a great fear or anguish, but has mastered it and now is quiet. Proud and grave he stood for a moment as he spoke to the guard, and Pippin gazing at him saw how closely he resembled his brother Boromir – whom Pippin had liked from the first, admiring the great man's lordly but kindly manner. Yet suddenly for Faramir his heart was strangely moved with a feeling that he had not known before. Here was one with an air of high nobility such as Aragorn at times revealed, less high perhaps, yet also less incalculable and remote: one of the Kings of Men born into a later time, but touched with the wisdom and sadness of the Elder Race. He knew now why Beregond spoke his name with love. He was a captain that men would follow, that he would follow, even under the shadow of the black wings.

'Faramir!' he cried aloud with the others. 'Faramir!' And Faramir, catching his strange voice among the clamour of the men of the City, turned and looked down at him and was amazed.

'Whence come you?' he said. 'A halfling, and in the livery of the Tower! Whence . . . ?'

But with that Gandalf stepped to his side and spoke. 'He came with me from the land of the Halflings,' he said. 'He came with me. But let us not tarry here. There is much to say and to do, and you are weary. He shall come with us. Indeed he must, for if he does not forget his new duties more easily than I do, he must attend on his lord again within this hour. Come, Pippin, follow us!'

So at length they came to the private chamber of the Lord of the City. There deep seats were set about a brazier of charcoal; and wine was brought; and there Pippin, hardly noticed, stood behind the chair of Denethor and felt his weariness little, so eagerly did he listen to all that was said.

When Faramir had taken white bread and drunk a draught of wine, he sat upon a low chair at his father's left hand. Removed a little upon the other side sat Gandalf in a chair of carven wood; and he seemed at first to be asleep. For at the beginning Faramir spoke only of the errand upon which he had been sent out ten days before, and he brought tidings of Ithilien and of movements of the Enemy and his allies; and he told of the fight on the road when the men of Harad and their great beast were overthrown: a captain reporting to his master such matters as had often been heard before, small things of border-war that now seemed useless and petty, shorn of their renown.

Then suddenly Faramir looked at Pippin. 'But now we come to strange matters,' he said. 'For this is not the first halfling that I have seen walking out of northern legends into the Southlands.'

At that Gandalf sat up and gripped the arms of his chair; but he said nothing, and with a look stopped the exclamation on Pippin's lips. Denethor looked at their faces and nodded his head, as though in sign that he had read much there before it was spoken. Slowly, while the others sat silent and still, Faramir told his tale, with his eyes for the most part on Gandalf, though now and again his glance strayed to Pippin, as if to refresh his memory of others that he had seen.

As his story was unfolded of his meeting with Frodo and his servant and of the events at Henneth Annûn, Pippin became aware that Gandalf's hands were trembling as they clutched the carven wood. White they seemed now and very old, and as he looked at them, suddenly with a thrill of fear

Pippin knew that Gandalf, Gandalf himself, was troubled, even afraid. The air of the room was close and still. At last when Faramir spoke of his parting with the travellers, and of their resolve to go to Cirith Ungol, his voice fell, and he shook his head and sighed. Then Gandalf sprang up.

'Cirith Ungol? Morgul Vale?' he said. 'The time, Faramir, the time? When did you part with them? When would they reach that accursed valley?'

'I parted with them in the morning two days ago,' said Faramir. 'It is fifteen leagues thence to the vale of the Morgul-duin, if they went straight south; and then they would be still five leagues westward of the accursed Tower. At swiftest they could not come there before today, and maybe they have not come there yet. Indeed I see what you fear. But the dark-ness is not due to their venture. It began yestereve, and all Ithilien was under shadow last night. It is clear to me that the Enemy has long planned an assault on us, and its hour had already been determined before ever the travellers left my keeping.'

Gandalf paced the floor. 'The morning of two days ago, nigh on three days of journey! How far is the place where you parted?'

'Some twenty-five leagues as a bird flies,' answered Fara-mir. 'But I could not come more swiftly. Yestereve I lay at Cair Andros, the long isle in the River northward which we hold in defence; and horses are kept on the hither bank. As the dark drew on I knew that haste was needed, so I rode thence with three others that could also be horsed. The rest of my company I sent south to strengthen the garrison at the fords of Osgiliath. I hope that I have not done ill?' He looked at his father.

'Ill?' cried Denethor, and his eyes flashed suddenly. 'Why do you ask? The men were under your command. Or do you ask for my judgement on all your deeds? Your bearing is lowly in my presence, yet it is long now since you turned from your own way at my counsel. See, you have spoken skilfully, as ever; but I, have I not seen your eye fixed on

Mithrandir, seeking whether you said well or too much? He has long had your heart in his keeping.

'My son, your father is old but not yet dotard. I can see and hear, as was my wont; and little of what you have half said or left unsaid is now hidden from me. I know the answer to many riddles. Alas, alas for Boromir!'

'If what I have done displeases you, my father,' said Faramir quietly, 'I wish I had known your counsel before the burden of so weighty a judgement was thrust on me.'

'Would that have availed to change your judgement?' said Denethor. 'You would still have done just so, I deem. I know you well. Ever your desire is to appear lordly and generous as a king of old, gracious, gentle. That may well befit one of high race, if he sits in power and peace. But in desperate hours gentleness may be repaid with death.'

'So be it,' said Faramir.

'So be it!' cried Denethor. 'But not with your death only, Lord Faramir: with the death also of your father, and of all your people, whom it is your part to protect now that Boromir is gone.'

'Do you wish then,' said Faramir, 'that our places had been exchanged?'

'Yes, I wish that indeed,' said Denethor. 'For Boromir was loyal to me and no wizard's pupil. He would have remembered his father's need, and would not have squandered what fortune gave. He would have brought me a mighty gift.'

For a moment Faramir's restraint gave way. 'I would ask you, my father, to remember why it was that I, not he, was in Ithilien. On one occasion at least your counsel has prevailed, not long ago. It was the Lord of the City that gave the errand to him.'

'Stir not the bitterness in the cup that I mixed for myself,' said Denethor. 'Have I not tasted it now many nights upon my tongue, foreboding that worse yet lay in the dregs? As now indeed I find. Would it were not so! Would that this thing had come to me!'

'Comfort yourself!' said Gandalf. 'In no case would Boromir have brought it to you. He is dead, and died well; may he sleep in peace! Yet you deceive yourself. He would have stretched out his hand to this thing, and taking it he would have fallen. He would have kept it for his own, and when he returned you would not have known your son.'

The face of Denethor set hard and cold. 'You found Boromir less apt to your hand, did you not?' he said softly. 'But I who was his father say that he would have brought it to me. You are wise, maybe, Mithrandir, yet with all your subtleties you have not all wisdom. Counsels may be found that are neither the webs of wizards nor the haste of fools. I have in this matter more lore and wisdom than you deem.'

'What then is your wisdom?' said Gandalf.

'Enough to perceive that there are two follies to avoid. To use this thing is perilous. At this hour, to send it in the hands of a witless halfling into the land of the Enemy himself, as you have done, and this son of mine, that is madness.'

'And the Lord Denethor what would he have done?'

'Neither. But most surely not for any argument would he have set this thing at a hazard beyond all but a fool's hope, risking our utter ruin, if the Enemy should recover what he lost. Nay, it should have been kept, hidden, hidden dark and deep. Not used, I say, unless at the uttermost end of need, but set beyond his grasp, save by a victory so final that what then befell would not trouble us, being dead.'

'You think, as is your wont, my lord, of Gondor only,' said Gandalf. 'Yet there are other men and other lives, and time still to be. And for me, I pity even his slaves.'

'And where will other men look for help, if Gondor falls?' answered Denethor. 'If I had this thing now in the deep vaults of this citadel, we should not then shake with dread under this gloom, fearing the worst, and our counsels would be undisturbed. If you do not trust me to endure the test, you do not know me yet.'

'Nonetheless I do not trust you,' said Gandalf. 'Had I done so, I could have sent this thing hither to your keeping and spared myself and others much anguish. And now hearing you speak I trust you less, no more than Boromir. Nay, stay your wrath! I do not trust myself in this, and I refused this thing, even as a freely given gift. You are strong and can still in some matters govern yourself, Denethor; yet if you had received this thing, it would have overthrown you. Were it buried beneath the roots of Mindolluin, still it would burn your mind away, as the darkness grows, and the yet worse things follow that soon shall come upon us.'

For a moment the eyes of Denethor glowed again as he faced Gandalf, and Pippin felt once more the strain between their wills; but now almost it seemed as if their glances were like blades from eye to eye, flickering as they fenced. Pippin trembled fearing some dreadful stroke. But suddenly Denethor relaxed and grew cold again. He shrugged his shoulders.

'If I had! If you had!' he said. 'Such words and ifs are vain. It has gone into the Shadow, and only time will show what doom awaits it, and us. The time will not be long. In what is left, let all who fight the Enemy in their fashion be at one, and keep hope while they may, and after hope still the hardihood to die free.' He turned to Faramir. 'What think you of the garrison at Osgiliath?'

'It is not strong,' said Faramir. 'I have sent the company of Ithilien to strengthen it, as I have said.'

'Not enough, I deem,' said Denethor. 'It is there that the first blow will fall. They will have need of some stout captain there.'

'There and elsewhere in many places,' said Faramir, and sighed. 'Alas for my brother, whom I too loved!' He rose. 'May I have your leave, father?' And then he swayed and leaned upon his father's chair.

'You are weary, I see,' said Denethor. 'You have ridden fast and far, and under shadows of evil in the air, I am told.'

'Let us not speak of that!' said Faramir.

'Then we will not,' said Denethor. 'Go now and rest as you may. Tomorrow's need will be sterner.'

All now took leave of the Lord of the City and went to rest while they still could. Outside there was a starless blackness as Gandalf, with Pippin beside him bearing a small torch, made his way to their lodging. They did not speak until they were behind closed doors. Then at last Pippin took Gandalf's hand.

'Tell me,' he said, 'is there any hope? For Frodo, I mean; or at least mostly for Frodo.'

Gandalf put his hand on Pippin's head. 'There never was much hope,' he answered. 'Just a fool's hope, as I have been told. And when I heard of Cirith Ungol——' He broke off and strode to the window, as if his eyes could pierce the night in the East. 'Cirith Ungol!' he muttered. 'Why that way, I wonder?' He turned. 'Just now, Pippin, my heart almost failed me, hearing that name. And yet in truth I believe that the news that Faramir brings has some hope in it. For it seems clear that our Enemy has opened his war at last and made the first move while Frodo was still free. So now for many days he will have his eye turned this way and that, away from his own land. And yet, Pippin, I feel from afar his haste and fear. He has begun sooner than he would. Something has happened to stir him.'

Gandalf stood for a moment in thought. 'Maybe,' he muttered. 'Maybe even your foolishness helped, my lad. Let me see: some five days ago now he would discover that we had thrown down Saruman, and had taken the Stone. Still what of that? We could not use it to much purpose, or without his knowing. Ah! I wonder. Aragorn? His time draws near. And he is strong and stern underneath, Pippin; bold, determined, able to take his own counsel and dare great risks at need. That may be it. He may have used the Stone and shown himself to the Enemy, challenging him, for this very purpose. I wonder. Well, we shall not know the answer till the Riders of Rohan come, if they do not come too late. There are evil days ahead. To sleep while we may!'

'But,' said Pippin.

'But what?' said Gandalf. 'Only one *but* will I allow tonight.'

'Gollum,' said Pippin. 'How on earth could they be going about *with* him, even following him? And I could see that Faramir did not like the place he was taking them to any more than you do. What is wrong?'

'I cannot answer that now,' said Gandalf. 'Yet my heart guessed that Frodo and Gollum would meet before the end. For good, or for evil. But of Cirith Ungol I will not speak tonight. Treachery, treachery I fear; treachery of that miserable creature. But so it must be. Let us remember that a traitor may betray himself and do good that he does not intend. It can be so, sometimes. Good night!'

The next day came with a morning like a brown dusk, and the hearts of men, lifted for a while by the return of Faramir, sank low again. The winged Shadows were not seen again that day, yet ever and anon, high above the city, a faint cry would come, and many who heard it would stand stricken with a passing dread, while the less stout-hearted quailed and wept.

And now Faramir was gone again. 'They give him no rest,' some murmured. 'The Lord drives his son too hard, and now he must do the duty of two, for himself and for the one that will not return.' And ever men looked northward, asking: 'Where are the Riders of Rohan?'

In truth Faramir did not go by his own choosing. But the Lord of the City was master of his Council, and he was in no mood that day to bow to others. Early in the morning the Council had been summoned. There all the captains judged that because of the threat in the South their force was too weak to make any stroke of war on their own part, unless perchance the Riders of Rohan yet should come. Meanwhile they must man the walls and wait.

'Yet,' said Denethor, 'we should not lightly abandon the outer defences, the Rammas made with so great a labour. And the Enemy must pay dearly for the crossing of the River.

That he cannot do, in force to assail the City, either north of Cair Andros because of the marshes, or southwards towards Lebennin because of the breadth of the River, that needs many boats. It is at Osgiliath that he will put his weight, as before when Boromir denied him the passage.'

'That was but a trial,' said Faramir. 'Today we may make the Enemy pay ten times our loss at the passage and yet rue the exchange. For he can afford to lose a host better than we to lose a company. And the retreat of those that we put out far afield will be perilous, if he wins across in force.'

'And what of Cair Andros?' said the Prince. 'That, too, must be held, if Osgiliath is defended. Let us not forget the danger on our left. The Rohirrim may come, and they may not. But Faramir has told us of great strength drawing ever to the Black Gate. More than one host may issue from it, and strike for more than one passage.'

'Much must be risked in war,' said Denethor. 'Cair Andros is manned, and no more can be sent so far. But I will not yield the River and the Pelennor unfought – not if there is a captain here who has still the courage to do his lord's will.'

Then all were silent. But at length Faramir said: 'I do not oppose your will, sire. Since you are robbed of Boromir, I will go and do what I can in his stead – if you command it.'

'I do so,' said Denethor.

'Then farewell!' said Faramir. 'But if I should return, think better of me!'

'That depends on the manner of your return,' said Denethor.

Gandalf it was that last spoke to Faramir ere he rode east. 'Do not throw your life away rashly or in bitterness,' he said. 'You will be needed here, for other things than war. Your father loves you, Faramir, and will remember it ere the end. Farewell!'

So now the Lord Faramir had gone forth again, and had taken with him such strength of men as were willing to go or could be spared. On the walls some gazed through the gloom towards the ruined city, and they wondered what chanced there, for nothing could be seen. And others, as ever, looked north and counted the leagues to Théoden in Rohan. 'Will he come? Will he remember our old alliance?' they said.

'Yes, he will come,' said Gandalf, 'even if he comes too late. But think! At best the Red Arrow cannot have reached him more than two days ago, and the miles are long from Edoras.'

It was night again ere news came. A man rode in haste from the fords, saying that a host had issued from Minas Morgul and was already drawing nigh to Osgiliath; and it had been joined by regiments from the South, Haradrim, cruel and tall. 'And we have learned,' said the messenger, 'that the Black Captain leads them once again, and the fear of him has passed before him over the River.'

With those ill-boding words the third day closed since Pippin came to Minas Tirith. Few went to rest, for small hope had any now that even Faramir could hold the fords for long.

The next day, though the darkness had reached its full and grew no deeper, it weighed heavier on men's hearts, and a great dread was on them. Ill news came soon again. The passage of Anduin was won by the Enemy. Faramir was retreating to the wall of the Pelennor, rallying his men to the Causeway Forts; but he was ten times outnumbered.

'If he wins back at all across the Pelennor, his enemies will be on his heels,' said the messenger. 'They have paid dear for the crossing, but less dearly than we hoped. The plan has been well laid. It is now seen that in secret they have long been building floats and barges in great number in East Osgiliath. They swarmed across like beetles. But it is the Black Captain that defeats us. Few will stand and abide even the rumour of his coming. His own folk quail at him, and they would slay themselves at his bidding.'

'Then I am needed there more than here,' said Gandalf, and rode off at once, and the glimmer of him faded soon from sight. And all that night Pippin alone and sleepless stood upon the wall and gazed eastward.

The bells of day had scarcely rung out again, a mockery in the unlightened dark, when far away he saw fires spring up, across in the dim spaces where the walls of the Pelennor stood. The watchmen cried aloud, and all men in the City stood to arms. Now ever and anon there was a red flash, and slowly through the heavy air dull rumbles could be heard.

'They have taken the wall!' men cried. 'They are blasting breaches in it. They are coming!'

'Where is Faramir?' cried Beregond in dismay. 'Say not that he has fallen!'

It was Gandalf that brought the first tidings. With a handful of horsemen he came in the middle morning, riding as escort to a line of wains. They were filled with wounded men, all that could be saved from the wreck of the Causeway Forts. At once he went to Denethor. The Lord of the City sat now in a high chamber above the Hall of the White Tower with Pippin at his side; and through the dim windows, north and south and east, he bent his dark eyes, as if to pierce the shadows of doom that ringed him round. Most to the North he looked, and would pause at whiles to listen as if by some ancient art his ears might hear the thunder of hoofs on the plains far away.

'Is Faramir come?' he asked.

'No,' said Gandalf. 'But he still lived when I left him. Yet he is resolved to stay with the rearguard, lest the retreat over the Pelennor become a rout. He may, perhaps, hold his men together long enough, but I doubt it. He is pitted against a foe too great. For one has come that I feared.'

'Not – the Dark Lord?' cried Pippin, forgetting his place in his terror.

Denethor laughed bitterly. 'Nay, not yet, Master Peregrin! He will not come save only to triumph over me when all is won. He uses others as his weapons. So do all great lords, if they are wise, Master Halfling. Or why should I sit here in my tower and think, and watch, and wait, spending even my sons? For I can still wield a brand.'

He stood up and cast open his long black cloak, and behold! he was clad in mail beneath, and girt with a long sword, great-hilted in a sheath of black and silver. 'Thus have I walked, and thus now for many years have I slept,' he said, 'lest with age the body should grow soft and timid.'

'Yet now under the Lord of Barad-dûr the most fell of all his captains is already master of your outer walls,' said Gandalf. 'King of Angmar long ago, Sorcerer, Ringwraith, Lord of the Nazgûl, a spear of terror in the hand of Sauron, shadow of despair.'

'Then, Mithrandir, you had a foe to match you,' said Denethor. 'For myself, I have long known who is the chief captain of the hosts of the Dark Tower. Is this all that you have returned to say? Or can it be that you have withdrawn because you are overmatched?'

Pippin trembled, fearing that Gandalf would be stung to sudden wrath, but his fear was needless. 'It might be so,' Gandalf answered softly. 'But our trial of strength is not yet come. And if words spoken of old be true, not by the hand of man shall he fall, and hidden from the Wise is the doom that awaits him. However that may be, the Captain of Despair does not press forward, yet. He rules rather according to the wisdom that you have just spoken, from the rear, driving his slaves in madness on before.

'Nay, I came rather to guard the hurt men that can yet be healed; for the Rammas is breached far and wide, and soon the host of Morgul will enter in at many points. And I came chiefly to say this. Soon there will be battle on the fields. A sortie must be made ready. Let it be of mounted men. In them lies our brief hope, for in one thing only is the enemy still poorly provided: he has few horsemen.'

'And we also have few. Now would the coming of Rohan be in the nick of time,' said Denethor.

'We are likely to see other newcomers first,' said Gandalf.
'Fugitives from Cair Andros have already reached us. The
isle has fallen. Another army is come from the Black Gate,
crossing from the north-east.'

'Some have accused you, Mithrandir, of delighting to bear
ill news,' said Denethor, 'but to me this is no longer news:
it was known to me ere nightfall yesterday. As for the sortie,
I had already given thought to it. Let us go down.'

Time passed. At length watchers on the walls could see
the retreat of the out-companies. Small bands of weary and
often wounded men came first with little order; some were
running wildly as if pursued. Away to the eastward the distant
fires flickered, and now it seemed that here and there they
crept across the plain. Houses and barns were burning. Then
from many points little rivers of red flame came hurrying on,
winding through the gloom, converging towards the line of
the broad road that led from the City-gate to Osgiliath.

'The enemy,' men murmured. 'The dike is down. Here
they come pouring through the breaches! And they carry
torches, it seems. Where are our own folk?'

It drew now to evening by the hour, and the light was so
dim that even far-sighted men upon the Citadel could discern
little clearly out upon the fields, save only the burnings that
ever multiplied, and the lines of fire that grew in length and
speed. At last, less than a mile from the City, a more ordered
mass of men came into view, marching not running, still
holding together.

The watchers held their breath. 'Faramir must be there,'
they said. 'He can govern man and beast. He will make it
yet.'

Now the main retreat was scarcely two furlongs distant.
Out of the gloom behind a small company of horsemen galloped, all that was left of the rearguard. Once again they
turned at bay, facing the oncoming lines of fire. Then suddenly there was a tumult of fierce cries. Horsemen of the

enemy swept up. The lines of fire became flowing torrents, file upon file of Orcs bearing flames, and wild Southron men with red banners, shouting with harsh tongues, surging up, overtaking the retreat. And with a piercing cry out of the dim sky fell the winged shadows, the Nazgûl stooping to the kill.

The retreat became a rout. Already men were breaking away, flying wild and witless here and there, flinging away their weapons, crying out in fear, falling to the ground.

And then a trumpet rang from the Citadel, and Denethor at last released the sortie. Drawn up within the shadow of the Gate and under the looming walls outside they had waited for his signal: all the mounted men that were left in the City. Now they sprang forward, formed, quickened to a gallop, and charged with a great shout. And from the walls an answering shout went up; for foremost on the field rode the swan-knights of Dol Amroth with their Prince and his blue banner at their head.

'Amroth for Gondor!' they cried. 'Amroth to Faramir!'

Like thunder they broke upon the enemy on either flank of the retreat; but one rider outran them all, swift as the wind in the grass: Shadowfax bore him, shining, unveiled once more, a light starting from his upraised hand.

The Nazgûl screeched and swept away, for their Captain was not yet come to challenge the white fire of his foe. The hosts of Morgul intent on their prey, taken at unawares in wild career, broke, scattering like sparks in a gale. The out-companies with a great cheer turned and smote their pursuers. Hunters became the hunted. The retreat became an onslaught. The field was strewn with stricken orcs and men, and a reek arose of torches cast away, sputtering out in swirling smoke. The cavalry rode on.

But Denethor did not permit them to go far. Though the enemy was checked, and for the moment driven back, great forces were flowing in from the East. Again the trumpet rang, sounding the retreat. The cavalry of Gondor halted. Behind their screen the out-companies re-formed. Now steadily they came marching back. They reached the Gate of the City and entered, stepping proudly; and proudly the people of the City looked on them and cried their praise, and yet they were troubled in heart. For the companies were grievously reduced. Faramir had lost a third of his men. And where was he?

Last of all he came. His men passed in. The mounted knights returned, and at their rear the banner of Dol Amroth, and the Prince. And in his arms before him on his horse he bore the body of his kinsman, Faramir son of Denethor, found upon the stricken field.

'Faramir! Faramir!' men cried, weeping in the streets. But he did not answer, and they bore him away up the winding road to the Citadel and his father. Even as the Nazgûl had swerved aside from the onset of the White Rider, there came flying a deadly dart, and Faramir, as he held at bay a mounted champion of Harad, had fallen to the earth. Only the charge of Dol Amroth had saved him from the red southland swords that would have hewed him as he lay.

The Prince Imrahil brought Faramir to the White Tower, and he said: 'Your son has returned, lord, after great deeds,' and he told all that he had seen. But Denethor rose and looked on the face of his son and was silent. Then he bade them make a bed in the chamber and lay Faramir upon it and depart. But he himself went up alone into the secret room under the summit of the Tower; and many who looked up thither at that time saw a pale light that gleamed and flickered from the narrow windows for a while, and then flashed and went out. And when Denethor descended again he went to Faramir and sat beside him without speaking, but the face of the Lord was grey, more deathlike than his son's.

So now at last the City was besieged, enclosed in a ring of foes. The Rammas was broken, and all the Pelennor abandoned to the Enemy. The last word to come from outside the walls was brought by men flying down the northward road ere the Gate was shut. They were the remnant of the guard that was kept at that point where the way from Anórien and Rohan ran into the townlands. Ingold led them, the same who had admitted Gandalf and Pippin less than five days before, while the sun still rose and there was hope in the morning.

'There is no news of the Rohirrim,' he said. 'Rohan will not come now. Or if they come, it will not avail us. The new host that we had tidings of has come first, from over the River by way of Andros, it is said. They are strong: battalions of Orcs of the Eye, and countless companies of Men of a new sort that we have not met before. Not tall, but broad and grim, bearded like dwarves, wielding great axes. Out of some savage land in the wide East they come, we deem. They hold the northward road; and many have passed on into Anórien. The Rohirrim cannot come.'

The Gate was shut. All night watchmen on the walls heard the rumour of the enemy that roamed outside, burning field and tree, and hewing any man that they found abroad, living or dead. The numbers that had already passed over the River could not be guessed in the darkness, but when morning, or its dim shadow, stole over the plain, it was seen that even fear by night had scarcely over-counted them. The plain was dark with their marching companies, and as far as eyes could strain in the mirk there sprouted, like a foul fungus-growth, all about the beleaguered city great camps of tents, black or sombre red.

Busy as ants hurrying orcs were digging, digging lines of deep trenches in a huge ring, just out of bowshot from the walls; and as the trenches were made each was filled with fire, though how it was kindled or fed, by art or devilry, none could see. All day the labour went forward, while the men of Minas Tirith looked on, unable to hinder it. And as each length of trench was completed, they could see great wains approaching; and soon yet more companies of the enemy were swiftly setting up, each behind the cover of a trench, great engines for the casting of missiles. There were none

upon the City walls large enough to reach so far or to stay
the work.

At first men laughed and did not greatly fear such devices.
For the main wall of the City was of great height and marvel-
lous thickness, built ere the power and craft of Númenor
waned in exile; and its outward face was like to the Tower
of Orthanc, hard and dark and smooth, unconquerable by
steel or fire, unbreakable except by some convulsion that
would rend the very earth on which it stood.

'Nay,' they said, 'not if the Nameless One himself should
come, not even he could enter here while we yet live.' But
some answered: 'While we yet live? How long? He has a
weapon that has brought low many strong places since the
world began. Hunger. The roads are cut. Rohan will not
come.'

But the engines did not waste shot upon the indomitable
wall. It was no brigand or orc-chieftain that ordered the
assault upon the Lord of Mordor's greatest foe. A power and
mind of malice guided it. As soon as the great catapults were
set, with many yells and the creaking of rope and winch, they
began to throw missiles marvellously high, so that they passed
right above the battlement and fell thudding within the first
circle of the City; and many of them by some secret art burst
into flame as they came toppling down.

Soon there was great peril of fire behind the wall, and all
who could be spared were busy quelling the flames that
sprang up in many places. Then among the greater casts
there fell another hail, less ruinous but more horrible. All
about the streets and lanes behind the Gate it tumbled down,
small round shot that did not burn. But when men ran to
learn what it might be, they cried aloud or wept. For the
enemy was flinging into the City all the heads of those who
had fallen fighting at Osgiliath, or on the Rammas, or in the
fields. They were grim to look on; for though some were
crushed and shapeless, and some had been cruelly hewn, yet
many had features that could be told, and it seemed that they
had died in pain; and all were branded with the foul token

of the Lidless Eye. But marred and dishonoured as they were, it often chanced that thus a man would see again the face of someone that he had known, who had walked proudly once in arms, or tilled the fields, or ridden in upon a holiday from the green vales in the hills.

In vain men shook their fists at the pitiless foes that swarmed before the Gate. Curses they heeded not, nor understood the tongues of western men, crying with harsh voices like beasts and carrion-birds. But soon there were few left in Minas Tirith who had the heart to stand up and defy the hosts of Mordor. For yet another weapon, swifter than hunger, the Lord of the Dark Tower had: dread and despair.

The Nazgûl came again, and as their Dark Lord now grew and put forth his strength, so their voices, which uttered only his will and his malice, were filled with evil and horror. Ever they circled above the City, like vultures that expect their fill of doomed men's flesh. Out of sight and shot they flew, and yet were ever present, and their deadly voices rent the air. More unbearable they became, not less, at each new cry. At length even the stout-hearted would fling themselves to the ground as the hidden menace passed over them, or they would stand, letting their weapons fall from nerveless hands while into their minds a blackness came, and they thought no more of war; but only of hiding and of crawling, and of death.

During all this black day Faramir lay upon his bed in the chamber of the White Tower, wandering in a desperate fever; dying someone said, and soon 'dying' all men were saying upon the walls and in the streets. And by him his father sat, and said nothing, but watched, and gave no longer any heed to the defence.

No hours so dark had Pippin known, not even in the clutches of the Uruk-hai. It was his duty to wait upon the Lord, and wait he did, forgotten it seemed, standing by the door of the unlit chamber, mastering his own fears as best he could. And as he watched, it seemed to him that Denethor grew old before his eyes, as if something had snapped in his proud will, and his stern mind was overthrown. Grief maybe had wrought it, and remorse. He saw tears on that once tearless face, more unbearable than wrath.

'Do not weep, lord,' he stammered. 'Perhaps he will get well. Have you asked Gandalf?'

'Comfort me not with wizards!' said Denethor. 'The fool's hope has failed. The Enemy has found it, and now his power waxes; he sees our very thoughts, and all we do is ruinous.

'I sent my son forth, unthanked, unblessed, out into needless peril, and here he lies with poison in his veins. Nay, nay, whatever may now betide in war, my line too is ending, even the House of the Stewards has failed. Mean folk shall rule the last remnant of the Kings of Men, lurking in the hills until all are hounded out.'

Men came to the door crying for the Lord of the City. 'Nay, I will not come down,' he said. 'I must stay beside my son. He might still speak before the end. But that is near. Follow whom you will, even the Grey Fool, though his hope has failed. Here I stay.'

So it was that Gandalf took command of the last defence of the City of Gondor. Wherever he came men's hearts would lift again, and the winged shadows pass from memory. Tirelessly he strode from Citadel to Gate, from north to south about the wall; and with him went the Prince of Dol Amroth in his shining mail. For he and his knights still held themselves like lords in whom the race of Númenor ran true. Men that saw them whispered saying: 'Belike the old tales speak well; there is Elvish blood in the veins of that folk, for the people of Nimrodel dwelt in that land once long ago.' And then one would sing amid the gloom some staves of the Lay of Nimrodel, or other songs of the Vale of Anduin out of vanished years.

And yet – when they had gone, the shadows closed on men again, and their hearts went cold, and the valour of Gondor withered into ash. And so slowly they passed out of a dim day of fears into the darkness of a desperate night. Fires now raged unchecked in the first circle of the City, and the garrison upon the outer wall was already in many places cut off from retreat. But the faithful who remained there at their posts were few; most had fled beyond the second gate.

Far behind the battle the River had been swiftly bridged, and all day more force and gear of war had poured across. Now at last in the middle night the assault was loosed. The vanguard passed through the trenches of fire by many devious paths that had been left between them. On they came, reckless of their loss as they approached, still bunched and herded, within the range of bowmen on the wall. But indeed there were too few now left there to do them great damage, though the light of the fires showed up many a mark for archers of such skill as Gondor once had boasted. Then perceiving that the valour of the City was already beaten down, the hidden Captain put forth his strength. Slowly the great siege-towers built in Osgiliath rolled forward through the dark.

Messengers came again to the chamber in the White Tower, and Pippin let them enter, for they were urgent. Denethor turned his head slowly from Faramir's face, and looked at them silently.

'The first circle of the City is burning, lord,' they said. 'What are your commands? You are still the Lord and Steward. Not all will follow Mithrandir. Men are flying from the walls and leaving them unmanned.'

'Why? Why do the fools fly?' said Denethor. 'Better to burn sooner than late, for burn we must. Go back to your bonfire! And I? I will go now to my pyre. To my pyre! No tomb for Denethor and Faramir. No tomb! No long slow sleep of death embalmed. We will burn like heathen kings before ever a ship sailed hither from the West. The West has failed. Go back and burn!'

The messengers without bow or answer turned and fled.

Now Denethor stood up and released the fevered hand of Faramir that he had held. 'He is burning, already burning,' he said sadly. 'The house of his spirit crumbles.' Then stepping softly towards Pippin he looked down at him.

'Farewell!' he said. 'Farewell, Peregrin son of Paladin! Your service has been short, and now it is drawing to an end. I release you from the little that remains. Go now, and die in what way seems best to you. And with whom you will, even that friend whose folly brought you to this death. Send for my servants and then go. Farewell!'

'I will not say farewell, my lord,' said Pippin kneeling. And then suddenly hobbit-like once more, he stood up and looked the old man in the eyes. 'I will take your leave, sir,' he said; 'for I want to see Gandalf very much indeed. But he is no fool; and I will not think of dying until he despairs of life. But from my word and your service I do not wish to be released while you live. And if they come at last to the Citadel, I hope to be here and stand beside you and earn perhaps the arms that you have given me.'

'Do as you will, Master Halfling,' said Denethor. 'But my life is broken. Send for my servants!' He turned back to Faramir.

Pippin left him and called for the servants, and they came: six men of the household, strong and fair; yet they trembled at the summons. But in a quiet voice Denethor bade them lay warm coverlets on Faramir's bed and take it up. And they did so, and lifting up the bed they bore it from the chamber. Slowly they paced to trouble the fevered man as little as might be, and Denethor, now bending on a staff, followed them; and last came Pippin.

Out from the White Tower they walked, as if to a funeral, out into the darkness, where the overhanging cloud was lit beneath with flickers of dull red. Softly they paced the great courtyard, and at a word from Denethor halted beside the Withered Tree.

All was silent, save for the rumour of war in the City down below, and they heard the water dripping sadly from the dead branches into the dark pool. Then they went on through the Citadel gate, where the sentinel stared at them in wonder and dismay as they passed by. Turning westward they came at length to a door in the rearward wall of the sixth circle. Fen Hollen it was called, for it was kept ever shut save at times of funeral, and only the Lord of the City might use that way, or those who bore the token of the tombs and tended the houses of the dead. Beyond it went a winding road that descended in many curves down to the narrow land under the shadow of Mindolluin's precipice where stood the mansions of the dead Kings and of their Stewards.

A porter sat in a little house beside the way, and with fear in his eyes he came forth bearing a lantern in his hand. At the Lord's command he unlocked the door, and silently it swung back; and they passed through, taking the lantern from his hand. It was dark on the climbing road between ancient walls and many-pillared balusters looming in the swaying lantern-beam. Their slow feet echoed as they walked down, down, until at last they came to the Silent Street, Rath Dínen, between pale domes and empty halls and images of men long dead; and they entered into the House of the Stewards and set down their burden.

There Pippin, staring uneasily about him, saw that he was in a wide vaulted chamber, draped as it were with the great shadows that the little lantern threw upon its shrouded walls. And dimly to be seen were many rows of tables, carved of marble; and upon each table lay a sleeping form, hands folded, head pillowed upon stone. But one table near at hand stood broad and bare. Upon it at a sign from Denethor they laid Faramir and his father side by side, and covered them with one covering, and stood then with bowed heads as mourners beside a bed of death. Then Denethor spoke in a low voice.

'Here we will wait,' he said. 'But send not for the embalmers. Bring us wood quick to burn, and lay it all about us, and beneath; and pour oil upon it. And when I bid you thrust in a torch. Do this and speak no more to me. Farewell!'

'By your leave, lord!' said Pippin and turned and fled in terror from the deathly house. 'Poor Faramir!' he thought. 'I must find Gandalf. Poor Faramir! Quite likely he needs medicine more than tears. Oh, where can I find Gandalf? In the thick of things, I suppose; and he will have no time to spare for dying men or madmen.'

At the door he turned to one of the servants who had remained on guard there. 'Your master is not himself,' he said. 'Go slow! Bring no fire to this place while Faramir lives! Do nothing until Gandalf comes!'

'Who is the master of Minas Tirith?' the man answered. 'The Lord Denethor or the Grey Wanderer?'

'The Grey Wanderer or no one, it would seem,' said Pippin, and he sped back and up the winding way as swiftly as his feet would carry him, past the astonished porter, out through the door, and on, till he came near the gate of the Citadel. The sentinel hailed him as he went by, and he recognized the voice of Beregond.

'Whither do you run, Master Peregrin?' he cried.

'To find Mithrandir,' Pippin answered.

'The Lord's errands are urgent and should not be hindered by me,' said Beregond; 'but tell me quickly, if you may: what goes forward? Whither has my Lord gone? I have just come on duty, but I heard that he passed towards the Closed Door, and men were bearing Faramir before him.'

'Yes,' said Pippin, 'to the Silent Street.'

Beregond bowed his head to hide his tears. 'They said that he was dying,' he sighed, 'and now he is dead.'

'No,' said Pippin, 'not yet. And even now his death might be prevented, I think. But the Lord of the City, Beregond, has fallen before his city is taken. He is fey and dangerous.' Quickly he told of Denethor's strange words and deeds. 'I must find Gandalf at once.'

'Then you must go down to the battle.'

'I know. The Lord has given me leave. But, Beregond, if

THE SIEGE OF GONDOR

you can, do something to stop any dreadful thing happening.'

'The Lord does not permit those who wear the black and silver to leave their post for any cause, save at his own command.'

'Well, you must choose between orders and the life of Faramir,' said Pippin. 'And as for orders, I think you have a madman to deal with, not a lord. I must run. I will return if I can.'

He ran on, down, down towards the outer city. Men flying back from the burning passed him, and some seeing his livery turned and shouted, but he paid no heed. At last he was through the Second Gate, beyond which great fires leaped up between the walls. Yet it seemed strangely silent. No noise or shouts of battle or din of arms could be heard. Then suddenly there was a dreadful cry and a great shock, and a deep echoing boom. Forcing himself on against a gust of fear and horror that shook him almost to his knees, Pippin turned a corner opening on the wide place behind the City Gate. He stopped dead. He had found Gandalf; but he shrank back, cowering into a shadow.

Ever since the middle night the great assault had gone on. The drums rolled. To the north and to the south company upon company of the enemy pressed to the walls. There came great beasts, like moving houses in the red and fitful light, the *mûmakil* of the Harad dragging through the lanes amid the fires huge towers and engines. Yet their Captain cared not greatly what they did or how many might be slain: their purpose was only to test the strength of the defence and to keep the men of Gondor busy in many places. It was against the Gate that he would throw his heaviest weight. Very strong it might be, wrought of steel and iron, and guarded with towers and bastions of indomitable stone, yet it was the key, the weakest point in all that high and impenetrable wall.

The drums rolled louder. Fires leaped up. Great engines crawled across the field; and in the midst was a huge ram, great as a forest-tree a hundred feet in length, swinging on mighty chains. Long had it been forging in the dark smithies of Mordor, and its hideous head, founded of black steel, was shaped in the likeness of a ravening wolf; on it spells of ruin lay. Grond they named it, in memory of the Hammer of the Underworld of old. Great beasts drew it, orcs surrounded it, and behind walked mountain-trolls to wield it.

But about the Gate resistance still was stout, and there the knights of Dol Amroth and the hardiest of the garrison stood at bay. Shot and dart fell thick; siege-towers crashed or blazed suddenly like torches. All before the walls on either side of the Gate the ground was choked with wreck and with bodies of the slain; yet still driven as by a madness more and more came up.

Grond crawled on. Upon its housing no fire would catch; and though now and again some great beast that hauled it would go mad and spread stamping ruin among the orcs innumerable that guarded it, their bodies were cast aside from its path and others took their place.

Grond crawled on. The drums rolled wildly. Over the hills of slain a hideous shape appeared: a horseman, tall, hooded, cloaked in black. Slowly, trampling the fallen, he rode forth, heeding no longer any dart. He halted and held up a long pale sword. And as he did so a great fear fell on all, defender and foe alike; and the hands of men drooped to their sides, and no bow sang. For a moment all was still.

The drums rolled and rattled. With a vast rush Grond was hurled forward by huge hands. It reached the Gate. It swung. A deep boom rumbled through the City like thunder running in the clouds. But the doors of iron and posts of steel withstood the stroke.

Then the Black Captain rose in his stirrups and cried aloud in a dreadful voice, speaking in some forgotten tongue words of power and terror to rend both heart and stone.

Thrice he cried. Thrice the great ram boomed. And suddenly upon the last stroke the Gate of Gondor broke. As if stricken by some blasting spell it burst asunder: there was a flash of searing lightning, and the doors tumbled in riven fragments to the ground.

In rode the Lord of the Nazgûl. A great black shape against the fires beyond he loomed up, grown to a vast menace of despair. In rode the Lord of the Nazgûl, under the archway that no enemy ever yet had passed, and all fled before his face.

All save one. There waiting, silent and still in the space before the Gate, sat Gandalf upon Shadowfax: Shadowfax who alone among the free horses of the earth endured the terror, unmoving, steadfast as a graven image in Rath Dínen.

'You cannot enter here,' said Gandalf, and the huge shadow halted. 'Go back to the abyss prepared for you! Go back! Fall into the nothingness that awaits you and your Master. Go!'

The Black Rider flung back his hood, and behold! he had a kingly crown; and yet upon no head visible was it set. The red fires shone between it and the mantled shoulders vast and dark. From a mouth unseen there came a deadly laughter.

'Old fool!' he said. 'Old fool! This is my hour. Do you not know Death when you see it? Die now and curse in vain!' And with that he lifted high his sword and flames ran down the blade.

Gandalf did not move. And in that very moment, away behind in some courtyard of the City, a cock crowed. Shrill and clear he crowed, recking nothing of wizardry or war, welcoming only the morning that in the sky far above the shadows of death was coming with the dawn.

And as if in answer there came from far away another note. Horns, horns, horns. In dark Mindolluin's sides they dimly echoed. Great horns of the North wildly blowing. Rohan had come at last.

CHAPTER V

THE RIDE OF THE ROHIRRIM

It was dark and Merry could see nothing as he lay on the ground rolled in a blanket; yet though the night was airless and windless, all about him hidden trees were sighing softly. He lifted his head. Then he heard it again: a sound like faint drums in the wooded hills and mountain-steps. The throb would cease suddenly and then be taken up again at some other point, now nearer, now further off. He wondered if the watchmen had heard it.

He could not see them, but he knew that all round him were the companies of the Rohirrim. He could smell the horses in the dark, and could hear their shiftings and their soft stamping on the needle-covered ground. The host was bivouacked in the pine-woods that clustered about Eilenach Beacon, a tall hill standing up from the long ridges of the Druadan Forest that lay beside the great road in East Anórien.

Tired as he was Merry could not sleep. He had ridden now for four days on end, and the ever-deepening gloom had slowly weighed down his heart. He began to wonder why he had been so eager to come, when he had been given every excuse, even his lord's command, to stay behind. He wondered, too, if the old King knew that he had been disobeyed and was angry. Perhaps not. There seemed to be some understanding between Dernhelm and Elfhelm, the Marshal who commanded the *éored* in which they were riding. He and all his men ignored Merry and pretended not to hear if he spoke. He might have been just another bag that Dernhelm was carrying. Dernhelm was no comfort: he never spoke to anyone. Merry felt small, unwanted, and lonely. Now the time was anxious, and the host was in peril. They were less than a day's ride from the out-walls of Minas Tirith that encircled the townlands. Scouts had been sent ahead. Some had not returned. Others hastening back had reported that the road was held in force against them. A host of the enemy was encamped upon it, three miles west of Amon Dîn, and some strength of men was already thrusting along the road and was no more than three leagues away. Orcs were roving in the hills and woods along the roadside. The king and Éomer held council in the watches of the night.

Merry wanted somebody to talk to, and he thought of Pippin. But that only increased his restlessness. Poor Pippin, shut up in the great city of stone, lonely and afraid. Merry wished he was a tall Rider like Éomer and could blow a horn or something and go galloping to his rescue. He sat up, listening to the drums that were beating again, now nearer at hand. Presently he heard voices speaking low, and he saw dim half-shrouded lanterns passing through the trees. Men nearby began to move uncertainly in the dark.

A tall figure loomed up and stumbled over him, cursing the tree-roots. He recognized the voice of Elfhelm the Marshal.

'I am not a tree-root, Sir,' he said, 'nor a bag, but a bruised hobbit. The least you can do in amends is to tell me what is afoot.'

'Anything that can keep so in this devil's mirk,' answered Elfhelm. 'But my lord sends word that we must set ourselves in readiness: orders may come for a sudden move.'

'Is the enemy coming then?' asked Merry anxiously. 'Are those their drums? I began to think I was imagining them, as no one else seemed to take any notice of them.'

'Nay, nay,' said Elfhelm, 'the enemy is on the road not in the hills. You hear the Woses, the Wild Men of the Woods: thus they talk together from afar. They still haunt Druadan Forest, it is said. Remnants of an older time they be, living few and secretly, wild and wary as the beasts. They go not to war with Gondor or the Mark; but now they are troubled by the darkness and the coming of the orcs: they fear lest the Dark Years be returning, as seems likely enough. Let us be thankful that they are not hunting us: for they use poisoned arrows, it is said, and they are woodcrafty beyond compare. But they have offered their services to Théoden. Even now one of their headmen is being taken to the king. Yonder go the lights. So much I have heard but no more. And now I must busy myself with my lord's commands. Pack yourself up, Master Bag!' He vanished into the shadows.

Merry did not like this talk of wild men and poisoned darts, but quite apart from that a great weight of dread was on him. Waiting was unbearable. He longed to know what was going to happen. He got up and soon was walking warily in pursuit of the last lantern before it disappeared among the trees.

Presently he came to an open space where a small tent had been set up for the king under a great tree. A large lantern, covered above, was hanging from a bough and cast a pale circle of light below. There sat Théoden and Éomer, and before them on the ground sat a strange squat shape of a man, gnarled as an old stone, and the hairs of his scanty beard straggled on his lumpy chin like dry moss. He was short-legged and fat-armed, thick and stumpy, and clad only with grass about his waist. Merry felt that he had seen him before somewhere, and suddenly he remembered the Púkel-men of Dunharrow. Here was one of those old images brought to life, or maybe a creature descended in true line through endless years from the models used by the forgotten craftsmen long ago.

There was a silence as Merry crept nearer, and then the Wild Man began to speak, in answer to some question, it seemed. His voice was deep and guttural, yet to Merry's surprise he spoke the Common Speech, though in a halting fashion, and uncouth words were mingled with it.

'No, father of Horse-men,' he said, 'we fight not. Hunt only. Kill *gorgûn* in woods, hate orc-folk. You hate *gorgûn* too. We help as we can. Wild Men have long ears and long eyes; know all paths. Wild Men live here before Stone-houses; before Tall Men come up out of Water.'

'But our need is for aid in battle,' said Éomer. 'How will you and your folk help us?'

'Bring news,' said the Wild Man. 'We look out from hills. We climb big mountain and look down. Stone-city is shut. Fire burns there outside; now inside too. You wish to come there? Then you must be quick. But *gorgûn* and men out of far-away,' he waved a short gnarled arm eastward, 'sit on horse-road. Very many, more than Horse-men.'

'How do you know that?' said Éomer.

The old man's flat face and dark eyes showed nothing, but his voice was sullen with displeasure. 'Wild Men are wild, free, but not children,' he answered. 'I am great headman, Ghân-buri-Ghân. I count many things: stars in sky, leaves on trees, men in the dark. You have a score of scores counted ten times and five. They have more. Big fight, and who will win? And many more walk round walls of Stone-houses.'

'Alas! he speaks all too shrewdly,' said Théoden. 'And our scouts say that they have cast trenches and stakes across the road. We cannot sweep them away in sudden onset.'

'And yet we need great haste,' said Éomer. 'Mundburg is on fire!'

'Let Ghân-buri-Ghân finish!' said the Wild Man. 'More than one road he knows. He will lead you by road where no pits are, no *gorgûn* walk, only Wild Men and beasts. Many paths were made when Stonehouse-folk were stronger. They carved hills as hunters carve beast-flesh. Wild Men think they ate stone for food. They went through Drúadan to Rimmon with great wains. They go no longer. Road is forgotten, but not by Wild Men. Over hill and behind hill it lies still under grass and tree, there behind Rimmon and down to Dîn, and back at the end to Horse-men's road. Wild Men will show you that road. Then you will kill *gorgûn* and drive away bad dark with bright iron, and Wild Men can go back to sleep in the wild woods.'

Éomer and the king spoke together in their own tongue. At length Théoden turned to the Wild Man. 'We will receive your offer,' he said. 'For though we leave a host of foes behind, what matter? If the Stone-city falls, then we shall have no returning. If it is saved, then the orc-host itself will be cut off. If you are faithful, Ghân-buri-Ghân, then we will give you rich reward, and you shall have the friendship of the Mark for ever.'

'Dead men are not friends to living men, and give them no gifts,' said the Wild Man. 'But if you live after the Darkness, then leave Wild Men alone in the woods and do not hunt them like beasts any more. Ghân-buri-Ghân will not lead you into trap. He will go himself with father of Horsemen, and if he leads you wrong, you will kill him.'

'So be it!' said Théoden.

'How long will it take to pass by the enemy and come back to the road?' asked Éomer. 'We must go at foot-pace, if you guide us; and I doubt not the way is narrow.'

'Wild Men go quick on feet,' said Ghân. 'Way is wide for four horses in Stonewain Valley yonder,' he waved his hand southwards; 'but narrow at beginning and at end. Wild Man could walk from here to Dîn between sunrise and noon.'

'Then we must allow at least seven hours for the leaders,' said Éomer; 'but we must reckon rather on some ten hours for all. Things unforeseen may hinder us, and if our host is all strung out, it will be long ere it can be set in order when we issue from the hills. What is the hour now?'

'Who knows?' said Théoden. 'All is night now.'

'It is all dark, but it is not all night,' said Ghân. 'When Sun comes we feel her, even when she is hidden. Already she climbs over East-mountains. It is the opening of day in the sky-fields.'

'Then we must set out as soon as may be,' said Éomer. 'Even so we cannot hope to come to Gondor's aid today.'

Merry waited to hear no more, but slipped away to get ready for the summons to the march. This was the last stage before the battle. It did not seem likely to him that many of them would survive it. But he thought of Pippin and the flames in Minas Tirith and thrust down his own dread.

All went well that day, and no sight or sound had they of the enemy waiting to waylay them. The Wild Men had put out a screen of wary hunters, so that no orc or roving spy should learn of the movements in the hills. The light was more dim than ever as they drew nearer to the beleaguered city, and the Riders passed in long files like dark shadows of men and horses. Each company was guided by a wild wood-man; but old Ghân walked beside the king. The start had been slower than was hoped, for it had taken time for the Riders, walking and leading their horses, to find paths over the thickly wooded ridges behind their camp and down into the hidden Stonewain Valley. It was late in the afternoon when the leaders came to wide grey thickets stretching beyond the eastward side of Amon Dîn, and masking a great gap in the line of hills that from Nardol to Dîn ran east and west. Through the gap the forgotten wain-road long ago had run down, back into the main horse-way from the City through Anórien; but now for many lives of men trees had had their way with it, and it had vanished, broken and buried under the leaves of uncounted years. But the thickets offered to the Riders their last hope of cover before they went into open battle; for beyond them lay the road and the plains of Anduin, while east and southwards the slopes were bare and rocky, as the writhen hills gathered themselves together and climbed up, bastion upon bastion, into the great mass and shoulders of Mindolluin.

The leading company was halted, and as those behind filed up out of the trough of the Stonewain Valley they spread out and passed to camping-places under the grey trees. The king summoned the captains to council. Éomer sent out scouts to spy upon the road; but old Ghân shook his head.

'No good to send Horse-men,' he said. 'Wild Men have already seen all that can be seen in the bad air. They will come soon and speak to me here.'

The captains came; and then out of the trees crept warily other púkel-shapes so like old Ghân that Merry could hardly tell them apart. They spoke to Ghân in a strange throaty language.

Presently Ghân turned to the king. 'Wild Men say many things,' he said. 'First, be wary! Still many men in camp beyond Dîn, an hour's walk yonder,' he waved his arm west towards the black beacon. 'But none to see between here and Stone-folk's new walls. Many busy there. Walls stand up no longer: *gorgûn* knock them down with earth-thunder and with clubs of black iron. They are unwary and do not look about them. They think their friends watch all roads!' At that old Ghân made a curious gurgling noise, and it seemed that he was laughing.

'Good tidings!' cried Éomer. 'Even in this gloom hope gleams again. Our Enemy's devices oft serve us in his despite. The accursed darkness itself has been a cloak to us. And now, lusting to destroy Gondor and throw it down stone from stone, his orcs have taken away my greatest fear. The out-wall could have been held long against us. Now we can sweep through – if once we win so far.'

'Once again I thank you, Ghân-buri-Ghân of the woods,' said Théoden. 'Good fortune go with you for tidings and for guidance!'

'Kill *gorgûn*! Kill orc-folk! No other words please Wild Men,' answered Ghân. 'Drive away bad air and darkness with bright iron!'

'To do these things we have ridden far,' said the king, 'and we shall attempt them. But what we shall achieve only tomorrow will show.'

Ghân-buri-Ghân squatted down and touched the earth with his horny brow in token of farewell. Then he got up as if to depart. But suddenly he stood looking up like some startled woodland animal snuffling a strange air. A light came in his eyes.

'Wind is changing!' he cried, and with that, in a twinkling as it seemed, he and his fellows had vanished into the glooms, never to be seen by any Rider of Rohan again. Not long after far away eastward the faint drums throbbed again. Yet to no heart in all the host came any fear that the Wild Men were unfaithful, strange and unlovely though they might appear.

'We need no further guidance,' said Elfhelm; 'for there are riders in the host who have ridden down to Mundburg in days of peace. I for one. When we come to the road it will veer south, and there will lie before us still seven leagues ere we reach the wall of the townlands. Along most of that way there is much grass on either side of the road. On that stretch the errand-riders of Gondor reckoned to make their greatest speed. We may ride it swiftly and without great rumour.'

'Then since we must look for fell deeds and the need of all our strength,' said Éomer, 'I counsel that we rest now, and set out hence by night, and so time our going that we come upon the fields when tomorrow is as light as it will be, or when our lord gives the signal.'

To this the king assented, and the captains departed. But soon Elfhelm returned. 'The scouts have found naught to report beyond the grey wood, lord,' he said, 'save two men only: two dead men and two dead horses.'

'Well?' said Éomer. 'What of it?'

'This, lord: they ·were errand-riders of Gondor; Hirgon was one maybe. At least his hand still clasped the Red Arrow, but his head was hewn off. And this also: it would seem by the signs that they were fleeing *westward* when they fell. As I read it, they found the enemy already on the out-wall, or assailing it, when they returned – and that would be two nights ago, if they used fresh horses from the posts, as is their wont. They could not reach the City and turned back.'

'Alas!' said Théoden. 'Then Denethor has heard no news of our riding and will despair of our coming.'

'*Need brooks no delay, yet late is better than never*,' said Éomer. 'And mayhap in this time shall the old saw be proved truer than ever before since men spoke with mouth.'

It was night. On either side of the road the host of Rohan was moving silently. Now the road passing about the skirts of Mindolluin turned southward. Far away and almost straight ahead there was a red glow under the black sky and the sides of the great mountain loomed dark against it. They were drawing near the Rammas of the Pelennor; but the day was not yet come.

The king rode in the midst of the leading company, his household-men about him. Elfhelm's *éored* came next; and now Merry noticed that Dernhelm had left his place and in the darkness was moving steadily forward, until at last he was riding just in rear of the king's guard. There came a check. Merry heard voices in front speaking softly. Out-riders had come back who had ventured forward almost to the wall. They came to the king.

'There are great fires, lord,' said one. 'The City is all set about with flame, and the field is full of foes. But all seem drawn off to the assault. As well as we could guess, there are few left upon the out-wall, and they are heedless, busy in destruction.'

'Do you remember the Wild Man's words, lord?' said another. 'I live upon the open Wold in days of peace; Wídfara is my name, and to me also the air brings messages. Already the wind is turning. There comes a breath out of the South; there is a sea-tang in it, faint though it be. The morning will bring new things. Above the reek it will be dawn when you pass the wall.'

'If you speak truly, Wídfara, then may you live beyond this day in years of blessedness!' said Théoden. He turned to the men of his household who were near, and he spoke now in a clear voice so that many also of the riders of the first *éored* heard him:

'Now is the hour come, Riders of the Mark, sons of Eorl! Foes and fire are before you, and your homes far behind. Yet, though you fight upon an alien field, the glory that you reap there shall be your own for ever. Oaths ye have taken: now fulfil them all, to lord and land and league of friendship!'

Men clashed spear upon shield.

'Éomer, my son! You lead the first *éored*,' said Théoden; 'and it shall go behind the king's banner in the centre.

Elfhelm, lead your company to the right when we pass the wall. And Grimbold shall lead his towards the left. Let the other companies behind follow these three that lead, as they have chance. Strike wherever the enemy gathers. Other plans we cannot make, for we know not yet how things stand upon the field. Forth now, and fear no darkness!'

The leading company rode off as swiftly as they could, for it was still deep dark, whatever change Wídfara might forebode. Merry was riding behind Dernhelm, clutching with the left hand while with the other he tried to loosen his sword in its sheath. He felt now bitterly the truth of the old king's words: *in such a battle what would you do, Meriadoc?* Just this,' he thought: 'encumber a rider, and hope at best to stay in my seat and not be pounded to death by galloping hoofs!'

It was no more than a league to where the out-walls had stood. They soon reached them; too soon for Merry. Wild cries broke out, and there was some clash of arms, but it was brief. The orcs busy about the walls were few and amazed, and they were quickly slain or driven off. Before the ruin of the north-gate in the Rammas the king halted again. The first *éored* drew up behind him and about him on either side. Dernhelm kept close to the king, though Elfhelm's company was away on the right. Grimbold's men turned aside and passed round to a great gap in the wall further eastward.

Merry peered from behind Dernhelm's back. Far away, maybe ten miles or more, there was a great burning, but between it and the Riders lines of fire blazed in a vast crescent, at the nearest point less than a league distant. He could make out little more on the dark plain, and as yet he neither saw any hope of morning, nor felt any wind, changed or unchanged.

Now silently the host of Rohan moved forward into the field of Gondor, pouring in slowly but steadily, like the rising tide through breaches in a dike that men have thought secure. But the mind and will of the Black Captain were bent wholly on the falling city, and as yet no tidings came to him warning that his designs held any flaw.

After a while the king led his men away somewhat east-ward, to come between the fires of the siege and the outer fields. Still they were unchallenged, and still Théoden gave no signal. At last he halted once again. The City was now nearer. A smell of burning was in the air and a very shadow of death. The horses were uneasy. But the king sat upon Snowmane, motionless, gazing upon the agony of Minas Tir-ith, as if stricken suddenly by anguish, or by dread. He seemed to shrink down, cowed by age. Merry himself felt as if a great weight of horror and doubt had settled on him. His heart beat slowly. Time seemed poised in uncertainty. They were too late! Too late was worse than never! Perhaps Théoden would quail, bow his old head, turn, slink away to hide in the hills.

Then suddenly Merry felt it at last, beyond doubt: a change. Wind was in his face! Light was glimmering. Far, far away, in the South the clouds could be dimly seen as remote grey shapes, rolling up, drifting: morning lay beyond them.

But at that same moment there was a flash, as if lightning had sprung from the earth beneath the City. For a searing second it stood dazzling far off in black and white, its topmost tower like a glittering needle; and then as the darkness closed again there came rolling over the fields a great *boom*.

At that sound the bent shape of the king sprang suddenly erect. Tall and proud he seemed again; and rising in his stirrups he cried in a loud voice, more clear than any there had ever heard a mortal man achieve before:

> *Arise, arise, Riders of Théoden!*
> *Fell deeds awake: fire and slaughter!*
> *spear shall be shaken, shield be splintered,*
> *a sword-day, a red day, ere the sun rises!*
> *Ride now, ride now! Ride to Gondor!*

With that he seized a great horn from Guthláf his banner-bearer, and he blew such a blast upon it that it burst asunder. And straightway all the horns in the host were lifted up in music, and the blowing of the horns of Rohan in that hour was like a storm upon the plain and a thunder in the mountains.

Ride now, ride now! Ride to Gondor!

Suddenly the king cried to Snowmane and the horse sprang away. Behind him his banner blew in the wind, white horse upon a field of green, but he outpaced it. After him thundered the knights of his house, but he was ever before them. Éomer rode there, the white horsetail on his helm floating in his speed, and the front of the first *éored* roared like a breaker foaming to the shore, but Théoden could not be overtaken. Fey he seemed, or the battle-fury of his fathers ran like new fire in his veins, and he was borne up on Snowmane like a god of old, even as Oromë the Great in the battle of the Valar when the world was young. His golden shield was uncovered, and lo! it shone like an image of the Sun, and the grass flamed into green about the white feet of his steed. For morning came, morning and a wind from the sea; and darkness was removed, and the hosts of Mordor wailed, and terror took them, and they fled, and died, and the hoofs of wrath rode over them. And then all the host of Rohan burst into song, and they sang as they slew, for the joy of battle was on them, and the sound of their singing that was fair and terrible came even to the City.

CHAPTER VI

THE BATTLE OF
THE PELENNOR FIELDS

But it was no orc-chieftain or brigand that led the assault upon Gondor. The darkness was breaking too soon, before the date that his Master had set for it: fortune had betrayed him for the moment, and the world had turned against him; victory was slipping from his grasp even as he stretched out his hand to seize it. But his arm was long. He was still in command, wielding great powers. King, Ringwraith, Lord of the Nazgûl, he had many weapons. He left the Gate and vanished.

Théoden King of the Mark had reached the road from the Gate to the River, and he turned towards the City that was now less than a mile distant. He slackened his speed a little, seeking new foes, and his knights came about him, and Dernhelm was with them. Ahead nearer the walls Elfhelm's men were among the siege-engines, hewing, slaying, driving their foes into the fire-pits. Well nigh all the northern half of the Pelennor was overrun, and there camps were blazing, orcs were flying towards the River like herds before the hunters; and the Rohirrim went hither and thither at their will. But they had not yet overthrown the siege, nor won the Gate. Many foes stood before it, and on the further half of the plain were other hosts still unfought. Southward beyond the road lay the main force of the Haradrim, and there their horsemen were gathered about the standard of their chieftain. And he looked out, and in the growing light he saw the banner of the king, and that it was far ahead of the battle with few men about it. Then he was filled with a red wrath and shouted aloud, and displaying his standard, black serpent upon scarlet, he came against the white horse and the green with great press of men; and the drawing of the scimitars of the Southrons was like a glitter of stars.

Then Théoden was aware of him, and would not wait for his onset, but crying to Snowmane he charged headlong to greet him. Great was the clash of their meeting. But the white fury of the Northmen burned the hotter, and more skilled was their knighthood with long spears and bitter. Fewer were they but they clove through the Southrons like a fire-bolt in a forest. Right through the press drove Théoden Thengel's son, and his spear was shivered as he threw down their chieftain. Out swept his sword, and he spurred to the standard, hewed staff and bearer; and the black serpent foundered. Then all that was left unslain of their cavalry turned and fled far away.

But lo! suddenly in the midst of the glory of the king his golden shield was dimmed. The new morning was blotted from the sky. Dark fell about him. Horses reared and screamed. Men cast from the saddle lay grovelling on the ground.

'To me! To me!' cried Théoden. 'Up Eorlingas! Fear no darkness!' But Snowmane wild with terror stood up on high, fighting with the air, and then with a great scream he crashed upon his side: a black dart had pierced him. The king fell beneath him.

The great shadow descended like a falling cloud. And behold! it was a winged creature: if bird, then greater than all other birds, and it was naked, and neither quill nor feather did it bear, and its vast pinions were as webs of hide between horned fingers; and it stank. A creature of an older world maybe it was, whose kind, lingering in forgotten mountains cold beneath the Moon, outstayed their day, and in hideous eyrie bred this last untimely brood, apt to evil. And the Dark Lord took it, and nursed it with fell meats, until it grew beyond the measure of all other things that fly; and he gave

it to his servant to be his steed. Down, down it came, and
then, folding its fingered webs, it gave a croaking cry, and
settled upon the body of Snowmane, digging in its claws,
stooping its long naked neck.

Upon it sat a shape, black-mantled, huge and threatening.
A crown of steel he bore, but between rim and robe naught
was there to see, save only a deadly gleam of eyes: the Lord
of the Nazgûl. To the air he had returned, summoning his
steed ere the darkness failed, and now he was come again,
bringing ruin, turning hope to despair, and victory to death.
A great black mace he wielded.

But Théoden was not utterly forsaken. The knights of his
house lay slain about him, or else mastered by the madness
of their steeds were borne far away. Yet one stood there still:
Dernhelm the young, faithful beyond fear; and he wept, for
he had loved his lord as a father. Right through the charge
Merry had been borne unharmed behind him, until the
Shadow came; and then Windfola had thrown them in his
terror, and now ran wild upon the plain. Merry crawled on
all fours like a dazed beast, and such a horror was on him
that he was blind and sick.

'King's man! King's man!' his heart cried within him. 'You
must stay by him. As a father you shall be to me, you said.'
But his will made no answer, and his body shook. He dared
not open his eyes or look up.

Then out of the blackness in his mind he thought that he
heard Dernhelm speaking; yet now the voice seemed strange,
recalling some other voice that he had known.

'Begone, foul dwimmerlaik, lord of carrion! Leave the dead
in peace!'

A cold voice answered: 'Come not between the Nazgûl
and his prey! Or he will not slay thee in thy turn. He will
bear thee away to the houses of lamentation, beyond all darkness, where thy flesh shall be devoured, and thy shrivelled
mind be left naked to the Lidless Eye.'

A sword rang as it was drawn. 'Do what you will; but I
will hinder it, if I may.'

'Hinder me? Thou fool. No living man may hinder me!'

Then Merry heard of all sounds in that hour the strangest. It seemed that Dernhelm laughed, and the clear voice was like the ring of steel. 'But no living man am I! You look upon a woman. Éowyn I am, Éomund's daughter. You stand between me and my lord and kin. Begone, if you be not deathless! For living or dark undead, I will smite you, if you touch him.'

The winged creature screamed at her, but the Ringwraith made no answer, and was silent, as if in sudden doubt. Very amazement for a moment conquered Merry's fear. He opened his eyes and the blackness was lifted from them. There some paces from him sat the great beast, and all seemed dark about it, and above it loomed the Nazgûl Lord like a shadow of despair. A little to the left facing them stood she whom he had called Dernhelm. But the helm of her secrecy had fallen from her, and her bright hair, released from its bonds, gleamed with pale gold upon her shoulders. Her eyes grey as the sea were hard and fell, and yet tears were on her cheek. A sword was in her hand, and she raised her shield against the horror of her enemy's eyes.

Éowyn it was, and Dernhelm also. For into Merry's mind flashed the memory of the face that he saw at the riding from Dunharrow: the face of one that goes seeking death, having no hope. Pity filled his heart and great wonder, and suddenly the slow-kindled courage of his race awoke. He clenched his hand. She should not die, so fair, so desperate! At least she should not die alone, unaided.

The face of their enemy was not turned towards him, but still he hardly dared to move, dreading lest the deadly eyes should fall on him. Slowly, slowly he began to crawl aside; but the Black Captain, in doubt and malice intent upon the woman before him, heeded him no more than a worm in the mud.

Suddenly the great beast beat its hideous wings, and the wind of them was foul. Again it leaped into the air, and then swiftly fell down upon Éowyn, shrieking, striking with beak and claw.

Still she did not blench: maiden of the Rohirrim, child of kings, slender but as a steel-blade, fair yet terrible. A swift stroke she dealt, skilled and deadly. The outstretched neck she clove asunder, and the hewn head fell like a stone. Backward she sprang as the huge shape crashed to ruin, vast wings outspread, crumpled on the earth; and with its fall the shadow passed away. A light fell about her, and her hair shone in the sunrise.

Out of the wreck rose the Black Rider, tall and threatening, towering above her. With a cry of hatred that stung the very ears like venom he let fall his mace. Her shield was shivered in many pieces, and her arm was broken; she stumbled to her knees. He bent over her like a cloud, and his eyes glittered; he raised his mace to kill.

But suddenly he too stumbled forward with a cry of bitter pain, and his stroke went wide, driving into the ground. Merry's sword had stabbed him from behind, shearing through the black mantle, and passing up beneath the hauberk had pierced the sinew behind his mighty knee.

'Éowyn! Éowyn!' cried Merry. Then tottering, struggling up, with her last strength she drove her sword between crown and mantle, as the great shoulders bowed before her. The sword broke sparkling into many shards. The crown rolled away with a clang. Éowyn fell forward upon her fallen foe. But lo! the mantle and hauberk were empty. Shapeless they lay now on the ground, torn and tumbled; and a cry went up into the shuddering air, and faded to a shrill wailing, passing with the wind, a voice bodiless and thin that died, and was swallowed up, and was never heard again in that age of this world.

And there stood Meriadoc the hobbit in the midst of the slain, blinking like an owl in the daylight, for tears blinded him; and through a mist he looked on Éowyn's fair head, as she lay and did not move; and he looked on the face of the king, fallen in the midst of his glory. For Snowmane in his agony had rolled away from him again; yet he was the bane of his master.

Then Merry stooped and lifted his hand to kiss it, and lo! Théoden opened his eyes, and they were clear, and he spoke in a quiet voice though laboured.

'Farewell, Master Holbytla!' he said. 'My body is broken. I go to my fathers. And even in their mighty company I shall not now be ashamed. I felled the black serpent. A grim morn, and a glad day, and a golden sunset!'

Merry could not speak, but wept anew. 'Forgive me, lord,' he said at last, 'if I broke your command, and yet have done no more in your service than to weep at our parting.'

The old king smiled. 'Grieve not! It is forgiven. Great heart will not be denied. Live now in blessedness; and when you sit in peace with your pipe, think of me! For never now shall I sit with you in Meduseld, as I promised, or listen to your herb-lore.' He closed his eyes, and Merry bowed beside him. Presently he spoke again. 'Where is Éomer? For my eyes darken, and I would see him ere I go. He must be king after me. And I would send word to Éowyn. She, she would not have me leave her, and now I shall not see her again, dearer than daughter.'

'Lord, lord,' began Merry brokenly, 'she is———'; but at that moment there was a great clamour, and all about them horns and trumpets were blowing. Merry looked round: he had forgotten the war, and all the world beside, and many hours it seemed since the king rode to his fall, though in truth it was only a little while. But now he saw that they were in danger of being caught in the very midst of the great battle that would soon be joined.

New forces of the enemy were hastening up the road from the River; and from under the walls came the legions of Morgul; and from the southward fields came footmen of Harad with horsemen before them, and behind them rose the huge backs of the *mûmakil* with war-towers upon them. But northward the white crest of Éomer led the great front of the Rohirrim which he had again gathered and marshalled; and out of the City came all the strength of men that was in it, and the silver swan of Dol Amroth was borne in the van, driving the enemy from the Gate.

For a moment the thought flitted through Merry's mind: 'Where is Gandalf? Is he not here? Could he not have saved the king and Éowyn?' But thereupon Éomer rode up in haste, and with him came the knights of the household that still lived and had now mastered their horses. They looked in wonder at the carcase of the fell beast that lay there; and their steeds would not go near. But Éomer leaped from the saddle, and grief and dismay fell upon him as he came to the king's side and stood there in silence.

Then one of the knights took the king's banner from the hand of Guthláf the banner-bearer who lay dead, and he lifted it up. Slowly Théoden opened his eyes. Seeing the banner he made a sign that it should be given to Éomer.

'Hail, King of the Mark!' he said. 'Ride now to victory! Bid Éowyn farewell!' And so he died, and knew not that Éowyn lay near him. And those who stood by wept, crying: 'Théoden King! Théoden King!'

But Éomer said to them:

> Mourn not overmuch! Mighty was the fallen,
> meet was his ending. When his mound is raised,
> women then shall weep. War now calls us!

Yet he himself wept as he spoke. 'Let his knights remain here,' he said, 'and bear his body in honour from the field, lest the battle ride over it! Yea, and all these other of the king's men that lie here.' And he looked at the slain, recalling their names. Then suddenly he beheld his sister Éowyn as she lay, and he knew her. He stood a moment as a man who is pierced in the midst of a cry by an arrow through the heart; and then his face went deathly white, and a cold fury rose in him, so that all speech failed him for a while. A fey mood took him.

'Éowyn, Éowyn!' he cried at last. 'Éowyn, how come you here? What madness or devilry is this? Death, death, death! Death take us all!'

Then without taking counsel or waiting for the approach of the men of the City, he spurred headlong back to the front of the great host, and blew a horn, and cried aloud for the onset. Over the field rang his clear voice calling: 'Death! Ride, ride to ruin and the world's ending!'

And with that the host began to move. But the Rohirrim sang no more. *Death* they cried with one voice loud and terrible, and gathering speed like a great tide their battle swept about their fallen king and passed, roaring away southwards.

And still Meriadoc the hobbit stood there blinking through his tears, and no one spoke to him, indeed none seemed to heed him. He brushed away the tears, and stooped to pick up the green shield that Éowyn had given him, and he slung it at his back. Then he looked for his sword that he had let fall; for even as he struck his blow his arm was numbed, and now he could only use his left hand. And behold! there lay his weapon, but the blade was smoking like a dry branch that has been thrust in a fire; and as he watched it, it writhed and withered and was consumed.

So passed the sword of the Barrow-downs, work of Western-esse. But glad would he have been to know its fate who wrought it slowly long ago in the North-kingdom when the Dúnedain were young, and chief among their foes was the dread realm of Angmar and its sorcerer king. No other blade, not though mightier hands had wielded it, would have dealt that foe a wound so bitter, cleaving the undead flesh, breaking the spell that knit his unseen sinews to his will.

Men now raised the king, and laying cloaks upon spear-truncheons they made shift to bear him away towards the City; and others lifted Éowyn gently up and bore her after him. But the men of the king's household they could not yet bring from the field; for seven of the king's knights had fallen there, and Déorwine their chief was among them. So they laid them apart from their foes and the fell beast and set spears about them. And afterwards when all was over men returned and made a fire there and burned the carcase of the beast; but for Snowmane they dug a grave and set up a stone upon which was carved in the tongues of Gondor and the Mark:

> *Faithful servant yet master's bane,*
> *Lightfoot's foal, swift Snowmane.*

Green and long grew the grass on Snowmane's Howe, but ever black and bare was the ground where the beast was burned.

Now slowly and sadly Merry walked beside the bearers, and he gave no more heed to the battle. He was weary and full of pain, and his limbs trembled as with a chill. A great rain came out of the Sea, and it seemed that all things wept for Théoden and Éowyn, quenching the fires in the City with grey tears. It was through a mist that presently he saw the van of the men of Gondor approaching. Imrahil, Prince of Dol Amroth, rode up and drew rein before them.

'What burden do you bear, Men of Rohan?' he cried.

'Théoden King,' they answered. 'He is dead. But Éomer King now rides in the battle: he with the white crest in the wind.'

Then the prince went from his horse, and knelt by the bier in honour of the king and his great onset; and he wept. And rising he looked then on Éowyn and was amazed. 'Surely, here is a woman?' he said. 'Have even the women of the Rohirrim come to war in our need?'

'Nay! One only,' they answered. 'The Lady Éowyn is she, sister of Éomer; and we knew naught of her riding until this hour, and greatly we rue it.'

Then the prince seeing her beauty, though her face was pale and cold, touched her hand as he bent to look more closely on her. 'Men of Rohan!' he cried. 'Are there no leeches among you? She is hurt, to the death maybe, but I deem that she yet lives.' And he held the bright-burnished vambrace that was upon his arm before her cold lips, and behold! a little mist was laid on it hardly to be seen.

'Haste now is needed,' he said, and he sent one riding back swiftly to the City to bring aid. But he bowing low to the fallen, bade them farewell, and mounting rode away into battle.

And now the fighting waxed furious on the fields of the Pelennor; and the din of arms rose upon high, with the crying of men and the neighing of horses. Horns were blown and trumpets were braying, and the *mûmakil* were bellowing as they were goaded to war. Under the south walls of the City the footmen of Gondor now drove against the legions of Morgul that were still gathered there in strength. But the horsemen rode eastward to the succour of Éomer: Húrin the Tall, Warden of the Keys, and the Lord of Lossarnach, and Hirluin of the Green Hills, and Prince Imrahil the fair with his knights all about him.

Not too soon came their aid to the Rohirrim; for fortune had turned against Éomer, and his fury had betrayed him. The great wrath of his onset had utterly overthrown the front of his enemies, and great wedges of his Riders had passed clear through the ranks of the Southrons, discomfiting their horsemen and riding their footmen to ruin. But wherever the *mûmakil* came there the horses would not go, but blenched and swerved away; and the great monsters were unfought, and stood like towers of defence, and the Haradrim rallied about them. And if the Rohirrim at their onset were thrice outnumbered by the Haradrim alone, soon their case became worse; for new strength came now streaming to the field out of Osgiliath. There they had been mustered for the sack of the City and the rape of Gondor, waiting on the call of their Captain. He now was destroyed; but Gothmog the lieutenant of Morgul had flung them into the fray; Easterlings with axes,

and Variags of Khand, Southrons in scarlet, and out of Far
Harad black men like half-trolls with white eyes and red
tongues. Some now hastened up behind the Rohirrim, others
held westward to hold off the forces of Gondor and prevent
their joining with Rohan.

It was even as the day thus began to turn against Gondor
and their hope wavered that a new cry went up in the City,
it being then mid-morning, and a great wind blowing, and
the rain flying north, and the sun shining. In that clear air
watchmen on the walls saw afar a new sight of fear, and their
last hope left them.

For Anduin, from the bend at the Harlond, so flowed that
from the City men could look down it lengthwise for some
leagues, and the far-sighted could see any ships that
approached. And looking thither they cried in dismay; for
black against the glittering stream they beheld a fleet borne
up on the wind: dromunds, and ships of great draught with
many oars, and with black sails bellying in the breeze.

'The Corsairs of Umbar!' men shouted. 'The Corsairs of
Umbar! Look! The Corsairs of Umbar are coming! So
Belfalas is taken, and the Ethir, and Lebennin is gone. The
Corsairs are upon us! It is the last stroke of doom!'

And some without order, for none could be found to command them in the City, ran to the bells and tolled the alarm;
and some blew the trumpets sounding the retreat. 'Back to
the walls!' they cried. 'Back to the walls! Come back to the
City before all are overwhelmed!' But the wind that sped the
ships blew all their clamour away.

The Rohirrim indeed had no need of news or alarm. All
too well they could see for themselves the black sails. For
Éomer was now scarcely a mile from the Harlond, and a
great press of his first foes was between him and the haven
there, while new foes came swirling behind, cutting him off
from the Prince. Now he looked to the River, and hope died
in his heart, and the wind that he had blessed he now called
accursed. But the hosts of Mordor were enheartened, and
filled with a new lust and fury they came yelling to the onset.

Stern now was Éomer's mood, and his mind clear again. He let blow the horns to rally all men to his banner that could come thither; for he thought to make a great shield-wall at the last, and stand, and fight there on foot till all fell, and do deeds of song on the fields of Pelennor, though no man should be left in the West to remember the last King of the Mark. So he rode to a green hillock and there set his banner, and the White Horse ran rippling in the wind.

> *Out of doubt, out of dark to the day's rising*
> *I came singing in the sun, sword unsheathing.*
> *To hope's end I rode and to heart's breaking:*
> *Now for wrath, now for ruin and a red nightfall!*

These staves he spoke, yet he laughed as he said them. For once more lust of battle was on him; and he was still unscathed, and he was young, and he was king: the lord of a fell people. And lo! even as he laughed at despair he looked out again on the black ships, and he lifted up his sword to defy them.

And then wonder took him, and a great joy; and he cast his sword up in the sunlight and sang as he caught it. And all eyes followed his gaze, and behold! upon the foremost ship a great standard broke, and the wind displayed it as she turned towards the Harlond. There flowered a White Tree, and that was for Gondor; but Seven Stars were about it, and a high crown above it, the signs of Elendil that no lord had borne for years beyond count. And the stars flamed in the sunlight, for they were wrought of gems by Arwen daughter of Elrond; and the crown was bright in the morning, for it was wrought of mithril and gold.

Thus came Aragorn son of Arathorn, Elessar, Isildur's heir, out of the Paths of the Dead, borne upon a wind from the Sea to the kingdom of Gondor; and the mirth of the Rohirrim was a torrent of laughter and a flashing of swords, and the joy and wonder of the City was a music of trumpets and a ringing of bells. But the hosts of Mordor were seized with bewilderment, and a great wizardry it seemed to them that their own ships should be filled with their foes; and a black dread fell on them, knowing that the tides of fate had turned against them and their doom was at hand.

East rode the knights of Dol Amroth driving the enemy before them: troll-men and Variags and orcs that hated the sunlight. South strode Éomer and men fled before his face, and they were caught between the hammer and the anvil. For now men leaped from the ships to the quays of the Harlond and swept north like a storm. There came Legolas, and Gimli wielding his axe, and Halbarad with the standard, and Elladan and Elrohir with stars on their brow, and the dour-handed Dúnedain, Rangers of the North, leading a great valour of the folk of Lebennin and Lamedon and the fiefs of the South. But before all went Aragorn with the Flame of the West, Andúril like a new fire kindled, Narsil reforged as deadly as of old; and upon his brow was the Star of Elendil.

And so at length Éomer and Aragorn met in the midst of the battle, and they leaned on their swords and looked on one another and were glad.

'Thus we meet again, though all the hosts of Mordor lay between us,' said Aragorn. 'Did I not say so at the Hornburg?'

'So you spoke,' said Éomer, 'but hope oft deceives, and I knew not then that you were a man foresighted. Yet twice blessed is help unlooked for, and never was a meeting of friends more joyful.' And they clasped hand in hand. 'Nor indeed more timely,' said Éomer. 'You come none too soon, my friend. Much loss and sorrow has befallen us.'

'Then let us avenge it, ere we speak of it!' said Aragorn, and they rode back to battle together.

Hard fighting and long labour they had still; for the Southrons were bold men and grim, and fierce in despair; and the Easterlings were strong and war-hardened and asked for no quarter. And so in this place and that, by burned homestead or barn, upon hillock or mound, under wall or on field, still they gathered and rallied and fought until the day wore away.

Then the Sun went at last behind Mindolluin and filled all the sky with a great burning, so that the hills and the mountains were dyed as with blood; fire glowed in the River, and the grass of the Pelennor lay red in the nightfall. And in that hour the great Battle of the field of Gondor was over; and not one living foe was left within the circuit of the Rammas. All were slain save those who fled to die, or to drown in the red foam of the River. Few ever came eastward to Morgul or Mordor; and to the land of the Haradrim came only a tale from far off: a rumour of the wrath and terror of Gondor.

Aragorn and Éomer and Imrahil rode back towards the Gate of the City, and they were now weary beyond joy or sorrow. These three were unscathed, for such was their fortune and the skill and might of their arms, and few indeed had dared to abide them or look on their faces in the hour of their wrath. But many others were hurt or maimed or dead upon the field. The axes hewed Forlong as he fought alone and unhorsed; and both Duilin of Morthond and his brother were trampled to death when they assailed the *mûmakil*, leading their bowmen close to shoot at the eyes of the monsters. Neither Hirluin the fair would return to Pinnath Gelin, nor Grimbold to Grimslade, nor Halbarad to the Northlands, dour-handed Ranger. No few had fallen, renowned or nameless, captain or soldier; for it was a great battle and the full count of it no tale has told. So long afterward a maker in Rohan said in his song of the Mounds of Mundburg:

> *We heard of the horns in the hills ringing,*
> *the swords shining in the South-kingdom.*
> *Steeds went striding to the Stoningland*
> *as wind in the morning. War was kindled.*
> *There Théoden fell, Thengling mighty,*
> *to his golden halls and green pastures*
> *in the Northern fields never returning,*

high lord of the host. Harding and Guthláf,
Dúnhere and Déorwine, doughty Grimbold,
Herefara and Herubrand, Horn and Fastred,
fought and fell there in a far country:
in the Mounds of Mundburg under mould they lie
with their league-fellows, lords of Gondor.
Neither Hirluin the Fair to the hills by the sea,
nor Forlong the old to the flowering vales
ever, to Arnach, to his own country
returned in triumph; nor the tall bowmen,
Derufin and Duilin, to their dark waters,
meres of Morthond under mountain-shadows.
Death in the morning and at day's ending
lords took and lowly. Long now they sleep
under grass in Gondor by the Great River.
Grey now as tears, gleaming silver,
red then it rolled, roaring water:
foam dyed with blood flamed at sunset;
as beacons mountains burned at evening;
red fell the dew in Rammas Echor.

CHAPTER VII

THE PYRE OF DENETHOR

When the dark shadow at the Gate withdrew Gandalf still sat motionless. But Pippin rose to his feet, as if a great weight had been lifted from him; and he stood listening to the horns, and it seemed to him that they would break his heart with joy. And never in after years could he hear a horn blown in the distance without tears starting in his eyes. But now suddenly his errand returned to his memory, and he ran forward. At that moment Gandalf stirred and spoke to Shadowfax, and was about to ride through the Gate.

'Gandalf, Gandalf!' cried Pippin, and Shadowfax halted.

'What are you doing here?' said Gandalf. 'Is it not a law in the City that those who wear the black and silver must stay in the Citadel, unless their lord gives them leave?'

'He has,' said Pippin. 'He sent me away. But I am frightened. Something terrible may happen up there. The Lord is out of his mind, I think. I am afraid he will kill himself, and kill Faramir too. Can't you do something?'

Gandalf looked through the gaping Gate, and already on the fields he heard the gathering sound of battle. He clenched his hand. 'I must go,' he said. 'The Black Rider is abroad, and he will yet bring ruin on us. I have no time.'

'But Faramir!' cried Pippin. 'He is not dead, and they will burn him alive, if someone does not stop them.'

'Burn him alive?' said Gandalf. 'What is this tale? Be quick!'

'Denethor has gone to the Tombs,' said Pippin, 'and he has taken Faramir, and he says we are all to burn, and he will not wait, and they are to make a pyre and burn him on it, and Faramir as well. And he has sent men to fetch wood and oil. And I have told Beregond, but I'm afraid he won't dare to leave his post: he is on guard. And what can he do anyway?' So Pippin poured out his tale, reaching up and touching Gandalf's knee with trembling hands. 'Can't you save Faramir?'

'Maybe I can,' said Gandalf; 'but if I do, then others will die, I fear. Well, I must come, since no other help can reach him. But evil and sorrow will come of this. Even in the heart of our stronghold the Enemy has power to strike us: for his will it is that is at work.'

Then having made up his mind he acted swiftly; and catching up Pippin and setting him before him, he turned Shadow-fax with a word. Up the climbing streets of Minas Tirith they clattered, while the noise of war rose behind them. Everywhere men were rising from their despair and dread, seizing their weapons, crying one to another: 'Rohan has come!' Captains were shouting, companies were mustering; many already were marching down to the Gate.

They met the Prince Imrahil, and he called to them: 'Whither now, Mithrandir? The Rohirrim are fighting on the fields of Gondor! We must gather all the strength that we can find.'

'You will need every man and more,' said Gandalf. 'Make all haste. I will come when I can. But I have an errand to the Lord Denethor that will not wait. Take command in the Lord's absence!'

They passed on; and as they climbed and drew near to the Citadel they felt the wind blowing in their faces, and they caught the glimmer of morning far away, a light growing in the southern sky. But it brought little hope to them, not knowing what evil lay before them, fearing to come too late.

'Darkness is passing,' said Gandalf, 'but it still lies heavy on this City.'

At the gate of the Citadel they found no guard. 'Then Beregond has gone,' said Pippin more hopefully. They turned away and hastened along the road to the Closed Door.

It stood wide open, and the porter lay before it. He was slain and his key had been taken.

'Work of the Enemy!' said Gandalf. 'Such deeds he loves: friend at war with friend; loyalty divided in confusion of hearts.' Now he dismounted and bade Shadowfax return to his stable. 'For, my friend,' he said, 'you and I should have ridden to the fields long ago, but other matters delay me. Yet come swiftly if I call!'

They passed the Door and walked on down the steep winding road. Light was growing, and the tall columns and carven figures beside the way went slowly by like grey ghosts.

Suddenly the silence was broken, and they heard below them cries and the ringing of swords: such sounds as had not been heard in the hallowed places since the building of the City. At last they came to Rath Dínen and hastened towards the House of the Stewards, looming in the twilight under its great dome.

'Stay! Stay!' cried Gandalf, springing forward to the stone stair before the door. 'Stay this madness!'

For there were the servants of Denethor with swords and torches in their hands; but alone in the porch upon the topmost step stood Beregond, clad in the black and silver of the Guard; and he held the door against them. Two of them had already fallen to his sword, staining the hallows with their blood; and the others cursed him, calling him outlaw and traitor to his master.

Even as Gandalf and Pippin ran forward, they heard from within the house of the dead the voice of Denethor crying: 'Haste, haste! Do as I have bidden! Slay me this renegade! Or must I do so myself?' Thereupon the door which Beregond held shut with his left hand was wrenched open, and there behind him stood the Lord of the City, tall and fell; a light like flame was in his eyes, and he held a drawn sword.

But Gandalf sprang up the steps, and the men fell back from him and covered their eyes; for his coming was like the incoming of a white light into a dark place, and he came with great anger. He lifted up his hand, and in the very stroke, the sword of Denethor flew up and left his grasp and fell behind him in the shadows of the house; and Denethor stepped backward before Gandalf as one amazed.

'What is this, my lord?' said the wizard. 'The houses of the dead are no places for the living. And why do men fight here in the Hallows when there is war enough before the Gate? Or has our Enemy come even to Rath Dínen?'

'Since when has the Lord of Gondor been answerable to thee?' said Denethor. 'Or may I not command my own servants?'

'You may,' said Gandalf. 'But others may contest your will, when it is turned to madness and evil. Where is your son, Faramir?'

'He lies within,' said Denethor, 'burning, already burning. They have set a fire in his flesh. But soon all shall be burned. The West has failed. It shall all go up in a great fire, and all shall be ended. Ash! Ash and smoke blown away on the wind!'

Then Gandalf seeing the madness that was on him feared that he had already done some evil deed, and he thrust forward, with Beregond and Pippin behind him, while Denethor gave back until he stood beside the table within. But there they found Faramir, still dreaming in his fever, lying upon the table. Wood was piled under it, and high all about it, and all was drenched with oil, even the garments of Faramir and the coverlets; but as yet no fire had been set to the fuel. Then Gandalf revealed the strength that lay hid in him, even as the light of his power was hidden under his grey mantle. He leaped up on to the faggots, and raising the sick man lightly he sprang down again, and bore him towards the door. But as he did so Faramir moaned and called on his father in his dream.

Denethor started as one waking from a trance, and the flame died in his eyes, and he wept; and he said: 'Do not take my son from me! He calls for me.'

'He calls,' said Gandalf, 'but you cannot come to him yet. For he must seek healing on the threshold of death, and maybe find it not. Whereas your part is to go out to the battle of your City, where maybe death awaits you. This you know in your heart.'

'He will not wake again,' said Denethor. 'Battle is vain. Why should we wish to live longer? Why should we not go to death side by side?'

'Authority is not given to you, Steward of Gondor, to order the hour of your death,' answered Gandalf. 'And only the heathen kings, under the domination of the Dark Power, did thus, slaying themselves in pride and despair, murdering their kin to ease their own death.' Then passing through the door he took Faramir from the deadly house and laid him on the bier on which he had been brought, and which had now been set in the porch. Denethor followed him, and stood trembling, looking with longing on the face of his son. And for a moment, while all were silent and still, watching the Lord in his throes, he wavered.

'Come!' said Gandalf. 'We are needed. There is much that you can yet do.'

Then suddenly Denethor laughed. He stood up tall and proud again, and stepping swiftly back to the table he lifted from it the pillow on which his head had lain. Then coming to the doorway he drew aside the covering, and lo! he had between his hands a *palantír*. And as he held it up, it seemed to those that looked on that the globe began to glow with an inner flame, so that the lean face of the Lord was lit as with a red fire, and it seemed cut out of hard stone, sharp with black shadows, noble, proud, and terrible. His eyes glittered.

'Pride and despair!' he cried. 'Didst thou think that the eyes of the White Tower were blind? Nay, I have seen more than thou knowest, Grey Fool. For thy hope is but ignorance. Go then and labour in healing! Go forth and fight! Vanity. For a little space you may triumph on the field, for a day. But against the Power that now arises there is no victory. To this City only the first finger of its hand has yet been stretched. All the East is moving. And even now the wind of thy hope cheats thee and wafts up Anduin a fleet with black sails. The West has failed. It is time for all to depart who would not be slaves.'

'Such counsels will make the Enemy's victory certain indeed,' said Gandalf.

'Hope on then!' laughed Denethor. 'Do I not know thee, Mithrandir? Thy hope is to rule in my stead, to stand behind every throne, north, south, or west. I have read thy mind and its policies. Do I not know that you commanded this halfling here to keep silence? That you brought him hither to be a spy within my very chamber? And yet in our speech together I have learned the names and purpose of all thy companions. So! With the left hand thou wouldst use me for a little while as a shield against Mordor, and with the right bring up this Ranger of the North to supplant me.

'But I say to thee, Gandalf Mithrandir, I will not be thy tool! I am Steward of the House of Anárion. I will not step down to be the dotard chamberlain of an upstart. Even were his claim proved to me, still he comes but of the line of Isildur. I will not bow to such a one, last of a ragged house long bereft of lordship and dignity.'

'What then would you have,' said Gandalf, 'if your will could have its way?'

'I would have things as they were in all the days of my life,' answered Denethor, 'and in the days of my longfathers before me: to be the Lord of this City in peace, and leave my chair to a son after me, who would be his own master and no wizard's pupil. But if doom denies this to me, then I will have *naught*: neither life diminished, nor love halved, nor honour abated.'

'To me it would not seem that a Steward who faithfully surrenders his charge is diminished in love or in honour,' said Gandalf. 'And at the least you shall not rob your son of his choice while his death is still in doubt.'

At those words Denethor's eyes flamed again, and taking the Stone under his arm he drew a knife and strode towards the bier. But Beregond sprang forward and set himself before Faramir.

'So!' cried Denethor. 'Thou hadst already stolen half my son's love. Now thou stealest the hearts of my knights also, so that they rob me wholly of my son at the last. But in this at least thou shalt not defy my will: to rule my own end.'

'Come hither!' he cried to his servants. 'Come, if you are not all recreant!' Then two of them ran up the steps to him. Swiftly he snatched a torch from the hand of one and sprang back into the house. Before Gandalf could hinder him he thrust the brand amid the fuel, and at once it crackled and roared into flame.

Then Denethor leaped upon the table, and standing there wreathed in fire and smoke he took up the staff of his stewardship that lay at his feet and broke it on his knee. Casting the pieces into the blaze he bowed and laid himself on the table, clasping the *palantír* with both hands upon his breast. And it was said that ever after, if any man looked in that Stone, unless he had a great strength of will to turn it to other purpose, he saw only two aged hands withering in flame.

Gandalf in grief and horror turned his face away and closed the door. For a while he stood in thought, silent upon the threshold, while those outside heard the greedy roaring of the fire within. And then Denethor gave a great cry, and afterwards spoke no more, nor was ever again seen by mortal men.

'So passes Denethor, son of Ecthelion,' said Gandalf. Then he turned to Beregond and the Lord's servants that stood there aghast. 'And so pass also the days of Gondor that you have known; for good or evil they are ended. Ill deeds have been done here; but let now all enmity that lies between you be put away, for it was contrived by the Enemy and works his will. You have been caught in a net of warring duties that you did not weave. But think, you servants of the Lord, blind in your obedience, that but for the treason of Beregond Faramir, Captain of the White Tower, would now also be burned.

'Bear away from this unhappy place your comrades who

have fallen. And we will bear Faramir, Steward of Gondor, to a place where he can sleep in peace, or die if that be his doom.'

Then Gandalf and Beregond taking up the bier bore it away towards the Houses of Healing, while behind them walked Pippin with downcast head. But the servants of the Lord stood gazing as stricken men at the house of the dead; and even as Gandalf came to the end of Rath Dínen there was a great noise. Looking back they saw the dome of the house crack and smokes issue forth; and then with a rush and rumble of stone it fell in a flurry of fire; but still unabated the flames danced and flickered among the ruins. Then in terror the servants fled and followed Gandalf.

At length they came back to the Steward's Door, and Beregond looked with grief at the porter. 'This deed I shall ever rue,' he said; 'but a madness of haste was on me, and he would not listen, but drew sword against me.' Then taking the key that he had wrested from the slain man he closed the door and locked it. 'This should now be given to the Lord Faramir,' he said.

'The Prince of Dol Amroth is in command in the absence of the Lord,' said Gandalf; 'but since he is not here, I must take this on myself. I bid you keep the key and guard it, until the City is set in order again.'

Now at last they passed into the high circles of the City, and in the light of morning they went their way towards the Houses of Healing; and these were fair houses set apart for the care of those who were grievously sick, but now they were prepared for the tending of men hurt in battle or dying. They stood not far from the Citadel-gate, in the sixth circle, nigh to its southward wall, and about them was a garden and a greensward with trees, the only such place in the City. There dwelt the few women that had been permitted to remain in Minas Tirith, since they were skilled in healing or in the service of the healers.

But even as Gandalf and his companions came carrying

the bier to the main door of the Houses, they heard a great cry that went up from the field before the Gate and rising shrill and piercing into the sky passed, and died away on the wind. So terrible was the cry that for a moment all stood still, and yet when it had passed, suddenly their hearts were lifted up in such a hope as they had not known since the darkness came out of the East; and it seemed to them that the light grew clear and the sun broke through the clouds.

But Gandalf's face was grave and sad, and bidding Beregond and Pippin to take Faramir into the Houses of Healing, he went up on to the walls nearby; and there like a figure carven in white he stood in the new sun and looked out. And he beheld with the sight that was given to him all that had befallen; and when Éomer rode out from the forefront of his battle and stood beside those who lay upon the field, he sighed, and he cast his cloak about him again, and went from the walls. And Beregond and Pippin found him standing in thought before the door of the Houses when they came out.

They looked at him, and for a while he was silent. At last he spoke. 'My friends,' he said, 'and all you people of this city and of the Western lands! Things of great sorrow and renown have come to pass. Shall we weep or be glad? Beyond hope the Captain of our foes has been destroyed, and you have heard the echo of his last despair. But he has not gone without woe and bitter loss. And that I might have averted but for the madness of Denethor. So long has the reach of our Enemy become! Alas! but now I perceive how his will was able to enter into the very heart of the City.

'Though the Stewards deemed that it was a secret kept only by themselves, long ago I guessed that here in the White Tower, one at least of the Seven Seeing Stones was preserved. In the days of his wisdom Denethor would not presume to use it to challenge Sauron, knowing the limits of his own strength. But his wisdom failed; and I fear that as the peril of his realm grew he looked in the Stone and was deceived: far too often, I guess, since Boromir departed. He was too great to be subdued to the will of the Dark Power, he saw nonetheless only those things which that Power permitted him to see. The knowledge which he obtained was, doubtless, often of service to him; yet the vision of the great might of Mordor that was shown to him fed the despair of his heart until it overthrew his mind.'

'Now I understand what seemed so strange to me!' said Pippin, shuddering at his memories as he spoke. 'The Lord went away from the room where Faramir lay; and it was only when he returned that I first thought he was changed, old and broken.'

'It was in the very hour that Faramir was brought to the Tower that many of us saw a strange light in the topmost chamber,' said Beregond. 'But we have seen that light before, and it has long been rumoured in the City that the Lord would at times wrestle in thought with his Enemy.'

'Alas! then I have guessed rightly,' said Gandalf. 'Thus the will of Sauron entered into Minas Tirith; and thus I have been delayed here. And here I shall still be forced to remain, for I shall soon have other charges, not Faramir only.

'Now I must go down to meet those who come. I have seen a sight upon the field that is very grievous to my heart, and greater sorrow may yet come to pass. Come with me, Pippin! But you, Beregond, should return to the Citadel and tell the chief of the Guard there what has befallen. It will be his duty, I fear, to withdraw you from the Guard; but say to him that, if I may give him counsel, you should be sent to the Houses of Healing, to be the guard and servant of your captain, and to be at his side when he awakes – if that shall ever be again. For by you he was saved from the fire. Go now! I shall return soon.'

With that he turned away and went with Pippin down towards the lower city. And even as they hastened on their way the wind brought a grey rain, and all the fires sank, and there arose a great smoke before them.

CHAPTER VIII

THE HOUSES OF HEALING

A mist was in Merry's eyes of tears and weariness when they drew near the ruined Gate of Minas Tirith. He gave little heed to the wreck and slaughter that lay about all. Fire and smoke and stench was in the air; for many engines had been burned or cast into the fire-pits, and many of the slain also, while here and there lay many carcases of the great Southron monsters, half-burned, or broken by stone-cast, or shot through the eyes by the valiant archers of Morthond. The flying rain had ceased for a time, and the sun gleamed up above; but all the lower city was still wrapped in a smouldering reek.

Already men were labouring to clear a way through the jetsam of battle; and now out from the Gate came some bearing litters. Gently they laid Éowyn upon soft pillows; but the king's body they covered with a great cloth of gold, and they bore torches about him, and their flames, pale in the sunlight, were fluttered by the wind.

So Théoden and Éowyn came to the City of Gondor, and all who saw them bared their heads and bowed; and they passed through the ash and fume of the burned circle, and went on and up along the streets of stone. To Merry the ascent seemed agelong, a meaningless journey in a hateful dream, going on and on to some dim ending that memory cannot seize.

Slowly the lights of the torches in front of him flickered and went out, and he was walking in a darkness; and he thought: 'This is a tunnel leading to a tomb; there we shall stay forever.' But suddenly into his dream there fell a living voice.

'Well, Merry! Thank goodness I have found you!'

He looked up and the mist before his eyes cleared a little. There was Pippin! They were face to face in a narrow lane, and but for themselves it was empty. He rubbed his eyes.

'Where is the king?' he said. 'And Éowyn?' Then he stumbled and sat down on a doorstep and began to weep again.

'They have gone up into the Citadel,' said Pippin. 'I think you must have fallen asleep on your feet and taken the wrong turning. When we found that you were not with them, Gandalf sent me to look for you. Poor old Merry! How glad I am to see you again! But you are worn out, and I won't bother you with any talk. But tell me, are you hurt, or wounded?'

'No,' said Merry. 'Well, no, I don't think so. But I can't use my right arm, Pippin, not since I stabbed him. And my sword burned all away like a piece of wood.'

Pippin's face was anxious. 'Well, you had better come with me as quick as you can,' he said. 'I wish I could carry you. You aren't fit to walk any further. They shouldn't have let you walk at all; but you must forgive them. So many dreadful things have happened in the City, Merry, that one poor hobbit coming in from the battle is easily overlooked.'

'It's not always a misfortune being overlooked,' said Merry. 'I was overlooked just now by – no, no, I can't speak of it. Help me, Pippin! It's all going dark again, and my arm is so cold.'

'Lean on me, Merry lad!' said Pippin. 'Come now! Foot by foot. It's not far.'

'Are you going to bury me?' said Merry.

'No, indeed!' said Pippin, trying to sound cheerful, though his heart was wrung with fear and pity. 'No, we are going to the Houses of Healing.'

They turned out of the lane that ran between tall houses and the outer wall of the fourth circle, and they regained the main street climbing up to the Citadel. Step by step they went, while Merry swayed and murmured as one in sleep.

'I'll never get him there,' thought Pippin. 'Is there no one to help me? I can't leave him here.' Just then to his surprise a boy came running up behind, and as he passed he recognized Bergil Beregond's son.

'Hullo, Bergil!' he called. 'Where are you going? Glad to see you again, and still alive!'

'I am running errands for the Healers,' said Bergil. 'I cannot stay.'

'Don't!' said Pippin. 'But tell them up there that I have a sick hobbit, a *perian* mind you, come from the battle-field. I don't think he can walk so far. If Mithrandir is there, he will be glad of the message.' Bergil ran on.

'I'd better wait here,' thought Pippin. So he let Merry sink gently down on to the pavement in a patch of sunlight, and then he sat down beside him, laying Merry's head in his lap. He felt his body and limbs gently, and took his friend's hands in his own. The right hand felt icy to the touch.

It was not long before Gandalf himself came in search of them. He stooped over Merry and caressed his brow; then he lifted him carefully. 'He should have been borne in honour into this city,' he said. 'He has well repaid my trust; for if Elrond had not yielded to me, neither of you would have set out; and then far more grievous would the evils of this day have been.' He sighed. 'And yet here is another charge on my hands, while all the time the battle hangs in the balance.'

So at last Faramir and Éowyn and Meriadoc were laid in beds in the Houses of Healing; and there they were tended well. For though all lore was in these latter days fallen from its fullness of old, the leechcraft of Gondor was still wise, and skilled in the healing of wound and hurt, and all such sickness as east of the Sea mortal men were subject to. Save old age only. For that they had found no cure; and indeed the span of their lives had now waned to little more than that of other men, and those among them who passed the tale of five score years with vigour were grown few, save in some houses of purer blood. But now their art and knowledge were baffled; for there were many sick of a malady that would not be healed; and they called it the Black Shadow, for it came from the Nazgûl. And those who were stricken with it fell slowly into an ever deeper dream, and then passed to silence and a deadly cold, and so died. And it seemed to the tenders of the sick that on the Halfling and on the Lady of Rohan this malady lay heavily. Still at whiles as the morning wore away they would speak, murmuring in their dreams; and the watchers listened to all that they said, hoping perhaps to learn something that would help them to understand their hurts. But soon they began to fall down into the darkness, and as the sun turned west a grey shadow crept over their faces. But Faramir burned with a fever that would not abate.

Gandalf went from one to the other full of care, and he was told all that the watchers could hear. And so the day passed, while the great battle outside went on with shifting hopes and strange tidings; and still Gandalf waited and watched and did not go forth; till at last the red sunset filled all the sky, and the light through the windows fell on the grey faces of the sick. Then it seemed to those who stood by that in the glow the faces flushed softly as with health returning, but it was only a mockery of hope.

Then an old wife, Ioreth, the eldest of the women who served in that house, looking on the fair face of Faramir, wept, for all the people loved him. And she said: 'Alas! if he should die. Would that there were kings in Gondor, as there were once upon a time, they say! For it is said in old lore: *The hands of the king are the hands of a healer.* And so the rightful king could ever be known.'

And Gandalf, who stood by, said: 'Men may long remember your words, Ioreth! For there is hope in them. Maybe a king has indeed returned to Gondor; or have you not heard the strange tidings that have come to the City?'

'I have been too busy with this and that to heed all the crying and shouting,' she answered. 'All I hope is that those murdering devils do not come to this House and trouble the sick.'

Then Gandalf went out in haste, and already the fire in

the sky was burning out, and the smouldering hills were fading, while ash-grey evening crept over the fields.

Now as the sun went down Aragorn and Éomer and Imrahil drew near the City with their captains and knights; and when they came before the Gate Aragorn said:

'Behold the Sun setting in a great fire! It is a sign of the end and fall of many things, and a change in the tides of the world. But this City and realm has rested in the charge of the Stewards for many long years, and I fear that if I enter it unbidden, then doubt and debate may arise, which should not be while this war is fought. I will not enter in, nor make any claim, until it be seen whether we or Mordor shall prevail. Men shall pitch my tents upon the field, and here I will await the welcome of the Lord of the City.'

But Éomer said: 'Already you have raised the banner of the Kings and displayed the tokens of Elendil's House. Will you suffer these to be challenged?'

'No,' said Aragorn. 'But I deem the time unripe; and I have no mind for strife except with our Enemy and his servants.'

And the Prince Imrahil said: 'Your words, lord, are wise, if one who is a kinsman of the Lord Denethor may counsel you in this matter. He is strong-willed and proud, but old; and his mood has been strange since his son was stricken down. Yet I would not have you remain like a beggar at the door.'

'Not a beggar,' said Aragorn. 'Say a captain of the Rangers, who are unused to cities and houses of stone.' And he commanded that his banner should be furled; and he did off the Star of the North Kingdom and gave it to the keeping of the sons of Elrond.

Then the Prince Imrahil and Éomer of Rohan left him and passed through the City and the tumult of the people, and mounted to the Citadel; and they came to the Hall of the Tower, seeking the Steward. But they found his chair empty, and before the dais lay Théoden King of the Mark upon a

bed of state; and twelve torches stood about it, and twelve
guards, knights both of Rohan and Gondor. And the hangings of the bed were of green and white, but upon the king
was laid the great cloth of gold up to his breast, and upon
that his unsheathed sword, and at his feet his shield. The
light of the torches shimmered in his white hair like sun in
the spray of a fountain, but his face was fair and young, save
that a peace lay on it beyond the reach of youth; and it
seemed that he slept.

When they had stood silent for a time beside the king,
Imrahil said: 'Where is the Steward? And where also is
Mithrandir?'

And one of the guards answered: 'The Steward of Gondor
is in the Houses of Healing.'

But Éomer said: 'Where is the Lady Éowyn, my sister; for
surely she should be lying beside the king, and in no less
honour? Where have they bestowed her?'

And Imrahil said: 'But the Lady Éowyn was yet living
when they bore her hither. Did you not know?'

Then hope unlooked-for came so suddenly to Éomer's
heart, and with it the bite of care and fear renewed, that he
said no more, but turned and went swiftly from the hall; and
the Prince followed him. And when they came forth evening
had fallen and many stars were in the sky. And there came
Gandalf on foot and with him one cloaked in grey; and they
met before the doors of the Houses of Healing. And they
greeted Gandalf and said: 'We seek the Steward, and men
say that he is in this House. Has any hurt befallen him? And
the Lady Éowyn, where is she?'

And Gandalf answered: 'She lies within and is not dead,
but is near death. But the Lord Faramir was wounded by an
evil dart, as you have heard, and he is now the Steward; for
Denethor has departed, and his house is in ashes.' And they
were filled with grief and wonder at the tale that he told.

But Imrahil said: 'So victory is shorn of gladness, and it is
bitter bought, if both Gondor and Rohan are in one day
bereft of their lords. Éomer rules the Rohirrim. Who shall

rule the City meanwhile? Shall we not send now for the Lord Aragorn?'

And the cloaked man spoke and said: 'He is come.' And they saw as he stepped into the light of the lantern by the door that it was Aragorn, wrapped in the grey cloak of Lórien above his mail, and bearing no other token than the green stone of Galadriel. 'I have come because Gandalf begs me to do so,' he said. 'But for the present I am but the Captain of the Dúnedain of Arnor; and the Lord of Dol Amroth shall rule the City until Faramir awakes. But it is my counsel that Gandalf should rule us all in the days that follow and in our dealings with the Enemy.' And they agreed upon that.

Then Gandalf said: 'Let us not stay at the door, for the time is urgent. Let us enter! For it is only in the coming of Aragorn that any hope remains for the sick that lie in the House. Thus spake Ioreth, wise-woman of Gondor: *The hands of the king are the hands of a healer, and so shall the rightful king be known.*'

Then Aragorn entered first and the others followed. And there at the door were two guards in the livery of the Citadel: one tall, but the other scarce the height of a boy; and when he saw them he cried aloud in surprise and joy.

'Strider! How splendid! Do you know, I guessed it was you in the black ships. But they were all shouting *corsairs* and wouldn't listen to me. How did you do it?'

Aragorn laughed, and took the hobbit by the hand. 'Well met indeed!' he said. 'But there is not time yet for travellers' tales.'

But Imrahil said to Éomer: 'Is it thus that we speak to our kings? Yet maybe he will wear his crown in some other name!'

And Aragorn hearing him, turned and said: 'Verily, for in the high tongue of old I am *Elessar*, the Elfstone, and *Envinyatar*, the Renewer': and he lifted from his breast the green stone that lay there. 'But Strider shall be the name of my house, if that be ever established. In the high tongue it will not sound so ill, and *Telcontar* I will be and all the heirs of my body.'

And with that they passed into the House; and as they went towards the rooms where the sick were tended Gandalf told of the deeds of Éowyn and Meriadoc. 'For,' he said, 'long have I stood by them, and at first they spoke much in their dreaming, before they sank into the deadly darkness. Also it is given to me to see many things far off.'

Aragorn went first to Faramir, and then to the Lady Éowyn, and last to Merry. When he had looked on the faces of the sick and seen their hurts he sighed. 'Here I must put forth all such power and skill as is given to me,' he said. 'Would that Elrond were here, for he is the eldest of all our race, and has the greater power.'

And Éomer seeing that he was both sorrowful and weary said: 'First you must rest, surely, and at the least eat a little?'

But Aragorn answered: 'Nay, for these three, and most soon for Faramir, time is running out. All speed is needed.'

Then he called to Ioreth and he said: 'You have store in this House of the herbs of healing?'

'Yes, lord,' she answered; 'but not enough, I reckon, for all that will need them. But I am sure I do not know where we shall find more; for all things are amiss in these dreadful days, what with fires and burnings, and the lads that run errands so few, and all the roads blocked. Why, it is days out of count since ever a carrier came in from Lossarnach to the market! But we do our best in this House with what we have, as I am sure your lordship will know.'

'I will judge that when I see,' said Aragorn. 'One thing also is short, time for speech. Have you *athelas*?'

'I do not know, I am sure, lord,' she answered, 'at least not by that name. I will go and ask of the herb-master; he knows all the old names.'

'It is also called *kingsfoil*,' said Aragorn; 'and maybe you know it by that name, for so the country-folk call it in these latter days.'

'Oh that!' said Ioreth. 'Well, if your lordship had named

it at first I could have told you. No, we have none of it, I am sure. Why, I have never heard that it had any great virtue; and indeed I have often said to my sisters when we came upon it growing in the woods: "kingsfoil", I said, "'tis a strange name, and I wonder why 'tis called so; for if I were a king, I would have plants more bright in my garden". Still it smells sweet when bruised, does it not? If sweet is the right word: wholesome, maybe, is nearer.'

'Wholesome verily,' said Aragorn. 'And now, dame, if you love the Lord Faramir, run as quick as your tongue and get me kingsfoil, if there is a leaf in the City.'

'And if not,' said Gandalf, 'I will ride to Lossarnach with Ioreth behind me, and she shall take me to the woods, but not to her sisters. And Shadowfax shall show her the meaning of haste.'

When Ioreth was gone, Aragorn bade the other women to make water hot. Then he took Faramir's hand in his, and laid the other hand upon the sick man's brow. It was drenched with sweat; but Faramir did not move or make any sign, and seemed hardly to breathe.

'He is nearly spent,' said Aragorn turning to Gandalf. 'But this comes not from the wound. See! that is healing. Had he been smitten by some dart of the Nazgûl, as you thought, he would have died that night. This hurt was given by some Southron arrow, I would guess. Who drew it forth? Was it kept?'

'I drew it forth,' said Imrahil, 'and staunched the wound. But I did not keep the arrow, for we had much to do. It was, as I remember, just such a dart as the Southrons use. Yet I believed that it came from the Shadows above, for else his fever and sickness were not to be understood; since the wound was not deep or vital. How then do you read the matter?'

'Weariness, grief for his father's mood, a wound, and over all the Black Breath,' said Aragorn. 'He is a man of staunch will, for already he had come close under the Shadow before ever he rode to battle on the out-walls. Slowly the dark must have crept on him, even as he fought and strove to hold his outpost. Would that I could have been here sooner!'

Thereupon the herb-master entered. 'Your lordship asked for *kingsfoil*, as the rustics name it,' he said; 'or *athelas* in the noble tongue, or to those who know somewhat of the Valinorean . . .'

'I do so,' said Aragorn, 'and I care not whether you say now *asëa aranion* or *kingsfoil*, so long as you have some.'

'Your pardon lord!' said the man. 'I see you are a lore-master, not merely a captain of war. But alas! sir, we do not keep this thing in the Houses of Healing, where only the gravely hurt or sick are tended. For it has no virtue that we know of, save perhaps to sweeten a fouled air, or to drive away some passing heaviness. Unless, of course, you give heed to rhymes of old days which women such as our good Ioreth still repeat without understanding.

> *When the black breath blows*
> *and death's shadow grows*
> *and all lights pass,*
> *come athelas! come athelas!*
> *Life to the dying*
> *In the king's hand lying!*

It is but a doggrel, I fear, garbled in the memory of old wives. Its meaning I leave to your judgement, if indeed it has any. But old folk still use an infusion of the herb for headaches.'

'Then in the name of the king, go and find some old man of less lore and more wisdom who keeps some in his house!' cried Gandalf.

Now Aragorn knelt beside Faramir, and held a hand upon his brow. And those that watched felt that some great struggle was going on. For Aragorn's face grew grey with weariness; and ever and anon he called the name of Faramir, but each time more faintly to their hearing, as if Aragorn himself was removed from them, and walked afar in some dark vale, calling for one that was lost.

And at last Bergil came running in, and he bore six leaves in a cloth. 'It is kingsfoil, Sir,' he said; 'but not fresh, I fear. It must have been culled two weeks ago at the least. I hope it will serve, Sir?' Then looking at Faramir he burst into tears.

But Aragorn smiled. 'It will serve,' he said. 'The worst is now over. Stay and be comforted!' Then taking two leaves, he laid them on his hands and breathed on them, and then he crushed them, and straightway a living freshness filled the room, as if the air itself awoke and tingled, sparkling with joy. And then he cast the leaves into the bowls of steaming water that were brought to him, and at once all hearts were lightened. For the fragrance that came to each was like a memory of dewy mornings of unshadowed sun in some land of which the fair world in Spring is itself but a fleeting memory. But Aragorn stood up as one refreshed, and his eyes smiled as he held a bowl before Faramir's dreaming face.

'Well now! Who would have believed it?' said Ioreth to a woman that stood beside her. 'The weed is better than I thought. It reminds me of the roses of Imloth Melui when I was a lass, and no king could ask for better.'

Suddenly Faramir stirred, and he opened his eyes, and he looked on Aragorn who bent over him; and a light of knowledge and love was kindled in his eyes, and he spoke softly. 'My lord, you called me. I come. What does the king command?'

'Walk no more in the shadows, but awake!' said Aragorn. 'You are weary. Rest a while, and take food, and be ready when I return.'

'I will, lord,' said Faramir. 'For who would lie idle when the king has returned?'

'Farewell then for a while!' said Aragorn. 'I must go to others who need me.' And he left the chamber with Gandalf and Imrahil; but Beregond and his son remained behind,

unable to contain their joy. As he followed Gandalf and shut
the door Pippin heard Ioreth exclaim:

'King! Did you hear that? What did I say? The hands of
a healer, I said.' And soon the word had gone out from the
House that the king was indeed come among them, and after
war he brought healing; and the news ran through the City.

But Aragorn came to Éowyn, and he said: 'Here there is
a grievous hurt and a heavy blow. The arm that was broken
has been tended with due skill, and it will mend in time, if
she has the strength to live. It is the shield-arm that is maimed;
but the chief evil comes through the sword-arm. In that there
now seems no life, although it is unbroken.

'Alas! For she was pitted against a foe beyond the strength
of her mind or body. And those who will take a weapon to
such an enemy must be sterner than steel, if the very shock
shall not destroy them. It was an evil doom that set her in
his path. For she is a fair maiden, fairest lady of a house of
queens. And yet I know not how I should speak of her. When
I first looked on her and perceived her unhappiness, it seemed
to me that I saw a white flower standing straight and proud,
shapely as a lily, and yet knew that it was hard, as if wrought
by elf-wrights out of steel. Or was it, maybe, a frost that had
turned its sap to ice, and so it stood, bitter-sweet, still fair to
see, but stricken, soon to fall and die? Her malady begins far
back before this day, does it not, Éomer?'

'I marvel that you should ask me, lord,' he answered. 'For
I hold you blameless in this matter, as in all else; yet I knew
not that Éowyn, my sister, was touched by any frost, until
she first looked on you. Care and dread she had, and shared
with me, in the days of Wormtongue and the king's bewitch-
ment; and she tended the king in growing fear. But that did
not bring her to this pass!'

'My friend,' said Gandalf, 'you had horses, and deeds of
arms, and the free fields; but she, born in the body of a maid,
had a spirit and courage at least the match of yours. Yet she
was doomed to wait upon an old man, whom she loved as a

father, and watch him falling into a mean dishonoured dot-
age; and her part seemed to her more ignoble than that of
the staff he leaned on.

'Think you that Wormtongue had poison only for Théoden's ears? *Dotard! What is the house of Eorl but a thatched
barn where brigands drink in the reek, and their brats roll on the
floor among their dogs?* Have you not heard those words
before? Saruman spoke them, the teacher of Wormtongue.
Though I do not doubt that Wormtongue at home wrapped
their meaning in terms more cunning. My lord, if your sister's
love for you, and her will still bent to her duty, had not
restrained her lips, you might have heard even such things
as these escape them. But who knows what she spoke to the
darkness, alone, in the bitter watches of the night, when all
her life seemed shrinking, and the walls of her bower closing
in about her, a hutch to trammel some wild thing in?'

Then Éomer was silent, and looked on his sister, as if
pondering anew all the days of their past life together. But
Aragorn said: 'I saw also what you saw, Éomer. Few other
griefs amid the ill chances of this world have more bitterness
and shame for a man's heart than to behold the love of a
lady so fair and brave that cannot be returned. Sorrow and
pity have followed me ever since I left her desperate in Dunharrow and rode to the Paths of the Dead; and no fear upon
that way was so present as the fear for what might befall her.
And yet, Éomer, I say to you that she loves you more truly
than me; for you she loves and knows; but in me she loves
only a shadow and a thought: a hope of glory and great
deeds, and lands far from the fields of Rohan.

'I have, maybe, the power to heal her body, and to recall
her from the dark valley. But to what she will awake: hope,
or forgetfulness, or despair, I do not know. And if to despair,
then she will die, unless other healing comes which I cannot
bring. Alas! for her deeds have set her among the queens of
great renown.'

Then Aragorn stooped and looked in her face, and it was
indeed white as a lily, cold as frost, and hard as graven stone.

But he bent and kissed her on the brow, and called her softly, saying:

'Éowyn Éomund's daughter, awake! For your enemy has passed away!'

She did not stir, but now she began again to breathe deeply, so that her breast rose and fell beneath the white linen of the sheet. Once more Aragorn bruised two leaves of *athelas* and cast them into steaming water; and he laved her brow with it, and her right arm lying cold and nerveless on the coverlet.

Then, whether Aragorn had indeed some forgotten power of Westernesse, or whether it was but his words of the Lady Éowyn that wrought on them, as the sweet influence of the herb stole about the chamber it seemed to those who stood by that a keen wind blew through the window, and it bore no scent, but was an air wholly fresh and clean and young, as if it had not before been breathed by any living thing and came new-made from snowy mountains high beneath a dome of stars, or from shores of silver far away washed by seas of foam.

'Awake, Éowyn, Lady of Rohan!' said Aragorn again, and he took her right hand in his and felt it warm with life returning. 'Awake! The shadow is gone and all darkness is washed clean!' Then he laid her hand in Éomer's and stepped away. 'Call her!' he said, and he passed silently from the chamber.

'Éowyn, Éowyn!' cried Éomer amid his tears. But she opened her eyes and said: 'Éomer! What joy is this? For they said that you were slain. Nay, but that was only the dark voices in my dream. How long have I been dreaming?'

'Not long, my sister,' said Éomer. 'But think no more on it!'

'I am strangely weary,' she said. 'I must rest a little. But tell me, what of the Lord of the Mark? Alas! Do not tell me that that was a dream; for I know that it was not. He is dead as he foresaw.'

'He is dead,' said Éomer, 'but he bade me say farewell to Éowyn, dearer than daughter. He lies now in great honour in the Citadel of Gondor.'

'That is grievous,' she said. 'And yet it is good beyond all that I dared hope in the dark days, when it seemed that the House of Eorl was sunk in honour less than any shepherd's cot. And what of the king's esquire, the Halfling? Éomer, you shall make him a knight of the Riddermark, for he is valiant!'

'He lies nearby in this House, and I will go to him,' said Gandalf. 'Éomer shall stay here for a while. But do not speak yet of war or woe, until you are made whole again. Great gladness it is to see you wake again to health and hope, so valiant a lady!'

'To health?' said Éowyn. 'It may be so. At least while there is an empty saddle of some fallen Rider that I can fill, and there are deeds to do. But to hope? I do not know.'

Gandalf and Pippin came to Merry's room, and there they found Aragorn standing by the bed. 'Poor old Merry!' cried Pippin, and he ran to the bedside, for it seemed to him that his friend looked worse and a greyness was in his face, as if a weight of years of sorrow lay on him; and suddenly a fear seized Pippin that Merry would die.

'Do not be afraid,' said Aragorn. 'I came in time, and I have called him back. He is weary now, and grieved, and he has taken a hurt like the Lady Éowyn, daring to smite that deadly thing. But these evils can be amended, so strong and gay a spirit is in him. His grief he will not forget; but it will not darken his heart, it will teach him wisdom.'

Then Aragorn laid his hand on Merry's head, and passing his hand gently through the brown curls, he touched the eyelids, and called him by name. And when the fragrance of *athelas* stole through the room, like the scent of orchards, and of heather in the sunshine full of bees, suddenly Merry awoke, and he said:

'I am hungry. What is the time?'

'Past supper-time now,' said Pippin; 'though I daresay I could bring you something, if they will let me.'

'They will indeed,' said Gandalf. 'And anything else that

this Rider of Rohan may desire, if it can be found in Minas
Tirith, where his name is in honour.'

'Good!' said Merry. 'Then I would like supper first, and
after that a pipe.' At that his face clouded. 'No, not a pipe.
I don't think I'll smoke again.'

'Why not?' said Pippin.

'Well,' answered Merry slowly. 'He is dead. It has brought
it all back to me. He said he was sorry he had never had a
chance of talking herb-lore with me. Almost the last thing he
ever said. I shan't ever be able to smoke again without think-
ing of him, and that day, Pippin, when he rode up to Isengard
and was so polite.'

'Smoke then, and think of him!' said Aragorn. 'For he was
a gentle heart and a great king and kept his oaths; and he
rose out of the shadows to a last fair morning. Though your
service to him was brief, it should be a memory glad and
honourable to the end of your days.'

Merry smiled. 'Well then,' he said, 'if Strider will provide
what is needed, I will smoke and think. I had some of
Saruman's best in my pack, but what became of it in the
battle, I am sure I don't know.'

'Master Meriadoc,' said Aragorn, 'if you think that I have
passed through the mountains and the realm of Gondor with
fire and sword to bring herbs to a careless soldier who throws
away his gear, you are mistaken. If your pack has not been
found, then you must send for the herb-master of this House.
And he will tell you that he did not know that the herb you
desire had any virtues, but that it is called *westmansweed* by
the vulgar, and *galenas* by the noble, and other names in other
tongues more learned, and after adding a few half-forgotten
rhymes that he does not understand, he will regretfully inform
you that there is none in the House, and he will leave you
to reflect on the history of tongues. And so now must I. For
I have not slept in such a bed as this, since I rode from
Dunharrow, nor eaten since the dark before dawn.'

Merry seized his hand and kissed it. 'I am frightfully sorry,'
he said. 'Go at once! Ever since that night at Bree we have

been a nuisance to you. But it is the way of my people to use light words at such times and say less than they mean. We fear to say too much. It robs us of the right words when a jest is out of place.'

'I know that well, or I would not deal with you in the same way,' said Aragorn. 'May the Shire live for ever unwithered!' And kissing Merry he went out, and Gandalf went with him.

Pippin remained behind. 'Was there ever any one like him?' he said. 'Except Gandalf, of course. I think they must be related. My dear ass, your pack is lying by your bed, and you had it on your back when I met you. He saw it all the time, of course. And anyway I have some stuff of my own. Come on now! Longbottom Leaf it is. Fill up while I run and see about some food. And then let's be easy for a bit. Dear me! We Tooks and Brandybucks, we can't live long on the heights.'

'No,' said Merry. 'I can't. Not yet, at any rate. But at least, Pippin, we can now see them, and honour them. It is best to love first what you are fitted to love, I suppose: you must start somewhere and have some roots, and the soil of the Shire is deep. Still there are things deeper and higher; and not a gaffer could tend his garden in what he calls peace but for them, whether he knows about them or not. I am glad that I know about them, a little. But I don't know why I am talking like this. Where is that leaf? And get my pipe out of my pack, if it isn't broken.'

Aragorn and Gandalf went now to the Warden of the Houses of Healing, and they counselled him that Faramir and Éowyn should remain there and still be tended with care for many days.

'The Lady Éowyn,' said Aragorn, 'will wish soon to rise and depart; but she should not be permitted to do so, if you can in any way restrain her, until at least ten days be passed.'

'As for Faramir,' said Gandalf, 'he must soon learn that his father is dead. But the full tale of the madness of Denethor should not be told to him, until he is quite healed and has duties to do. See that Beregond and the *perian* who were present do not speak to him of these things yet!'

'And the other *perian*, Meriadoc, who is under my care, what of him?' said the Warden.

'It is likely that he will be fit to arise tomorrow, for a short while,' said Aragorn. 'Let him do so, if he wishes. He may walk a little in the care of his friends.'

'They are a remarkable race,' said the Warden, nodding his head. 'Very tough in the fibre, I deem.'

At the doors of the Houses many were already gathered to see Aragorn, and they followed after him; and when at last he had supped, men came and prayed that he would heal their kinsmen or their friends whose lives were in peril through hurt or wound, or who lay under the Black Shadow. And Aragorn arose and went out, and he sent for the sons of Elrond, and together they laboured far into the night. And word went through the City: 'The King is come again indeed.' And they named him Elfstone, because of the green stone that he wore, and so the name which it was foretold at his birth that he should bear was chosen for him by his own people.

And when he could labour no more, he cast his cloak about him, and slipped out of the City, and went to his tent just ere dawn and slept for a little. And in the morning the banner of Dol Amroth, a white ship like a swan upon blue water, floated from the Tower, and men looked up and wondered if the coming of the King had been but a dream.

CHAPTER IX

THE LAST DEBATE

The morning came after the day of battle, and it was fair with light clouds and the wind turning westward. Legolas and Gimli were early abroad, and they begged leave to go up into the City; for they were eager to see Merry and Pippin.

'It is good to learn that they are still alive,' said Gimli; 'for they cost us great pains in our march over Rohan, and I would not have such pains all wasted.'

Together the Elf and the Dwarf entered Minas Tirith, and folk that saw them pass marvelled to see such companions; for Legolas was fair of face beyond the measure of Men, and he sang an elven-song in a clear voice as he walked in the morning; but Gimli stalked beside him, stroking his beard and staring about him.

'There is some good stone-work here,' he said as he looked at the walls; 'but also some that is less good, and the streets could be better contrived. When Aragorn comes into his own, I shall offer him the service of stonewrights of the Mountain, and we will make this a town to be proud of.'

'They need more gardens,' said Legolas. 'The houses are dead, and there is too little here that grows and is glad. If Aragorn comes into his own, the people of the Wood shall bring him birds that sing and trees that do not die.'

At length they came to the Prince Imrahil, and Legolas looked at him and bowed low; for he saw that here indeed was one who had elven-blood in his veins. 'Hail, lord!' he said. 'It is long since the people of Nimrodel left the woodlands of Lórien, and yet still one may see that not all sailed from Amroth's haven west over water.'

'So it is said in the lore of my land,' said the Prince; 'yet never has one of the fair folk been seen there for years beyond count. And I marvel to see one here now in the midst of sorrow and war. What do you seek?'

'I am one of the Nine Companions who set out with Mithrandir from Imladris,' said Legolas; 'and with this Dwarf, my friend, I came with the Lord Aragorn. But now we wish to see our friends, Meriadoc and Peregrin, who are in your keeping, we are told.'

'You will find them in the Houses of Healing, and I will lead you thither,' said Imrahil.

'It will be enough if you send one to guide us, lord,' said Legolas. 'For Aragorn sends this message to you. He does not wish to enter the City again at this time. Yet there is need for the captains to hold council at once, and he prays that you and Éomer of Rohan will come down to his tents, as soon as may be. Mithrandir is already there.'

'We will come,' said Imrahil; and they parted with courteous words.

'That is a fair lord and a great captain of men,' said Legolas. 'If Gondor has such men still in these days of fading, great must have been its glory in the days of its rising.'

'And doubtless the good stone-work is the older and was wrought in the first building,' said Gimli. 'It is ever so with the things that Men begin: there is a frost in Spring, or a blight in Summer, and they fail of their promise.'

'Yet seldom do they fail of their seed,' said Legolas. 'And that will lie in the dust and rot to spring up again in times and places unlooked-for. The deeds of Men will outlast us, Gimli.'

'And yet come to naught in the end but might-have-beens, I guess,' said the Dwarf.

'To that the Elves know not the answer,' said Legolas.

With that the servant of the Prince came and led them to the Houses of Healing; and there they found their friends in the garden, and their meeting was a merry one. For a while they walked and talked, rejoicing for a brief space in peace and rest under the morning high up in the windy circles of the City. Then when Merry became weary, they went and sat upon the wall with the greensward of the Houses of Healing behind them; and away southward before them was the Anduin glittering in the sun, as it flowed away, out of the sight even of Legolas, into the wide flats and green haze of Lebennin and South Ithilien.

And now Legolas fell silent, while the others talked, and he looked out against the sun, and as he gazed he saw white sea-birds beating up the River.

'Look!' he cried. 'Gulls! They are flying far inland. A wonder they are to me and a trouble to my heart. Never in all my life had I met them, until we came to Pelargir, and there I heard them crying in the air as we rode to the battle of the ships. Then I stood still, forgetting war in Middle-earth; for their wailing voices spoke to me of the Sea. The Sea! Alas! I have not yet beheld it. But deep in the hearts of all my kindred lies the sea-longing, which it is perilous to stir. Alas! for the gulls. No peace shall I have again under beech or under elm.'

'Say not so!' said Gimli. 'There are countless things still to see in Middle-earth, and great works to do. But if all the fair folk take to the Havens, it will be a duller world for those who are doomed to stay.'

'Dull and dreary indeed!' said Merry. 'You must not go to the Havens, Legolas. There will always be some folk, big or little, and even a few wise dwarves like Gimli, who need you. At least I hope so. Though I feel somehow that the worst of this war is still to come. How I wish it was all over, and well over!'

'Don't be so gloomy!' cried Pippin. 'The Sun is shining, and here we are together for a day or two at least. I want to hear more about you all. Come, Gimli! You and Legolas have mentioned your strange journey with Strider about a dozen times already this morning. But you haven't told me anything about it.'

'The Sun may shine here,' said Gimli, 'but there are mem-

ories of that road that I do not wish to recall out of the
darkness. Had I known what was before me, I think that not
for any friendship would I have taken the Paths of the Dead.'

'The Paths of the Dead?' said Pippin. 'I heard Aragorn
say that, and I wondered what he could mean. Won't you
tell us some more?'

'Not willingly,' said Gimli. 'For upon that road I was put
to shame: Gimli Glóin's son, who had deemed himself more
tough than Men, and hardier under earth than any Elf. But
neither did I prove; and I was held to the road only by the
will of Aragorn.'

'And by the love of him also,' said Legolas. 'For all those
who come to know him come to love him after his own
fashion, even the cold maiden of the Rohirrim. It was at early
morn of the day ere you came there, Merry, that we left
Dunharrow, and such a fear was on all the folk that none
would look on our going, save the Lady Éowyn, who lies
now hurt in the House below. There was grief at that parting,
and I was grieved to behold it.'

'Alas! I had heart only for myself,' said Gimli. 'Nay! I will
not speak of that journey.'

He fell silent; but Pippin and Merry were so eager for news
that at last Legolas said: 'I will tell you enough for your peace;
for I felt not the horror, and I feared not the shadows of
Men, powerless and frail as I deemed them.'

Swiftly then he told of the haunted road under the mountains, and the dark tryst at Erech, and the great ride thence,
ninety leagues and three, to Pelargir on Anduin. 'Four days
and nights, and on into a fifth, we rode from the Black Stone,'
he said. 'And lo! in the darkness of Mordor my hope rose;
for in that gloom the Shadow Host seemed to grow stronger
and more terrible to look upon. Some I saw riding, some
striding, yet all moving with the same great speed. Silent they
were, but there was a gleam in their eyes. In the uplands
of Lamedon they overtook our horses, and swept round us,
and would have passed us by, if Aragorn had not forbidden
them.

'At his command they fell back. "Even the shades of Men are obedient to his will," I thought. "They may serve his needs yet!"

'One day of light we rode, and then came the day without dawn, and still we rode on, and Ciril and Ringló we crossed; and on the third day we came to Linhir above the mouth of Gilrain. And there men of Lamedon contested the fords with fell folk of Umbar and Harad who had sailed up the river. But defenders and foes alike gave up the battle and fled when we came, crying out that the King of the Dead was upon them. Only Angbor, Lord of Lamedon, had the heart to abide us; and Aragorn bade him gather his folk and come behind, if they dared, when the Grey Host had passed.

'"At Pelargir the Heir of Isildur will have need of you," he said.

'Thus we crossed over Gilrain, driving the allies of Mordor in rout before us; and then we rested a while. But soon Aragorn arose, saying: "Lo! already Minas Tirith is assailed. I fear that it will fall ere we come to its aid." So we mounted again before night had passed and went on with all the speed that our horses could endure over the plains of Lebennin.'

Legolas paused and sighed, and turning his eyes southward softly he sang:

> Silver flow the streams from Celos to Erui
> In the green fields of Lebennin!
> Tall grows the grass there. In the wind from the Sea
> The white lilies sway,
> And the golden bells are shaken of mallos and alfirin
> In the green fields of Lebennin,
> In the wind from the Sea!

'Green are those fields in the songs of my people; but they were dark then, grey wastes in the blackness before us. And over the wide land, trampling unheeded the grass and the flowers, we hunted our foes through a day and a night, until we came at the bitter end to the Great River at last.

'Then I thought in my heart that we drew near to the Sea; for wide was the water in the darkness, and sea-birds innumerable cried on its shores. Alas for the wailing of the gulls! Did not the Lady tell me to beware of them? And now I cannot forget them.'

'For my part I heeded them not,' said Gimli; 'for we came then at last upon battle in earnest. There at Pelargir lay the main fleet of Umbar, fifty great ships and smaller vessels beyond count. Many of those that we pursued had reached the havens before us, and brought their fear with them; and some of the ships had put off, seeking to escape down the River or to reach the far shore; and many of the smaller craft were ablaze. But the Haradrim, being now driven to the brink, turned at bay, and they were fierce in despair; and they laughed when they looked on us, for they were a great army still.

'But Aragorn halted and cried with a great voice: "Now come! By the Black Stone I call you!" And suddenly the Shadow Host that had hung back at the last came up like a grey tide, sweeping all away before it. Faint cries I heard, and dim horns blowing, and a murmur as of countless far voices: it was like the echo of some forgotten battle in the Dark Years long ago. Pale swords were drawn; but I know not whether their blades would still bite, for the Dead needed no longer any weapon but fear. None would withstand them.

'To every ship they came that was drawn up, and then they passed over the water to those that were anchored; and all the mariners were filled with a madness of terror and leaped overboard, save the slaves chained to the oars. Reckless we rode among our fleeing foes, driving them like leaves, until we came to the shore. And then to each of the great ships that remained Aragorn sent one of the Dúnedain, and they comforted the captives that were aboard, and bade them put aside fear and be free.

'Ere that dark day ended none of the enemy were left to resist us; all were drowned, or were flying south in the hope to find their own lands upon foot. Strange and wonderful I thought it that the designs of Mordor should be overthrown by such wraiths of fear and darkness. With its own weapons was it worsted!'

'Strange indeed,' said Legolas. 'In that hour I looked on Aragorn and thought how great and terrible a Lord he might have become in the strength of his will, had he taken the Ring to himself. Not for naught does Mordor fear him. But nobler is his spirit than the understanding of Sauron; for is he not of the children of Lúthien? Never shall that line fail, though the years may lengthen beyond count.'

'Beyond the eyes of the Dwarves are such foretellings,' said Gimli. 'But mighty indeed was Aragorn that day. Lo! all the black fleet was in his hands; and he chose the greatest ship to be his own, and he went up into it. Then he let sound a great concourse of trumpets taken from the enemy; and the Shadow Host withdrew to the shore. There they stood silent, hardly to be seen, save for a red gleam in their eyes that caught the glare of the ships that were burning. And Aragorn spoke in a loud voice to the Dead Men, crying:

' "Hear now the words of the Heir of Isildur! Your oath is fulfilled. Go back and trouble not the valleys ever again! Depart and be at rest!"

'And thereupon the King of the Dead stood out before the host and broke his spear and cast it down. Then he bowed low and turned away; and swiftly the whole grey host drew off and vanished like a mist that is driven back by a sudden wind; and it seemed to me that I awoke from a dream.

'That night we rested while others laboured. For there were many captives set free, and many slaves released who had been folk of Gondor taken in raids; and soon also there was a great gathering of men out of Lebennin and the Ethir, and Angbor of Lamedon came up with all the horsemen that he could muster. Now that the fear of the Dead was removed they came to aid us and to look on the Heir of Isildur; for the rumour of that name had run like fire in the dark.

'And that is near the end of our tale. For during that evening and night many ships were made ready and manned; and in the morning the fleet set forth. Long past it now seems, yet it was but the morn of the day ere yesterday, the sixth since we rode from Dunharrow. But still Aragorn was driven by fear that time was too short.

' "It is forty leagues and two from Pelargir to the landings at the Harlond," he said. "Yet to the Harlond we must come tomorrow or fail utterly."

'The oars were now wielded by free men, and manfully they laboured; yet slowly we passed up the Great River, for we strove against its stream, and though that is not swift down in the South, we had no help of wind. Heavy would my heart have been, for all our victory at the havens, if Legolas had not laughed suddenly.

' "Up with your beard, Durin's son!" he said. "For thus is it spoken: *Oft hope is born, when all is forlorn.*" But what hope he saw from afar he would not tell. When night came it did but deepen the darkness, and our hearts were hot, for away in the North we saw a red glow under the cloud, and Aragorn said: "Minas Tirith is burning."

'But at midnight hope was indeed born anew. Sea-crafty men of the Ethir gazing southward spoke of a change coming with a fresh wind from the Sea. Long ere day the masted ships hoisted sail, and our speed grew, until dawn whitened the foam at our prows. And so it was, as you know, that we came in the third hour of the morning with a fair wind and the Sun unveiled, and we unfurled the great standard in battle. It was a great day and a great hour, whatever may come after.'

'Follow what may, great deeds are not lessened in worth,' said Legolas. 'Great deed was the riding of the Paths of the Dead, and great it shall remain, though none be left in Gondor to sing of it in the days that are to come.'

'And that may well befall,' said Gimli. 'For the faces of Aragorn and Gandalf are grave. Much I wonder what counsels they are taking in the tents there below. For my part, like Merry, I wish that with our victory the war was now over. Yet whatever is still to do, I hope to have a part in it, for the honour of the folk of the Lonely Mountain.'

'And I for the folk of the Great Wood,' said Legolas, 'and for the love of the Lord of the White Tree.'

Then the companions fell silent, but a while they sat there in the high place, each busy with his own thoughts, while the Captains debated.

When the Prince Imrahil had parted from Legolas and Gimli, at once he sent for Éomer; and he went down with him from the City, and they came to the tents of Aragorn that were set up on the field not far from the place where King Théoden had fallen. And there they took counsel together with Gandalf and Aragorn and the sons of Elrond.

'My lords,' said Gandalf, 'listen to the words of the Steward of Gondor before he died: *You may triumph on the fields of the Pelennor for a day, but against the Power that has now arisen there is no victory.* I do not bid you despair, as he did, but to ponder the truth in these words.

'The Stones of Seeing do not lie, and not even the Lord of Barad-dûr can make them do so. He can, maybe, by his will choose what things shall be seen by weaker minds, or cause them to mistake the meaning of what they see. Nonetheless it cannot be doubted that when Denethor saw great forces arrayed against him in Mordor, and more still being gathered, he saw that which truly is.

'Hardly has our strength sufficed to beat off the first great assault. The next will be greater. This war then is without final hope, as Denethor perceived. Victory cannot be achieved by arms, whether you sit here to endure siege after siege, or march out to be overwhelmed beyond the River. You have only a choice of evils; and prudence would counsel you to strengthen such strong places as you have, and there await the onset; for so shall the time before your end be made a little longer.'

'Then you would have us retreat to Minas Tirith, or Dol

Amroth, or to Dunharrow, and there sit like children on
sand-castles when the tide is flowing?' said Imrahil.

'That would be no new counsel,' said Gandalf. 'Have you
not done this and little more in all the days of Denethor? But
no! I said this would be prudent. I do not counsel prudence.
I said victory could not be achieved by arms. I still hope for
victory, but not by arms. For into the midst of all these
policies comes the Ring of Power, the foundation of Barad-
dûr, and the hope of Sauron.

'Concerning this thing, my lords, you now all know enough
for the understanding of our plight, and of Sauron's. If he
regains it, your valour is vain, and his victory will be swift
and complete: so complete that none can foresee the end of
it while this world lasts. If it is destroyed, then he will fall;
and his fall will be so low that none can foresee his arising
ever again. For he will lose the best part of the strength that
was native to him in his beginning, and all that was made or
begun with that power will crumble, and he will be maimed
for ever, becoming a mere spirit of malice that gnaws itself
in the shadows, but cannot again grow or take shape. And
so a great evil of this world will be removed.

'Other evils there are that may come; for Sauron is himself
but a servant or emissary. Yet it is not our part to master all
the tides of the world, but to do what is in us for the succour
of those years wherein we are set, uprooting the evil in the
fields that we know, so that those who live after may have
clean earth to till. What weather they shall have is not ours
to rule.

'Now Sauron knows all this, and he knows that this pre-
cious thing which he lost has been found again; but he does
not yet know where it is, or so we hope. And therefore he is
now in great doubt. For if we have found this thing, there
are some among us with strength enough to wield it. That
too he knows. For do I not guess rightly, Aragorn, that you
have shown yourself to him in the Stone of Orthanc?'

'I did so ere I rode from the Hornburg,' answered Aragorn.
'I deemed that the time was ripe, and that the Stone had

come to me for just such a purpose. It was then ten days since the Ring-bearer went east from Rauros, and the Eye of Sauron, I thought, should be drawn out from his own land. Too seldom has he been challenged since he returned to his Tower. Though if I had foreseen how swift would be his onset in answer, maybe I should not have dared to show myself. Bare time was given me to come to your aid.'

'But how is this?' asked Éomer. 'All is vain, you say, if he has the Ring. Why should he think it not vain to assail us, if we have it?'

'He is not yet sure,' said Gandalf, 'and he has not built up his power by waiting until his enemies are secure, as we have done. Also we could not learn how to wield the full power all in a day. Indeed it can be used only by one master alone, not by many; and he will look for a time of strife, ere one of the great among us makes himself master and puts down the others. In that time the Ring might aid him, if he were sudden.

'He is watching. He sees much and hears much. His Nazgûl are still abroad. They passed over this field ere the sunrise, though few of the weary and sleeping were aware of them. He studies the signs: the Sword that robbed him of his treasure re-made; the winds of fortune turning in our favour, and the defeat unlooked-for of his first assault; the fall of his great Captain.

'His doubt will be growing, even as we speak here. His Eye is now straining towards us, blind almost to all else that is moving. So we must keep it. Therein lies all our hope. This, then, is my counsel. We have not the Ring. In wisdom or great folly it has been sent away to be destroyed, lest it destroy us. Without it we cannot by force defeat his force. But we must at all costs keep his Eye from his true peril. We cannot achieve victory by arms, but by arms we can give the Ring-bearer his only chance, frail though it be.

'As Aragorn has begun, so we must go on. We must push Sauron to his last throw. We must call out his hidden strength, so that he shall empty his land. We must march out to meet him at once. We must make ourselves the bait, though his jaws should close on us. He will take that bait, in hope and in greed, for he will think that in such rashness he sees the pride of the new Ringlord: and he will say: "So! he pushes out his neck too soon and too far. Let him come on, and behold I will have him in a trap from which he cannot escape. There I will crush him, and what he has taken in his insolence shall be mine again for ever."

'We must walk open-eyed into that trap, with courage, but small hope for ourselves. For, my lords, it may well prove that we ourselves shall perish utterly in a black battle far from the living lands; so that even if Barad-dûr be thrown down, we shall not live to see a new age. But this, I deem, is our duty. And better so than to perish nonetheless – as we surely shall, if we sit here – and know as we die that no new age shall be.'

They were silent for a while. At length Aragorn spoke. 'As I have begun, so I will go on. We come now to the very brink, where hope and despair are akin. To waver is to fall. Let none now reject the counsels of Gandalf, whose long labours against Sauron come at last to their test. But for him all would long ago have been lost. Nonetheless I do not yet claim to command any man. Let others choose as they will.'

Then said Elrohir: 'From the North we came with this purpose, and from Elrond our father we brought this very counsel. We will not turn back.'

'As for myself,' said Éomer, 'I have little knowledge of these deep matters; but I need it not. This I know, and it is enough, that as my friend Aragorn succoured me and my people, so I will aid him when he calls. I will go.'

'As for me,' said Imrahil, 'the Lord Aragorn I hold to be my liege-lord, whether he claim it or no. His wish is to me a command. I will go also. Yet for a while I stand in the place of the Steward of Gondor, and it is mine to think first of its people. To prudence some heed must still be given. For we must prepare against all chances, good as well as evil. Now, it may be that we shall triumph, and while there is any hope of this, Gondor must be protected. I would not have us return with victory to a City in ruins and a land ravaged behind us. And yet we learn from the Rohirrim that there is an army still unfought upon our northern flank.'

'That is true,' said Gandalf. 'I do not counsel you to leave the City all unmanned. Indeed the force that we lead east need not be great enough for any assault in earnest upon Mordor, so long as it be great enough to challenge battle. And it must move soon. Therefore I ask the Captains: what force could we muster and lead out in two days' time at the latest? And they must be hardy men that go willingly, knowing their peril.'

'All are weary, and very many have wounds light or grievous,' said Éomer, 'and we have suffered much loss of our horses, and that is ill to bear. If we must ride soon, then I cannot hope to lead even two thousands, and yet leave as many for the defence of the City.'

'We have not only to reckon with those who fought on this field,' said Aragorn. 'New strength is on the way from the southern fiefs, now that the coasts have been rid. Four thousands I sent marching from Pelargir through Lossarnach two days ago; and Angbor the fearless rides before them. If we set out in two days more, they will draw nigh ere we depart. Moreover many were bidden to follow me up the River in any craft they could gather; and with this wind they will soon be at hand, indeed several ships have already come to the Harlond. I judge that we could lead out seven thousands of horse and foot, and yet leave the City in better defence than it was when the assault began.'

'The Gate is destroyed,' said Imrahil, 'and where now is the skill to rebuild it and set it up anew?'

'In Erebor in the Kingdom of Dáin there is such skill,' said Aragorn; 'and if all our hopes do not perish, then in time I will send Gimli Glóin's son to ask for wrights of the Mountain. But men are better than gates, and no gate will endure against our Enemy if men desert it.'

*   *   *

This then was the end of the debate of the lords: that they should set forth on the second morning from that day with seven thousands, if these might be found; and the great part of this force should be on foot, because of the evil lands into which they would go. Aragorn should find some two thousands of those that he had gathered to him in the South; but Imrahil should find three and a half thousands; and Éomer five hundreds of the Rohirrim who were unhorsed but themselves warworthy, and he himself should lead five hundreds of his best Riders on horse; and another company of five hundred horse there should be, among which should ride the sons of Elrond with the Dúnedain and the knights of Dol Amroth: all told six thousand foot and a thousand horse. But the main strength of the Rohirrim that remained horsed and able to fight, some three thousand under the command of Elfhelm, should waylay the West Road against the enemy that was in Anórien. And at once swift riders were sent out to gather what news they could northwards; and eastwards from Osgiliath and the road to Minas Morgul.

And when they had reckoned up all their strength and taken thought for the journeys they should make and the roads they should choose, Imrahil suddenly laughed aloud.

'Surely,' he cried, 'this is the greatest jest in all the history of Gondor: that we should ride with seven thousands, scarce as many as the vanguard of its army in the days of its power, to assail the mountains and the impenetrable gate of the Black Land! So might a child threaten a mail-clad knight with a bow of string and green willow! If the Dark Lord knows so much as you say, Mithrandir, will he not rather smile than fear, and with his little finger crush us like a fly that tries to sting him?'

'No, he will try to trap the fly and take the sting,' said Gandalf. 'And there are names among us that are worth more than a thousand mail-clad knights apiece. No, he will not smile.'

'Neither shall we,' said Aragorn. 'If this be jest, then it is too bitter for laughter. Nay, it is the last move in a great jeopardy, and for one side or the other it will bring the end of the game.' Then he drew Andúril and held it up glittering in the sun. 'You shall not be sheathed again until the last battle is fought,' he said.

CHAPTER X

THE BLACK GATE OPENS

Two days later the army of the West was all assembled on the Pelennor. The host of Orcs and Easterlings had turned back out of Anórien, but harried and scattered by the Rohirrim they had broken and fled with little fighting towards Cair Andros; and with that threat destroyed and new strength arriving out of the South the City was as well manned as might be. Scouts reported that no enemies remained upon the roads east as far as the Cross-roads of the Fallen King. All now was ready for the last throw.

Legolas and Gimli were to ride again together in the company of Aragorn and Gandalf, who went in the van with the Dúnedain and the sons of Elrond. But Merry to his shame was not to go with them.

'You are not fit for such a journey,' said Aragorn. 'But do not be ashamed. If you do no more in this war, you have already earned great honour. Peregrin shall go and represent the Shirefolk; and do not grudge him his chance of peril, for though he has done as well as his fortune allowed him, he has yet to match your deed. But in truth all now are in like danger. Though it may be our part to find a bitter end before the Gate of Mordor, if we do so, then you will come also to a last stand, either here or wherever the black tide overtakes you. Farewell!'

And so despondently Merry now stood and watched the mustering of the army. Bergil was with him, and he also was downcast; for his father was to march leading a company of the Men of the City: he could not rejoin the Guard until his case was judged. In that same company Pippin was also to go, as a soldier of Gondor. Merry could see him not far off, a small but upright figure among the tall men of Minas Tirith.

At last the trumpets rang and the army began to move. Troop by troop, and company by company, they wheeled and went off eastward. And long after they had passed away out of sight down the great road to the Causeway, Merry stood there. The last glint of the morning sun on spear and helm twinkled and was lost, and still he remained with bowed head and heavy heart, feeling friendless and alone. Everyone that he cared for had gone away into the gloom that hung over the distant eastern sky; and little hope at all was left in his heart that he would ever see any of them again.

As if recalled by his mood of despair, the pain in his arm returned, and he felt weak and old, and the sunlight seemed thin. He was roused by the touch of Bergil's hand.

'Come, Master Perian!' said the lad. 'You are still in pain, I see. I will help you back to the Healers. But do not fear! They will come back. The Men of Minas Tirith will never be overcome. And now they have the Lord Elfstone, and Beregond of the Guard too.'

Ere noon the army came to Osgiliath. There all the workers and craftsmen that could be spared were busy. Some were strengthening the ferries and boat-bridges that the enemy had made and in part destroyed when they fled; some gathered stores and booty; and others on the eastern side across the River were throwing up hasty works of defence.

The vanguard passed on through the ruins of Old Gondor, and over the wide River, and on up the long straight road that in the high days had been made to run from the fair Tower of the Sun to the tall Tower of the Moon, which now was Minas Morgul in its accursed vale. Five miles beyond Osgiliath they halted, ending their first day's march.

But the horsemen pressed on and ere evening they came to the Cross-roads and the great ring of trees, and all was silent. No sign of any enemy had they seen, no cry or call had been heard, no shaft had sped from rock or thicket by the way, yet ever as they went forward they felt the watchfulness of the land increase. Tree and stone, blade and leaf were listening. The darkness had been dispelled, and far away westward sunset was on the Vale of Anduin, and the white peaks of the mountains blushed in the blue air; but a shadow and a gloom brooded upon the Ephel Dúath.

Then Aragorn set trumpeters at each of the four roads that ran into the ring of trees, and they blew a great fanfare, and the heralds cried aloud: 'The Lords of Gondor have returned and all this land that is theirs they take back.' The hideous orc-head that was set upon the carven figure was cast down and broken in pieces, and the old king's head was raised and set in its place once more, still crowned with white and golden flowers; and men laboured to wash and pare away all the foul scrawls that orcs had put upon the stone.

Now in their debate some had counselled that Minas Morgul should first be assailed, and if they might take it, it should be utterly destroyed. 'And, maybe,' said Imrahil, 'the road that leads thence to the pass above will prove an easier way of assault upon the Dark Lord than his northern gate.'

But against this Gandalf had spoken urgently, because of the evil that dwelt in the valley, where the minds of living men would turn to madness and horror, and because also of the news that Faramir had brought. For if the Ring-bearer had indeed attempted that way, then above all they should not draw the Eye of Mordor thither. So the next day when the main host came up, they set a strong guard upon the Cross-roads to make some defence, if Mordor should send a force over the Morgul Pass, or should bring more men up from the South. For that guard they chose mostly archers who knew the ways of Ithilien and would lie hid in the woods and slopes about the meeting of the ways. But Gandalf and Aragorn rode with the vanguard to the entrance of Morgul Vale and looked on the evil city.

It was dark and lifeless; for the Orcs and lesser creatures of Mordor that had dwelt there had been destroyed in battle, and the Nazgûl were abroad. Yet the air of the valley was heavy with fear and enmity. Then they broke the evil bridge and set red flames in the noisome fields and departed.

The day after, being the third day since they set out from Minas Tirith, the army began its northward march along the road. It was some hundred miles by that way from the Cross-roads to the Morannon, and what might befall them before they came so far none knew. They went openly but heedfully, with mounted scouts before them on the road, and others on foot upon either side, especially on the eastward flank; for there lay dark thickets, and a tumbled land of rocky ghylls and crags, behind which the long grim slopes of the Ephel Dúath clambered up. The weather of the world remained fair, and the wind held in the west, but nothing could waft away the glooms and the sad mists that clung about the Mountains of Shadow; and behind them at whiles great smokes would arise and hover in the upper winds.

Ever and anon Gandalf let blow the trumpets, and the heralds would cry: 'The Lords of Gondor are come! Let all leave this land or yield them up!' But Imrahil said: 'Say not *The Lords of Gondor*. Say *The King Elessar*. For that is true, even though he has not yet sat upon the throne; and it will give the Enemy more thought, if the heralds use that name.' And thereafter thrice a day the heralds proclaimed the coming of the King Elessar. But none answered the challenge.

Nonetheless, though they marched in seeming peace, the hearts of all the army, from the highest to the lowest, were downcast, and with every mile that they went north foreboding of evil grew heavier on them. It was near the end of the second day of their march from the Cross-roads that they first met any offer of battle. For a strong force of Orcs and Easterlings attempted to take their leading companies in an ambush; and that was in the very place where Faramir had waylaid the men of Harad, and the road went in a deep cutting through an out-thrust of the eastward hills. But the Captains of the West were well warned by their scouts, skilled men from Henneth Annûn led by Mablung; and so the ambush was itself trapped. For horsemen went wide about westward and came up on the flank of the enemy and from behind, and they were destroyed or driven east into the hills.

But the victory did little to enhearten the captains. 'It is but a feint,' said Aragorn; 'and its chief purpose, I deem, was rather to draw us on by a false guess of our Enemy's weakness than to do us much hurt, yet.' And from that evening onward the Nazgûl came and followed every move of the army. They still flew high and out of sight of all save Legolas, and yet their presence could be felt, as a deepening of shadow and a dimming of the sun; and though the Ring-wraiths did not yet stoop low upon their foes and were silent, uttering no cry, the dread of them could not be shaken off.

So time and the hopeless journey wore away. Upon the fourth day from the Cross-roads and the sixth from Minas Tirith they came at last to the end of the living lands, and began to pass into the desolation that lay before the gates of the Pass of Cirith Gorgor; and they could descry the marshes and the desert that stretched north and west to the Emyn Muil. So desolate were those places and so deep the horror that lay on them that some of the host were unmanned, and they could neither walk nor ride further north.

Aragorn looked at them, and there was pity in his eyes rather than wrath; for these were young men from Rohan, from Westfold far away, or husbandmen from Lossarnach, and to them Mordor had been from childhood a name of evil, and yet unreal, a legend that had no part in their simple life; and now they walked like men in a hideous dream made true, and they understood not this war nor why fate should lead them to such a pass.

'Go!' said Aragorn. 'But keep what honour you may, and do not run! And there is a task which you may attempt and so be not wholly shamed. Take your way south-west till you come to Cair Andros, and if that is still held by enemies, as I think, then re-take it, if you can; and hold it to the last in defence of Gondor and Rohan!'

Then some being shamed by his mercy overcame their

fear and went on, and the others took new hope, hearing of a manful deed within their measure that they could turn to, and they departed. And so, since many men had already been left at the Cross-roads, it was with less than six thousands that the Captains of the West came at last to challenge the Black Gate and the might of Mordor.

They advanced now slowly, expecting at every hour some answer to their challenge, and they drew together, since it was but waste of men to send out scouts or small parties from the main host. At nightfall of the fifth day of the march from Morgul Vale they made their last camp, and set fires about it of such dead wood and heath as they could find. They passed the hours of night in wakefulness and they were aware of many things half-seen that walked and prowled all about them, and they heard the howling of wolves. The wind had died and all the air seemed still. They could see little, for though it was cloudless and the waxing moon was four nights old, there were smokes and fumes that rose out of the earth and the white crescent was shrouded in the mists of Mordor.

It grew cold. As morning came the wind began to stir again, but now it came from the North, and soon it freshened to a rising breeze. All the night-walkers were gone, and the land seemed empty. North amid their noisome pits lay the first of the great heaps and hills of slag and broken rock and blasted earth, the vomit of the maggot-folk of Mordor; but south and now near loomed the great rampart of Cirith Gorgor, and the Black Gate amidmost, and the two Towers of the Teeth tall and dark upon either side. For in their last march the Captains had turned away from the old road as it bent east, and avoided the peril of the lurking hills, and so now they were approaching the Morannon from the north-west, even as Frodo had done.

The two vast iron doors of the Black Gate under its frowning arch were fast closed. Upon the battlement nothing could be seen. All was silent but watchful. They were come to the last end of their folly, and stood forlorn and chill in the grey light of early day before towers and walls which their army could not assault with hope, not even if it had brought thither engines of great power, and the Enemy had no more force than would suffice for the manning of the gate and wall alone. Yet they knew that all the hills and rocks about the Morannon were filled with hidden foes, and the shadowy defile beyond was bored and tunnelled by teeming broods of evil things. And as they stood they saw all the Nazgûl gathered together, hovering above the Towers of the Teeth like vultures; and they knew that they were watched. But still the Enemy made no sign.

No choice was left them but to play their part to its end. Therefore Aragorn now set the host in such array as could best be contrived; and they were drawn up on two great hills of blasted stone and earth that orcs had piled in years of labour. Before them towards Mordor lay like a moat a great mire of reeking mud and foul-smelling pools. When all was ordered, the Captains rode forth towards the Black Gate with a great guard of horsemen and the banner and heralds and trumpeters. There was Gandalf as chief herald, and Aragorn with the sons of Elrond, and Éomer of Rohan, and Imrahil; and Legolas and Gimli and Peregrin were bidden to go also, so that all the enemies of Mordor should have a witness.

They came within cry of the Morannon, and unfurled the banner, and blew upon their trumpets; and the heralds stood out and sent their voices up over the battlement of Mordor.

'Come forth!' they cried. 'Let the Lord of the Black Land come forth! Justice shall be done upon him. For wrongfully he has made war upon Gondor and wrested its lands. Therefore the King of Gondor demands that he should atone for his evils, and depart then for ever. Come forth!'

There was a long silence, and from wall and gate no cry or sound was heard in answer. But Sauron had already laid his plans, and he had a mind first to play these mice cruelly before he struck to kill. So it was that, even as the Captains were about to turn away, the silence was broken suddenly. There came a long rolling of great drums like thunder in the mountains, and then a braying of horns that shook the very stones and stunned men's ears. And thereupon the door of the Black Gate was thrown open with a great clang, and out of it there came an embassy from the Dark Tower.

At its head there rode a tall and evil shape, mounted upon a black horse, if horse it was; for it was huge and hideous, and its face was a frightful mask, more like a skull than a living head, and in the sockets of its eyes and in its nostrils there burned a flame. The rider was robed all in black, and black was his lofty helm; yet this was no Ringwraith but a living man. The Lieutenant of the Tower of Barad-dûr he was, and his name is remembered in no tale; for he himself had forgotten it, and he said: 'I am the Mouth of Sauron.' But it is told that he was a renegade, who came of the race of those that are named the Black Númenoreans; for they established their dwellings in Middle-earth during the years of Sauron's domination, and they worshipped him, being enamoured of evil knowledge. And he entered the service of the Dark Tower when it first rose again, and because of his cunning he grew ever higher in the Lord's favour; and he learned great sorcery, and knew much of the mind of Sauron; and he was more cruel than any orc.

He it was that now rode out, and with him came only a small company of black-harnessed soldiery, and a single banner, black but bearing on it in red the Evil Eye. Now halting a few paces before the Captains of the West he looked them up and down and laughed.

'Is there anyone in this rout with authority to treat with me?' he asked. 'Or indeed with wit to understand me? Not thou at least!' he mocked, turning to Aragorn with scorn. 'It needs more to make a king than a piece of elvish glass, or a rabble such as this. Why, any brigand of the hills can show as good a following!'

Aragorn said naught in answer, but he took the other's eye and held it, and for a moment they strove thus; but soon,

though Aragorn did not stir nor move hand to weapon, the
other quailed and gave back as if menaced with a blow. 'I
am a herald and ambassador, and may not be assailed!' he
cried.

'Where such laws hold,' said Gandalf, 'it is also the custom
for ambassadors to use less insolence. But no one has threat-
ened you. You have naught to fear from us, until your errand
is done. But unless your master has come to new wisdom,
then with all his servants you will be in great peril.'

'So!' said the Messenger. 'Then thou art the spokesman,
old greybeard? Have we not heard of thee at whiles, and of
thy wanderings, ever hatching plots and mischief at a safe
distance? But this time thou hast stuck out thy nose too far,
Master Gandalf; and thou shalt see what comes to him who
sets his foolish webs before the feet of Sauron the Great. I
have tokens that I was bidden to show to thee – to thee in
especial, if thou shouldst dare to come.' He signed to one of
his guards, and he came forward bearing a bundle swathed
in black cloths.

The Messenger put these aside, and there to the wonder
and dismay of all the Captains he held up first the short
sword that Sam had carried, and next a grey cloak with an
elven-brooch, and last the coat of mithril-mail that Frodo
had worn wrapped in his tattered garments. A blackness came
before their eyes, and it seemed to them in a moment of
silence that the world stood still, but their hearts were dead
and their last hope gone. Pippin who stood behind Prince
Imrahil sprang forward with a cry of grief.

'Silence!' said Gandalf sternly, thrusting him back; but the
Messenger laughed aloud.

'So you have yet another of these imps with you!' he cried.
'What use you find in them I cannot guess; but to send them
as spies into Mordor is beyond even your accustomed folly.
Still, I thank him, for it is plain that this brat at least has seen
these tokens before, and it would be vain for you to deny
them now.'

'I do not wish to deny them,' said Gandalf. 'Indeed, I know

them all and all their history, and despite your scorn, foul Mouth of Sauron, you cannot say as much. But why do you bring them here?'

'Dwarf-coat, elf-cloak, blade of the downfallen West, and spy from the little rat-land of the Shire – nay, do not start! We know it well – here are the marks of a conspiracy. Now, maybe he that bore these things was a creature that you would not grieve to lose, and maybe otherwise: one dear to you, perhaps? If so, take swift counsel with what little wit is left to you. For Sauron does not love spies, and what his fate shall be depends now on your choice.'

No one answered him; but he saw their faces grey with fear and the horror in their eyes, and he laughed again, for it seemed to him that his sport went well. 'Good, good!' he said. 'He was dear to you, I see. Or else his errand was one that you did not wish to fail? It has. And now he shall endure the slow torment of years, as long and slow as our arts in the Great Tower can contrive, and never be released, unless maybe when he is changed and broken, so that he may come to you, and you shall see what you have done. This shall surely be unless you accept my Lord's terms.'

'Name the terms,' said Gandalf steadily, but those nearby saw the anguish in his face, and now he seemed an old and wizened man, crushed, defeated at last. They did not doubt that he would accept.

'These are the terms,' said the Messenger, and smiled as he eyed them one by one. 'The rabble of Gondor and its deluded allies shall withdraw at once beyond the Anduin, first taking oaths never again to assail Sauron the Great in arms, open or secret. All lands east of the Anduin shall be Sauron's for ever, solely. West of the Anduin as far as the Misty Mountains and the Gap of Rohan shall be tributary to Mordor, and men there shall bear no weapons, but shall have leave to govern their own affairs. But they shall help to rebuild Isengard which they have wantonly destroyed, and that shall be Sauron's, and there his lieutenant shall dwell: not Saruman, but one more worthy of trust.'

Looking in the Messenger's eyes they read his thought. He was to be that lieutenant, and gather all that remained of the West under his sway; he would be their tyrant and they his slaves.

But Gandalf said: 'This is much to demand for the delivery of one servant: that your Master should receive in exchange what he must else fight many a war to gain! Or has the field of Gondor destroyed his hope in war, so that he falls to haggling? And if indeed we rated this prisoner so high, what surety have we that Sauron, the Base Master of Treachery, will keep his part? Where is this prisoner? Let him be brought forth and yielded to us, and then we will consider these demands.'

It seemed then to Gandalf, intent, watching him as a man engaged in fencing with a deadly foe, that for the taking of a breath the Messenger was at a loss; yet swiftly he laughed again.

'Do not bandy words in your insolence with the Mouth of Sauron!' he cried. 'Surety you crave! Sauron gives none. If you sue for his clemency you must first do his bidding. These are his terms. Take them or leave them!'

'These we will take!' said Gandalf suddenly. He cast aside his cloak and a white light shone forth like a sword in that black place. Before his upraised hand the foul Messenger recoiled, and Gandalf coming seized and took from him the tokens: coat, cloak, and sword. 'These we will take in memory of our friend,' he cried. 'But as for your terms, we reject them utterly. Get you gone, for your embassy is over and death is near to you. We did not come here to waste words in treating with Sauron, faithless and accursed; still less with one of his slaves. Begone!'

Then the Messenger of Mordor laughed no more. His face was twisted with amazement and anger to the likeness of some wild beast that, as it crouches on its prey, is smitten on the muzzle with a stinging rod. Rage filled him and his mouth slavered, and shapeless sounds of fury came strangling from his throat. But he looked at the fell faces of the Captains and their deadly eyes, and fear overcame his wrath. He gave a great cry, and turned, leaped upon his steed, and with his company galloped madly back to Cirith Gorgor. But as they went his soldiers blew their horns in signal long arranged; and even before they came to the gate Sauron sprang his trap.

Drums rolled and fires leaped up. The great doors of the Black Gate swung back wide. Out of it streamed a great host as swiftly as swirling waters when a sluice is lifted.

The Captains mounted again and rode back, and from the host of Mordor there went up a jeering yell. Dust rose smothering the air, as from nearby there marched up an army of Easterlings that had waited for the signal in the shadows of Ered Lithui beyond the further Tower. Down from the hills on either side of the Morannon poured Orcs innumerable. The men of the West were trapped, and soon, all about the grey mounds where they stood, forces ten times and more than ten times their match would ring them in a sea of enemies. Sauron had taken the proffered bait in jaws of steel.

Little time was left to Aragorn for the ordering of his battle. Upon the one hill he stood with Gandalf, and there fair and desperate was raised the banner of the Tree and Stars. Upon the other hill hard by stood the banners of Rohan and Dol Amroth, White Horse and Silver Swan. And about each hill a ring was made facing all ways, bristling with spear and sword. But in the front towards Mordor where the first bitter assault would come there stood the sons of Elrond on the left with the Dúnedain about them, and on the right the Prince Imrahil with the men of Dol Amroth tall and fair, and picked men of the Tower of Guard.

The wind blew, and the trumpets sang, and arrows whined; but the sun now climbing towards the South was veiled in the reeks of Mordor, and through a threatening haze it gleamed, remote, a sullen red, as if it were the ending of the day, or the end maybe of all the world of light. And out of the gathering mirk the Nazgûl came with their cold voices crying words of death; and then all hope was quenched.

Pippin had bowed crushed with horror when he heard Gandalf reject the terms and doom Frodo to the torment of the Tower; but he had mastered himself, and now he stood beside Beregond in the front rank of Gondor with Imrahil's men. For it seemed best to him to die soon and leave the bitter story of his life, since all was in ruin.

'I wish Merry was here,' he heard himself saying, and quick thoughts raced through his mind, even as he watched the enemy come charging to the assault. 'Well, well, now at any rate I understand poor Denethor a little better. We might die together, Merry and I, and since die we must, why not? Well, as he is not here, I hope he'll find an easier end. But now I must do my best.'

He drew his sword and looked at it, and the intertwining shapes of red and gold; and the flowing characters of Númenor glinted like fire upon the blade. 'This was made for just such an hour,' he thought. 'If only I could smite that foul Messenger with it, then almost I should draw level with old Merry. Well, I'll smite some of this beastly brood before the end. I wish I could see cool sunlight and green grass again!'

Then even as he thought these things the first assault crashed into them. The orcs hindered by the mires that lay before the hills halted and poured their arrows into the defending ranks. But through them there came striding up, roaring like beasts, a great company of hill-trolls out of Gorgoroth. Taller and broader than Men they were, and they were clad only in close-fitting mesh of horny scales, or maybe that was their hideous hide; but they bore round bucklers huge and black and wielded heavy hammers in their knotted hands. Reckless they sprang into the pools and waded across, bellowing as they came. Like a storm they broke upon the line of the men of Gondor, and beat upon helm and head, and arm and shield, as smiths hewing the hot bending iron.

At Pippin's side Beregond was stunned and overborne, and
he fell; and the great troll-chief that smote him down bent
over him, reaching out a clutching claw; for these fell creatures would bite the throats of those that they threw down.

Then Pippin stabbed upwards, and the written blade of
Westernesse pierced through the hide and went deep into
the vitals of the troll, and his black blood came gushing out.
He toppled forward and came crashing down like a falling
rock, burying those beneath him. Blackness and stench and
crushing pain came upon Pippin, and his mind fell away into
a great darkness.

'So it ends as I guessed it would,' his thought said, even
as it fluttered away; and it laughed a little within him ere it
fled, almost gay it seemed to be casting off at last all doubt
and care and fear. And then even as it winged away into
forgetfulness it heard voices, and they seemed to be crying
in some forgotten world far above:

'The Eagles are coming! The Eagles are coming!'

For one moment more Pippin's thought hovered. 'Bilbo!'
it said. 'But no! That came in his tale, long long ago. This
is my tale, and it is ended now. Good-bye!' And his thought
fled far away and his eyes saw no more.

Also by J.R.R. Tolkien

The Hobbit

A great modern classic and the prelude to *The Lord of the Rings*.

Smaug certainly looked fast asleep, when Bilbo peeped once more from the entrance. He was just about to step out on to the floor when he caught a sudden thin ray of red from under the drooping lid of Smaug's left eye. He was only pretending to be asleep! He was watching the tunnel entrance . . .

Whisked away from his comfortable, unambitious life in his hobbit-hole in Bag End by Gandalf the wizard and a company of dwarves, Bilbo Baggins finds himself caught up in a plot to raid the treasure hoard of Smaug the Magnificent, a large and very dangerous dragon. Although quite reluctant to take part in this quest, Bilbo surprises even himself by his resourcefulness and his skill as a burglar!

'An exciting epic of travel and magical adventure' *Observer*

'A flawless masterpiece'   *The Times*

ISBN: 0 261 10221 4

Also by J.R.R. Tolkien,
edited by Christopher Tolkien

The Silmarillion

Tolkien's epic legendary precursor to *The Lord of the Rings*.

The Silmarilli were three perfect jewels, fashioned by
Fëanor, most gifted of the Elves, and within them was
imprisoned the last Light of the Two Trees of Valinor.
When the first Dark Lord, Morgoth, stole the jewels and
set them within an iron crown in the impenetrable fortress
of Angband, Fëanor and his kindred took up arms against
the great Enemy and waged a long and terrible war to
recover them.

The Silmarillion tells the story of the rebellion by Fëanor's
allies against the gods, their exile from Valinor and return
to Middle-earth. It is the history of the heroic First Age in
Tolkien's world, the ancient drama long before the time of
The Hobbit and *The Lord of the Rings*.

'At times rises to the greatness of true myth'
Financial Times

'A creation myth of singular beauty . . . magnificent'
Washington Post

ISBN: 0 261 10273 7

Also by J.R.R. Tolkien,
edited by Christopher Tolkien

Unfinished Tales

J.R.R. Tolkien's *Unfinished Tales* is a collection ranging
from the time of *The Silmarillion* – the Elder Days of
Middle-earth – to the end of the War of the Ring in *The
Lord of the Rings*. Its many treasures include Gandalf's
lively account of how he came to send the Dwarves to the
celebrated party at Bag-End, the emergence of the sea-god
Ulmo before the eyes of Tuor on the coast of Beleriand,
and a description of the military organisation of the Riders
of Rohan.

Lovers of Tolkien's mythology will also be fascinated to
read the only story from the long ages of Númenor before
its downfall, and all that is known of such matters as the
Five Wizards, the Palantíri, and the legend of Amroth.

The collection has been edited by Christopher Tolkien,
who provides a commentary placing each of the *Tales* in
the context of his father's work.

'Moments of mythic grandeur'   *Sunday Times*

'Another monument to the incredible imagination of
Tolkien'   *Sunday Telegraph*

ISBN: 0 261 10362 8

Also by J.R.R. Tolkien,
edited by Christopher Tolkien

The History of Middle-earth

When J.R.R. Tolkien died in 1973, he left behind him an enormous legacy of unpublished writings. In an unprecedented feat of literary study spanning 15 years, J.R.R. Tolkien's son and literary heir, Christopher Tolkien, has brought together his father's many unpublished stories and background notes, most of which were written long before even *The Hobbit* was conceived, to form the groundbreaking *The History of Middle-earth*. Combining his father's unique imagination with his own privileged insight, *The History of Middle-earth* is a series of 12 books no fan of *The Lord of the Rings* can afford to overlook.

The first two volumes contain the earliest concepts of Middle-earth and Valinor. Undertaking a great westward voyage over the ocean, a mariner named Eriol (a.k.a. Aelfwine) comes to the Lonely Isle, where he encounters Elves and learns from them their true history, the *Lost Tales of Elfinesse*. Written by Tolkien between 1916 and 1920, the *Tales* include his earliest accounts of Gods and Elves, Dwarves, Balrogs and Orcs; of the Silmarils and the Two Trees of Valinor; of Nargothrond and Gondolin; of the geography and cosmology of the invented world.

Each tale is followed by a commentary by Christopher Tolkien in the form of a short essay, together with the texts of associated poems and extensive information on names and vocabulary in the earliest Elvish languages.

The History of Middle-earth

The third, fourth and fifth volumes of *The History of Middle-earth* pull together Tolkien's pre-*Lord of the Rings* writing from 1920 up to the time when, at the end of 1937, he reluctantly set aside his work on the myths and heroic legends of Valinor and Middle-earth to begin *The Lord of the Rings*.

The Lays of Beleriand centres on the tales - told in verse - of two of the most crucial stories in Tolkien's world. *The Lay of the Children of Húrin* narrates on a grand scale the tragedy of Túrin Turambar, while the moving *Lay of Leithian* is the chief source of the tale of Beren and Lúthien, telling of the Quest of the Silmaril and the encounter with Morgoth in the subterranean fortress.

The Shaping of Middle-earth shows how Tolkien moulded the chronology of the First Age in *The Annals of Valinor* and *The Annals of Beleriand*, and include more of Aelfwine's voyage to the Lonely Isle. Also in the book are the original 'Silmarillion' of 1926, and the *Quenta Noldorinwa* of 1930 - the only version of the myths and legends of the First Age that J.R.R. Tolkien completed to their end.

The Lost Road and Other Writings examines the legend of the Downfall of Númenor and the central ideas of the World Made Round and the Straight Path into the vanished West. Also included are the abandoned time-travel story *The Lost Road* and an 'etymological dictionary' containing an extensive account of Elvish vocabularies

The History of Middle-earth

The following four volumes of *The History of Middle-earth* examine the creation of *The Lord of the Rings* from its inception to its finished form. At the core of these books are a great many early drafts and unpublished passages by Tolkien which add greatly to one's understanding of his great masterpiece.

The Return of the Shadow examines how Bilbo's 'magic' ring from *The Hobbit* evolved into the supremely dangerous Ruling Ring of the Dark Lord, the unforeseen moment when a Black Rider first rode into the Shire, and how the central characters underwent many changes of name and personality.

The Treason of Isengard traces the great expansion of the tale into new lands and new peoples south and east of the Misty Mountains. In brief outlines and pencilled drafts are seen the first entry of Galadriel, the earliest ideas of the history of Gondor, and the original meeting of Aragorn and Éowyn.

The War of the Ring takes up the story with the Battle of Helm's Deep, the journey of Frodo, Sam and Gollum to the Pass of Cirith Ungol, describes the war in Gondor, and ends with the parley between Gandalf and the ambassador of the dark Lord before the Black Gate of Mordor.

Sauron Defeated concludes the study of *The Lord of the Rings* with Frodo's rescue from the Tower of Cirith Ungol, and gives a very different account of the Scouring of the Shire. It includes the unpublished *Epilogue*, in which, years after the departure of Bilbo and Frodo, Sam attempts to answer his children's questions. The book also includes Tolkien's mysterious *The Notion Club Papers*, an account of the legends of Atlantis.

The History of Middle-earth

Volumes 10 and 11 take up the story of Tolkien's creativity from the time when he turned again to 'the Matter of the Elder Days' once *The Lord of the Rings* was at last completed, while the final volume returns to that work to examine the future history of Tolkien's world.

Morgoth's Ring examines the nature of the problems faced by Tolkien in his later years as he tried to reconcile new and radical ideas he had introduced at the heart of the mythology. The book includes the full text of the *Annals of Aman* and a study of later developments in the legends of Beleriand.

The War of the Jewels continues the account, returning to Middle-earth and the ruinous conflict of the High Elves and their allies with the power of the Dark Lord. The book contains the full text of the *Grey Annals*, the primary record of the War of the Jewels, and the tale of the disaster that occurred after Húrin's release from the fortress of Morgoth.

The Peoples of Middle-earth traces the evolution of the Appendices to *The Lord of the Rings*, which provide a comprehensive historical structure of the Second and Third Ages, including Calendars, Hobbit genealogies and the Westron language. The book concludes with two unique abandoned stories: *The New Shadow*, set in Gondor during the Fourth Age, and the tale of *Tal-elmar*, in which the coming of the dreaded Númenórean ships is seen through the eyes of men of Middle-earth in the Dark Years.

With the publication of this book, the long history of J.R.R. Tolkien's creation is completed and the enigmatic state of his work can be understood.

Also available by Brian Sibley
illustrated by John Howe

The Map of Tolkien's Middle-earth

This superb map will take you straight to the heart of
J.R.R. Tolkien's mythical world of Middle-earth. Redrawn
in full colour by artist John Howe from the original map
created by Christopher Tolkien, it is beautifully decorated
with scenes from *The Lord of the Rings*.

Trace the epic journey of Frodo and Sam through the
Misty Mountains and the Dead Marshes to Mount Doom;
Follow Aragorn to the great city of Minas Tirith; Discover
where Gandalf fought the Balrog on the peak of Zirak-
zigil.

The map shows how the geography created in such metic-
ulous detail by J.R.R. Tolkien is central to an understanding of his books. It comes with an illustrated explanatory
booklet written by Brian Sibley, creator of the highly
successful BBC radio dramatisation of *The Lord of the
Rings*.

The Map of Tolkien's Middle-earth is one of three comple-
mentary publications: also available are *There and Back
Again: The Map of The Hobbit* and *The Map of Tolkien's
Beleriand and the Lands to the North*.

ISBN: 0 261 10318 0